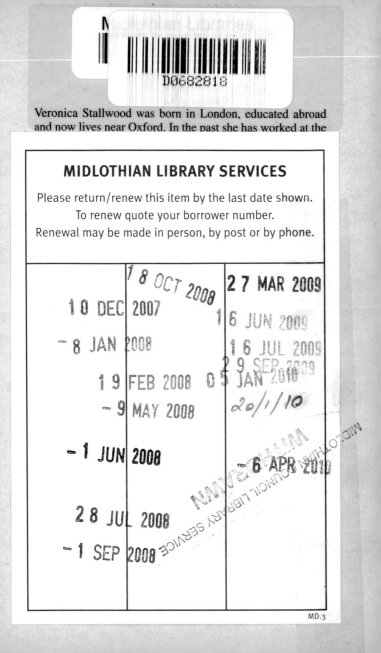

Veronica Stallwood was born in London, educated abroad and now lives near Oxford. In the past she has worked at the

Also by Veronica Stallwood and available from Headline

Deathspell
Death and the Oxford Box
Oxford Exit
Oxford Mourning
Oxford Fall
Oxford Knot
Oxford Blue
The Rainbow Sign

Oxford Shift

Veronica Stallwood

headline

First published in 1999
by HEADLINE BOOK PUBLISHING

First published in paperback in 2000
by HEADLINE BOOK PUBLISHING

10 9 8 7 6 5

ISBN 0 7472 6009 5

Printed and bound in Great Britain by
Clays Ltd, St Ives plc

HEADLINE BOOK PUBLISHING
A division of the Hodder Headline Group
338 Euston Road
London NW1 3BH
www.headline.co.uk
www.hodderheadline.com

For Hugh Griffith

1

Joyce

She knew there was something wrong as soon as she turned the key in the lock and pushed the door open. She was not an imaginative woman, but she felt the tremor of tension in the air, brushing like a cold breath against her cheek.

Instead of closing the door with a sharp click and calling out, 'It's only me!' as she usually did to announce her return, she stood on the doormat, looking down the hall at the closed doors, wondering which rooms were empty, which one held her new friend, Ruth.

She realized she had been holding her breath and now she let it go with a faint whistling sound. She listened again. There was something about the quality of the silence in the flat that told her that she wasn't alone. Someone else was here, but if it was Ruth, why hadn't she come to greet her with her big smile and her customary call of 'Kettle's on!'? She had been looking forward to a cup of tea all the way home from the shops.

'It's only me,' she said into the emptiness. But the words came out from her dry throat as a hoarse whisper and were swallowed by the emptiness of the hall. 'Are you there?'

She started to walk towards the kitchen, but paused after a few steps. This was Ruth's flat, not hers. Ruth's ownership was never stated, but it was understood. She, Joyce, was here by invitation, as a guest. She had been staying here for only three days and she couldn't take any liberties. Not that she would ever take anything for granted: she wasn't that sort of woman. She didn't like to enter the kitchen, let alone intrude in any of the other rooms, without Ruth's specific invitation to do so. 'Come and sit yourself down,' Ruth would say, hailing her as she entered the flat. And, 'I've bought us some chocolate biscuits,' Joyce would reply. A cup of tea and a chocolate biscuit: the idea seemed like heaven to her at this moment.

This was the first time she had felt herself a stranger, an interloper in the place. But she must pull herself together. It was ridiculous to feel so nervous. She put her shopping bag down and eased her aching arm.

She heard, or maybe she only imagined it, faint sounds from the other end of the flat. Ruth must be there. At any moment she would say, 'Come into the kitchen, Joyce. We'll have a cuppa.' Or, 'I've been doing a spot of shopping. Would you like to see what I've bought?' And, childlike, she would follow Ruth into her room and watch her unwrap the packages in their bright plastic bags. There was always a little something among them for Joyce.

But Ruth didn't emerge from her room, although the force of her personality, like an electric field, kept Joyce rooted to the spot, a third of the way into the flat. She shifted her weight from one foot to the other like an impatient child. She should explore the flat, she told herself, but then again, although Ruth was a wonderful person, and sweet and generous in so many ways, it didn't do to cross her, or to encroach on her privacy, or her 'space' as she called it.

It seemed as if she had been standing there for an hour, although it was probably only a minute or so, and then Joyce saw that one of the doors was open, as though by magic, as though no human agency had turned a handle, or

2

pushed it ajar. She blinked. It had certainly been closed just a few seconds before.

And, just as suddenly, Ruth was standing in the doorway, her stocky figure preventing any view of the living room behind her. Ruth wasn't grotesquely fat, or unusually tall – nothing like that. But even so, she was quite a bit taller than Joyce – maybe five foot eight or nine – and she was strongly, even powerfully built, so that if she stood four-square in a doorway, blocking your entrance, there was no way you would get past her unless she gave you permission. And yet, in spite of her physical presence, the expression on her face was mild. *Or maybe it's blank.* The thought struck Joyce for the first time. Maybe she just isn't showing me anything of what's inside her head. Ruth's eyes, very dark brown and shiny behind her glasses, stared back at Joyce. Like a lizard, thought Joyce, wondering why she was seeing her friend in this new light. Ruth's hair was the same, short and dark and curly, with a sprinkling of grey, brushed straight up and back from her face so that it looked as though an electric current had just passed through it. She was wearing the same cream blouse and tweed skirt, her shoulders were as broad, her hips as round, her legs as solid as usual. And yet there was something indefinably different about her. She held her white, capable hands clasped loosely in front of her stomach, palms upwards, as though demonstrating that she had nothing to hide.

'Yes?' asked Joyce nervously, remembering rare occasions from her childhood when she had been called to answer for her actions in front of the headmistress.

'I'm afraid there's been a slight unpleasantness,' said Ruth. 'We have to leave.'

'Leave?' Joyce was bewildered.

'Leave the flat,' said Ruth patiently.

'Leave the flat?' Joyce knew she sounded stupid, repeating

3

everything Ruth said. 'What sort of unpleasantness? Why do we have to go?'

'I can't explain now, I haven't got the time. And in any case, it isn't the sort of thing you'd wish to know about.'

Ruth knew well the kind of thing which Joyce preferred to know nothing about.

'I know it's inconvenient,' Ruth said in her well-behaved child's voice. 'And I do apologize for it. But I'm afraid that we really have to leave. And as soon as possible.'

'What's that on your face?' asked Joyce, wishing immediately that she hadn't spoken.

'Where?'

'Just by your ear.' The place you would miss if you were looking in a mirror to rub dirt off your face, and forgot to turn your head to one side.

Ruth rubbed at the mark. 'Nothing,' she said. 'It's nothing.'

'Only it looked like a spot of dried blood,' said Joyce.

'Nothing,' repeated Ruth firmly. 'Why don't you start to pack your things? It shouldn't take you long.' Ruth was smiling at her now, a bright smile that puffed out her cheeks and pushed her glasses up towards her eyebrows, giving her a startled expression.

'I haven't got a suitcase,' said Joyce weakly.

'Of course you haven't. How silly of me. Wait there –' this said as though it was an order rather than a request – 'and I'll fetch you one.'

Ruth disappeared into her bedroom for a moment and then reappeared holding a smart navy suitcase with wheels and a pull-up handle, the sort of suitcase that an air stewardess might use, it seemed to Joyce.

'How kind,' she said, overwhelmed by Ruth's generosity. Her own suitcase, the one she had left behind in her previous life, had been of checked green nylon, with worn corners and no wheels.

'Hurry along now, dear,' said Ruth, her face rearranged into its usual benign planes, her voice filled with the persuasiveness of a nurse wielding a hypodermic.

So Joyce took the navy-blue suitcase into her room, laid it on the bed and started to fold her belongings and place them neatly in the case. There weren't many of them, since she had left her former home in such a hurry. She had felt embarrassed, accepting the twenty-pound notes that Ruth had pressed into her unwilling hand when she first moved in. 'Buy yourself something decent to wear,' Ruth had said, and had squeezed Joyce's hand closed over the money, giving it a little pat to end the discussion. 'You deserve a treat.' Joyce had promised herself that she would pay the money back out of her pension, but it would take her a few weeks. She had suggested to Ruth that she might go back to her flat and pick up some of her own belongings, but dear Ruth had been quite short with her.

'You mustn't dream of going back,' she had said, and her voice had rasped unpleasantly. 'You've entered into a new life, and you must leave the old one behind. Aren't we told that we shouldn't ever try to pour the new wine into our nasty old bottles? No, we take the empties down to the recycling bin and we buy ourselves a new supply of full ones from Oddbins.' And she had beamed at Joyce and passed her a cup of tea, and told her all over again about the useful work they would be doing together, while Joyce tried to remember the exact words of Mark 2, xxii and whether Ruth had got them precisely right.

It's taking me no time at all to pack up my life, Joyce thought, as she folded her face flannel round her toothbrush. She wished she had her plastic-lined sponge bag with her. But she would just have to place her towel underneath them and hope that the damp wouldn't seep through to her underclothes.

When she had finished, she wheeled the case out into the hallway and stood by the front door, next to her neglected shopping bag, waiting for Ruth. Of course it would take her friend longer to get ready, since she had far more to pack up than Joyce did.

'Can I give you a hand, Ruth dear?' she called out to the closed doors.

'No need. I've nearly finished,' came Ruth's muffled reply. And then she opened the sitting-room door, poked her head out into the hall and added sharply, 'Don't you move, Joyce. Stay where you are.'

Joyce could hear furniture being shifted and large objects being dragged across the floor. She felt so old and useless standing there, just waiting while Ruth did all the work. Why wouldn't she let her help? Didn't she trust her to treat things properly? Ruth was such a perfectionist, she thought, as she looked around the hallway.

The paintwork on the front door was old and scratched, but even so, it had been scrubbed clean, and the lock and handle had been polished. The carpet that stretched down the hall, though covered in a vulgar, swirling pattern of yellow and orange sunflowers, was free of dust, and someone had scrubbed out the footprints of the years, leaving it a little paler in patches, but clean. Someone – the same someone – had washed the skirting boards, and cleaned the glass fingerplates on the doors. Joyce approved of all this. She and Ruth between them had brought the flat up to their own standards. They agreed absolutely about the importance of cleanliness and neatness. It was considered old-fashioned by many, no doubt, but Joyce knew that a well-kept house indicated a well-ordered conscience. Once you let go, once you let dirt and untidiness trespass in your life, you were on the slippery slope that led to immorality and damnation. And damnation was another word you daren't utter out loud in a modern, so-called liberal household.

But she and Ruth had had long and illuminating conversations about damnation. And they both knew without having to mention it that the washing-up should be done straightaway after each meal, before they sat and relaxed in their red armchairs. Washed and wiped and put away. Everything scrubbed clean and in its rightful place.

Ruth appeared briefly from one door, smiled at Joyce and disappeared into her own bedroom. It was amazing how fast she could move when she wanted to. She reappeared with a bulging black bin-liner in each hand and dropped them on the carpet next to Joyce.

'You are wearing your gloves, Joyce, aren't you?' she said.

'One of them,' said Joyce, who was holding the other in her hand.

'Put them both on, there's a good girl,' said Ruth, as though Joyce were five years old instead of nearly sixty years more than that. She watched as Joyce dutifully put on her second glove and then bustled away again.

'Nearly ready!' she called.

'Where are we going? Who will help us with our cases?' Joyce spoke aloud, but without expecting anyone to answer her. Always, in the past, there had been a man to answer such questions for her. How could two women on their own ever hope to deal with these practical matters?

Ruth materialized beside her. 'Don't worry about a thing,' she said. 'I've phoned for a car to take us to our new place.'

A car? wondered Joyce, looking down at the pile of belongings that was accumulating by the front door.

'More of a van, really,' said Ruth, depositing a large plastic bag of what looked like bedding on top of the heap.

Joyce heard the sound of running water from the kitchen,

watched Ruth appear with mop and bucket, wearing her blue rubber gloves.

'I should be helping you,' said Joyce ruefully, feeling useless as she stood next to her small suitcase.

'Just giving the place a last lick and polish,' called back Ruth, reappearing with a yellow duster in her hand this time, rubbing vigorously at the fingerplate on the front door, buffing up the door handle.

And then she was at Joyce's side, dressed in her beige coat and wearing a brown felt hat pulled well down on her forehead and covering her ears. Her hands were hidden in thick leather gloves.

It was little more than thirty minutes since she had told Joyce that they must leave the flat.

'There. That wasn't so bad now, was it?' she said.

As she spoke there was the sound of rapping on the front door.

'That'll be our transport,' said Ruth. 'Open the door, dear, and we'll be on our way.'

2

Kate

It's that time of year when the daylight starts to dim by three in the afternoon. By four Kate Ivory will have to switch on the lights, and by four-fifteen her thoughts will turn to tea and biscuits, and then to deciding how she'll spend the long evening. After four-thirty, when the sky darkens to a murky blue and the street lamps cast a sulphurous glow on the greasy pavement, serious work will be out of the question for the rest of the day.

Kate Ivory was staring idly out of the window, thinking that she should cut her grass for one final time that autumn, and perhaps plant a few bulbs in place of the tattered daisies and dandelions that decorated her lawn, before the frosts turned the ground to iron. But then, she reflected lazily, it was already well into November, so maybe it was better to leave the garden to itself until the spring.

Rain streaked the windows of her sitting room and gusts of wind rattled their frames, but nothing could spoil her feeling of contentment. The sofa where she had stretched out supported her exactly from her feet to her shoulders and was just the right shade of pink velvet to suit her mood. A dark green vase of freesias stood on the windowsill and in the background a CD was playing quietly to itself. Downstairs in her workroom, the inkjet printer was busy churning out the pages of her new, completed, novel. If she listened hard, she could hear the whine and snap as it reproduced line after line of her excellent prose on to crisp white paper. She could imagine the black lines of print snaking down the page, ready to captivate her regular readers. In short, it was wonderful to be back in her own house after the weeks she had been forced to spend away from it.

Some months before, there had been a tragedy here in the house in Agatha Street, and she had needed to escape for a while. She had hidden herself away in a friend's cottage in the country, but had come to realize that she was, after all, a strictly urban animal. I like to feel the concrete under my running shoes, she thought, not the mud of a bridle path. I like the distant growl of traffic and the sodium glare of street lamps. I even prefer the smell of diesel to that of silage. Half a mile away from my door here in Fridesley there are restaurants and cinemas and shops full of desirable clothes and interesting food. So much more exciting than a view of cows in a muddy field and the relentless chirping of small brown birds.

Perhaps I'll go into town tomorrow, she thought lazily, and buy myself some new clothes. Perhaps Roz and I can try the new fish restaurant in St Clement's. Perhaps I'll just lie here and do nothing at all.

From the next-door house she could hear the background noises of the Venn family as they went about their respective lives. From outside in the road came the clatter and whirr of skateboards. Cars passed, with the bass of their CD players thumping a heart-stirring rhythm the length of the street. A helicopter snarled overhead and in the distance she heard the wail of an ambulance siren on its way to the hospital. She loved it all. It meant that life (and occasionally death) was happening right outside her window. In the country, she had grown tired of the silence of growing crops, the rhythmic munching of cows in the adjacent field, and only the muted roar of a distant tractor to break the tedium. She had felt relieved when she had finally returned the keys of the borrowed cottage to her friend Callie and had set off with her two suitcases and her computer back to Fridesley. Her mother, Roz, had followed in her egg-yolk yellow Beetle, and she had even felt good about that, too.

On her return to her own house, invigorated by the urban buzz, she had decided to take control of her territory and claim it back from her ghosts. She had drawn sketches and studied paint charts, she had collected fabric samples. She had pulled up the hall carpet and taken it down to the tip. She and Roz had visited DIY warehouses and returned loaded with supplies. The two of them had passed through the house like a whirlwind.

Gone were the tasteful cream and barley colours. In their place she had put hyacinth blue, navy and pistachio green. She altered the lighting, she splashed out on large, bright framed prints. And thus she had completely transformed her entrance hall and staircase until there was nothing there to remind her of the past. She had repainted bedrooms and sitting room. She had only balked at kitchen and bathroom as being too time-consuming. Nearly everything was new and held no echoes of a tragedy. Only occasionally, at dusk perhaps, before she switched on the lights, familiar shadows might lie in wait for her on the stairs.

As if on cue, the door was pushed open and something small and ghostlike came sidling into the room.

Kate looked up apprehensively. 'Hello, Suse,' she said with relief, greeting the long-legged ginger cat.

Susanna, as though not entirely sure she could trust Kate, turned her head away and slipped into the narrow space between the sofa and the wall.

'I'm back for good, Suse, really,' coaxed Kate. She missed

the way Susanna used to sit on her knees and knead her thighs with her sharp claws, or leave trails of muddy paw-prints across the pristine pages of a manuscript. This polite, distant behaviour was unnerving. 'I'll never leave you again, I promise.' Susanna didn't reply, but set herself to scratching up the carpet and shredding the back of the sofa. Kate ignored the destruction. One day her cat might forgive her. In the meantime, she would have to be indulged.

On the table by Kate's elbow, the biography of Fanny Trollope was placed invitingly – it was so much easier to read other people's books than write her own, she had always found. She was also considering broaching an unopened packet of chocolate Hobnobs which she had saved for a secret and solitary binge. Fortunately for her waistline, her mother entered the room just before she could indulge herself.

'Hobnobs make you fat,' said Roz Ivory, opening the packet, helping herself to a couple of biscuits, and crunching noisily.

'Nothing makes *you* fat,' replied Kate, watching the crumbs drop on to the carpet.

'I know. Sickening, isn't it?' said Roz complacently, turning up the volume of the CD player and then curling herself into one of Kate's comfortable armchairs.

'I might go for a run,' said Kate.

'How boring of you,' yawned Roz.

'Running is an invigorating, life-enhancing exercise,' said Kate dogmatically.

'So is sex, but I don't see you doing much of that.'

Kate opened her mouth to reply, but at this moment, luckily for the fragile harmony of their relationship, they were interrupted by the ringing of the phone.

'I'll answer it,' said Kate.

'Hello, Kate. It's Emma here.'

'Hello, Emma. How are you?' Kate spoke cautiously. Emma and she had been on less than friendly terms since Kate had taken over Emma's writing class for a few weeks and had discovered a murderer lurking within its creative bosom. For some reason that was obscure to Kate, Emma had blamed her entirely for the way the cosy atmosphere in the class had been destroyed. Everything, apparently, had been fine until Kate appeared. This seemed illogical to Kate, but it was useless trying to argue with Emma, whose mind was as undisciplined and untidy as her house. Then, last year, Kate had helped Emma out at Bartlemas College here in Oxford when she was organizing a study fortnight on the subject of 'Gender and Genre'. And once more Kate had brought to light various dishonest dealings. It was odd how no one was grateful to her for her achievements this time either, and instead she was somehow blamed for trailing such sordid events in her wake. But maybe this phone call meant that Emma had forgiven her at last, or at least had started to forget.

'It's all impossible. I'm at my wits' end. I don't know what to do. And Christmas is approaching, too. I expect you've heard about Sam?'

Emma was gabbling and Kate sorted out the disjointed sentences and focused on the one she could understand. Reliable Sam. A woolly mammoth of a man, even-tempered and easy-going. Emma's husband and the father of their six children. Or was it seven by now? Kate had long since lost count. 'No,' she said. 'I've been away. What's happened to Sam? Tell me about it.'

'He was riding his bike along the Cowley Road. I told him he should always wear his helmet, I gave him a really nice fluorescent yellow one for his birthday, but he said it wouldn't matter for such a short journey, he was only going a few hundred yards. And it happened when he started to cycle round The Plain, ready to turn off into the High. He should have got off the bike and walked. That's what I always do, and that's what I tell the children to do, too. But Sam wouldn't listen to me, he said something about life being too safe these days and how one should resist the nanny state, take the occasional risk, and anyway he had always cycled round the roundabout without a helmet without anything awful happening to him, and why didn't I stop fussing and leave him alone. That's just tempting fate, isn't it?'

'What happened?'

'A lorry shot out of the Iffley Road. They're supposed to halt at the white line, but this one didn't bother. The driver said he wasn't expecting a cyclist to be moving at that speed and he just didn't see him. If he'd been wearing a fluorescent yellow helmet, the driver would have seen him all right, wouldn't he?'

Emma stopped and Kate heard gulping, spluttering noises at the other end of the phone. But surely she would have heard if Sam had been killed? 'How is he?' she asked, keeping her fingers crossed.

'He's out of intensive care, thank God. But he's got weeks to go before he comes home. They're moving him into the Maxwell Clinic tomorrow, which will be easier for us all to visit. But then there'll be more weeks of physiotherapy and rehabilitation. I just don't know what I'm going to do. You've got to help me, Kate.'

'But I'm no good with children. I don't even like them very much.' She looked over at her own mother, Roz, reclining decoratively in an armchair, drinking a margarita and reading the *Sporting Life*. Roz had come for an indeterminate stay, but Kate didn't think she was ready for granny-duty yet. 'And I don't think that Roz would be much good to you, either.'

'I know you're useless with children,' said Emma dismissively. 'You introduce them to bribery and very probably corruption as well. I wouldn't dream of asking you to cope with mine. And your mother is even worse, as far as I can make out. Look at the way she let you behave when you were young! Goodness only knows what the children would end up doing if one of you had charge of them for more than an hour or two. No, it's my mother.'

'You've lost me. Has she had an accident, too?'

'Oh, do *listen*, Kate! I'm going to be the main breadwinner when Sam's sick pay runs out, and she agreed to help with the housework and child-care.'

Sam worked for a charity, and Kate imagined that they couldn't afford much by way of sick pay, and not for the length of time that Emma had been implying.

'It was all working out beautifully. I've been getting plenty of teaching work, and Mummy was running the house and children like clockwork. And then she disappeared.'

'Ah.' Kate remembered Emma's house vividly. It had children and belongings strewn throughout its length. Music thumped from radios and CD players, and issued from the violins and recorders of untalented youngsters. More children squabbled over the choice of television programme. It gave Kate a headache just to think about it. If she'd been Emma's mother, she'd have disappeared, too. 'Perhaps she's taken a day or two off,' she suggested. 'I expect she needed a bit of a rest.'

'She wouldn't do that! Not without telling me first.'

'Did she leave a note?'

'No.'

'Has she taken anything with her? Suitcase, clothes, handbag?'

'I'm not sure.'

No, Kate could see that it might be difficult to ascertain

whether anything had been added to or subtracted from the heaps of discarded clothing, rollerblades, books, teddy bears, manuscripts and children that littered Emma's house.

'Though I haven't come across her handbag, certainly,' added Emma. 'I think I'd have noticed that.'

'What is it you want me to do?' asked Kate, with the unpleasant feeling that she was letting herself in for more than she wished to take on.

'We've always depended on Mummy. All my life she was the rock I could lean on. Daddy wasn't much use. He was a bit distant, and I didn't feel I could confide in him. But Mummy's different. The whole house revolved around her. And I want you to find her.'

'Why me?'

'Well, you like poking around and finding out things. Isn't that how you do the research for your books?'

'I wouldn't put it quite like that. But let me think about it. I do have commitments of my own, you know.'

'You've only got one of those historical novels of yours to write, after all. You must have produced a dozen of them and I'm sure you can write another one in your sleep by now. Will you ring me back?' Emma sounded quite desperate.

'I'll ring you back in an hour,' said Kate, giving herself time to consider whether she really wanted to work for Emma again. For the moment she would keep to herself the fact that she was basking in the brief glow of a completed manuscript and needn't begin a new book for another week at least. She would like to keep an option or two open for the present. She replaced her receiver.

'And what was all that about?' asked Roz, putting down her margarita and looking interested. 'Is someone offering us a job?'

3

Joyce

'There now, aren't we more comfy here?'

Ruth passed across the cup of tea, milky and sweetened with three spoonfuls of sugar. Joyce, who didn't normally take sugar in her tea, told herself she needed the energy, and swallowed it gratefully.

'The flat's very nice, certainly. And so well furnished.'

'I told you you'd like it.'

It was true that this place was nicer than their previous one, with a polished wood table and sideboard in the room as well as a respectable three-piece suite.

'Though really I hardly had time to settle myself into the old place before we moved on here,' Joyce added. 'Not that I'm complaining, of course.'

'All I need to make me happy is a comfortable chair,' announced Ruth. 'And this one suits me just right.'

The armchair in question was wide in the seat, rather like Ruth herself. Its arms were broad and the fabric a soft green. Ruth filled it as a jelly does a mould, and under her weight the seat drooped so close to the carpet that she would have great difficulty in rising to her feet. Not that Ruth was eager to stand up and move around, Joyce had noticed. Static, that was the word she would use to describe her since they had moved into this new flat. Or restful, she told herself reprovingly. Yes, that's what Ruth was: a very restful person.

'I woke up in the night,' Joyce said hesitantly.

'It always takes a few days to get used to a new bed,' said Ruth, whose gentle, even snores had vibrated continuously through the wall between their rooms from midnight until seven-thirty that morning. 'I expect you'll sleep like a top tonight, no problem at all.'

'Yes. But once I woke up, I lay awake worrying for hours.'

'You're not worried about anything special, are you, dear?' asked Ruth solicitously.

Joyce reminded herself that one meaning of the name 'Ruth' was 'compassion'. Such a fitting name for her friend. She was always so much more concerned for others' comfort than for her own. 'It's just that I found myself wondering why we had to move out of the house in Carpenter Street at such short notice,' she said.

She sat looking at Ruth, nervous that her misgivings had upset her friend. Ruth was so sensitive. But Ruth's benign expression didn't change.

'Don't you fuss over that. It's nothing to be concerned about. You'll soon be glad I made us pull up sticks and go.' Ruth heaved herself far enough out of the chair to reach across and pat her hand. 'I know it must be upsetting for you, all these changes coming one on top of another, but we'll soon get into our new routine, don't you fret.'

Thirty minutes! thought Joyce. We were out of there in thirty minutes! What could have forced us out in such a rush, with so little preparation? And not a word of explanation at the time, nor even a mention of it since they had moved into their new abode. No wonder she had lain there with the streetlight glaring through the curtains, wondering what had caused such an upheaval. But in the daylight, and with Ruth's reasonable words sounding soothingly in her ear, it didn't, after all, seem such an extraordinary thing. She trusted Ruth. She had to. She had met her at such an anxious time in her life, at a point where she was so confused and in desperate need of a friend. And Ruth, who was quite wonderful, had accepted her on the spot, and then taken her under her wing. Ruth's very solidity, as she sat encased in the green chair, her feet in their sensible lace-ups set squarely on the beige carpet, was a guarantee of her reliability. And over sixty years' practice at compliance with others' wishes meant that Joyce was not very good at arguing her own point of view.

'It is a very nice flat, certainly,' she said, reassuring herself as much as Ruth.

She looked around at the newly magnolia-painted room to reinforce the point. A pebble-dashed post-war semi had been converted into two flats, and theirs was the upstairs one, with two small bedrooms, a tiny kitchen and bathroom and a large, bright front room with a view across the park.

'The park isn't much to look at at this time of the year,' said Ruth, as though following her thoughts. 'But come February and March it'll be alive with daffodils and crocuses. You'll like that. There's nothing as cheering as a nice lively bunch of daffs, I always think.'

'And blossom on the trees. I love the sight of the pink blossom,' said Joyce. Ruth hadn't mentioned them, but Joyce imagined, too, the children who would run and shout and climb on the swings when the weather grew warmer.

'Perhaps we should get ourselves a little dog, so that you could take it for walks,' said Ruth.

'I don't think so. They can make such a mess, and their hairs get everywhere,' said Joyce, who believed that all animals belonged out of doors and had no place in a well-ordered home.

'It was time to move on, you'll see I'm right in the end,' said Ruth, shifting her weight forwards until she could stretch out a hand and help herself to a second custard cream. Her tone became more confiding. 'To tell you the truth, that place had been getting on my nerves. And the landlord was a right little bastard, if you'll excuse my language, dear.' The strong word sounded strange coming from Ruth's chaste, rosy lips.

'I'm sure you're right,' said Joyce, biting delicately into her third biscuit, and catching the crumbs neatly on her plate. 'What happened? Was he being a nuisance?' She hardly liked to imagine what kind of nuisance a man like Mr Bettony could be to a woman like Ruth.

'I'd complained about the roof,' said Ruth. 'I expect you'd noticed the damp patch on the bathroom ceiling when it rained.'

'I can't say I had. I'm not very good at practical things. I rely on my daughter and son-in-law for things like that. At least, I used to rely on them,' she corrected herself quickly.

'Well, the damp patch was there, and it was getting bigger. And he had the gall to tell me that if I wanted a few new tiles on the roof I could pay for them myself.'

'That doesn't seem right, certainly,' said Joyce. 'It's his responsibility to look after things like that. It's quite dreadful that he should ask you to pay.'

'I must admit that I lost my rag with him,' said Ruth meekly, not looking at all like someone who might lose their temper. 'I shouldn't have done that. It was wrong of me. And when he argued, I told him that he could keep his beastly flat, that I wouldn't stay there a minute longer.'

Joyce wondered for a moment whether 'beastly' was the exact word Ruth had used. 'I'm sure you were right,' she said. 'It doesn't do to let that sort of person gain the upper hand. But how did you find a new place so quickly?'

Ruth chewed thoughtfully on a mouthful of biscuit, then washed it down with her tea.

'Shall I add some hot water to this, or should we have a fresh pot, do you think?' she asked.

'It just needs a little top-up. I'll do it,' said Joyce, not wanting the major disturbance of raising Ruth from her chair, and she took the teapot out to the kitchen.

'I'll pour,' said Ruth, when she returned, and she did so, her plump pink hand curled elegantly round the handle. Such a refined person, thought Joyce. She's obviously come from a very nice background.

'Now, what were we talking about?' asked Ruth.

'The flat,' said Joyce. 'I was just wondering how you managed to find a new one at such short notice.'

'I'd been thinking of moving for some time,' said Ruth easily. 'I didn't really like that other place. And I'd been making a few enquiries of various acquaintances of mine, and I'd heard just that morning that this flat was free. Wasn't that lucky? There seemed no point in waiting around, so I arranged for us to move in straight away.'

Joyce wanted to ask about the lease, and when had Ruth signed it, but it seemed rude to be so inquisitive, so she held her tongue. Maybe in Ruth's world, among Ruth's friends and acquaintances, these things were managed differently from in her own staid past life.

Ruth smiled blandly at her across the table. Now that they were settled again, her face had lost its set, masklike quality and had regained its soft curves and upward-slanting lines. She always looked as though she had dusted her skin with peachy-pink powder that left her looking downy and vulnerable. It was a pity her lovely brown eyes were hidden behind the thick lenses of her glasses, for they were large and expressive. At least, they would be, Joyce was sure, if only she could see them properly.

'Will we be getting back to work soon?' she asked.

'Of course! We've just taken a few days' holiday,' said

Ruth comfortably. 'They'll be missing us, though. We'll see a few eager faces when we get back, I can tell you.'

'I do feel that my work is my salvation,' said Joyce.

'Quite right, dear. You have to cut yourself off from the wickedness of your former friends and acquaintances, and fill your mind with the Lord's words and works. Fast, pray, and spend your days in good deeds,' said Ruth, helping herself to the last chocolate biscuit. 'Don't look to left or right, just straight ahead at the path to the Light, that's what I say.'

'I do try,' said Joyce.

Ruth, so inactive today, would be transformed into a bustling, vigorous ball of energy when they returned to work.

'And of course, I do like to do what I can,' said Joyce. 'I like to dedicate my life to the Lord and to the work of his hands. I don't like to think I'm sitting here being lazy. I'm used to a busy life.'

'Don't worry, dear. You certainly contribute so very much.'

'And since you mention it, I'm a little worried about my contribution to our household expenses,' went on Joyce, who had been determined to raise this subject and now saw her chance.

'Don't let that worry you. It doesn't matter at all to me,' said Ruth, which wasn't what Joyce wanted to hear.

'But I should be paying half the rent of this flat. It's just that my pension is quite modest, and you haven't told me how much I owe you.' And she hadn't even begun to repay the money that Ruth had pressed into her hand that day.

'You keep your pension for your own personal requirements,' said Ruth. 'You need a bit of independence. You don't want to have to come running to me every time you want a new pair of tights or when the fancy takes you to eat a bar of chocolate, do you?'

Joyce struggled with her inherent good manners. She couldn't ask Ruth straight out how she was managing to pay for both of them. Suppose she ran into money difficulties? She compromised.

'You will let me know if there's anything I can do, won't you?' she said, hoping that Ruth understood what she was saying.

'Of course I will,' said Ruth. 'More tea, dear?'

'I shouldn't, really. I've had two cups already.'

'Go on, spoil yourself. There's plenty more where that came from. And then you can get out the ironing board and the spray starch and we'll make sure our uniforms are spruced up, ready for our return to work.'

'I'm looking forward so much to helping you again.'

'I'm sure you're a grand little ironer,' said Ruth. 'You deal with our uniforms and then you can help me with the fancy goods. I've got some lovely coloured tissue paper and shiny gold ribbon. I'll show you how it's done. It's all a matter of presentation, I've found. It makes such a difference, don't you think, when things look really nice?'

'Oh yes, appearances are so very important. I do agree with you,' said Joyce.

'It's the festive season, so we're making a special effort. I like to think that when one of my Sunshine Angels wheels her trolley into a ward, then hearts are uplifted to the Lord.'

'I will try to do my bit.'

'And you won't mind if I ask you to pop out for an hour or two this afternoon, will you? I've got someone coming in for a little business talk . . .'

Joyce had inadvertently raised her eyebrows and Ruth paused.

'Just a little chat about my pension,' she said. 'You wouldn't mind leaving me a little privacy, would you?'

'Of course not!' said Joyce hastily. 'A nice walk in the fresh air will do me good.' Ruth was so very much younger than she appeared that Joyce had trouble remembering that they weren't in fact contemporaries. But she supposed that it was only sensible for a woman in her thirties to sort out her pension, especially if she was self-employed. At least, Joyce assumed that Ruth was self-employed.

'Before you get going on the ironing, do you think you could pass me over my knitting,' said Ruth. 'I don't like to sit here with idle hands.'

Joyce took the knitting bag from the sideboard drawer. The garment Ruth was making, whatever it was, struck her as slightly repellent. Ruth favoured green plastic knitting needles and a yarn that looked faintly organic, as though it was spun from the entrails of sheep rather than from their fleece. The knitting appeared to grow in thickness as fast as it did in length, and Joyce couldn't imagine what it would eventually become. The thought that Ruth might be making something for her occurred to her briefly, but she dismissed it. Ruth's many generous actions were always directed at those who were truly in need.

4

Kate

'What was all that about?' Roz had put down her margarita and was looking interested. 'Is someone offering us a job?'

'That was Emma Dolby.'

'I'm sure you've mentioned that name to me before, but I've forgotten in what connection.'

'She lives in Headington with her husband and about a dozen children. When she isn't cooking meals or washing nappies she writes stories to amuse other people's children. She must be quite good at it since she gets them published, which isn't easy. She also runs an evening class for would-be writers, and does a bit of adult teaching in her spare time. And she has some connection with Bartlemas College – I think she must have been an undergraduate there – as she was helping to organize a study fortnight last year.'

'Was that the time someone fell off the tower with a funny name?'

'The Tower of Grace, it was called. That's the one.'

'And you're sounding acid about poor Emma because you're jealous of her Oxford education.'

'Possibly,' admitted Kate.

'It's time you prised that particular chip off your shoulder. You could have gone to university if you'd really wanted to.'

'Could I? I don't remember much encouragement from my schoolteachers at the time.'

'You weren't very keen on doing what was expected of you, admit it. And knowing your usual habit of exaggeration, I bet Emma has four children at the most.'

'I think it's probably five by now. She and Sam breed like rabbits.'

'You can't blame Emma because you're not married with children, either. You need to make your mind up about what you really want from life, and if the answer is "babies", then you should do something about it before you get too old, or you'll turn into a bitter old maid.'

'Thank you for your advice.'

'Is that what you'd describe as "a voice dripping with ice"?'

'I wouldn't dream of using such a cliché.'

'Really? I thought it was rather a telling phrase, and most appropriate for your tone of voice. Well, tell me what Emma wanted.'

'Sam – her husband – has been knocked off his bicycle and is still in hospital. She's trying to look after the kids and earn a decent living by taking on more teaching, presumably as well as writing children's stories. But the linchpin of the whole operation is her mother, who is a dependable type, still in sturdy middle-age, and who was looking after the children while Emma got on with her work. I'm expanding a little on what Emma said, you understand, but I think I've got it about right. And now she's mislaid her mother and she wants me to find her.'

'I should think we'd be quite good at that. What did you say to her?'

'You know what I said. You were listening. And what's with this "we"?'

'You'll need me to help you. What would you know about the thought-processes of the grandmother, the angst of the older generation?'

Kate laughed. It was difficult to see Roz as belonging to anything other than a youth culture, and a disreputable one at that. And angst wasn't usually a word to be found in her vocabulary. 'I should think I know at least as much as you do about the older generation. I can't see that you'd contribute anything at all to this search.'

'I'd be a second pair of feet,' said Roz. 'I can walk the streets and look as well as you can. I can ask questions. I can be very nearly as objectionable as you to total strangers. What more do you want?'

'Can you make me one of your margaritas? And do they really mix with chocolate biscuits?'

'Everything mixes with chocolate biscuits. It's one of the basic rules of gastronomy.'

It was a pity Emma didn't have Roz's sense of humour. She needed to lighten up and stop being so deadly serious about everything. Perhaps it was the result of that expensive Oxford education. There might well be advantages to the lightweight education that she, and Roz before her, had received. Even before Sam's accident, Emma tended to be deeply earnest about her life. But then, she was unlikely to abandon her raft of children when they were barely out of childhood to go gallivanting around the world, the way that Roz had.

Kate said, 'I must think how to approach Emma on the subject of money when I ring her back. I gather she can't afford much, but we professionals have our principles. We can't go offering our services for free, not even to friends.'

'Quite right,' approved Roz. 'If we don't find her mother for her she'll be unable to earn her living, so we must be worth hard cash to her. And remind her that this fee will have to feed and clothe two of us.'

'I think I might omit that part of the bargain. It'll be our little secret for the moment. I'll break it to her gently, after a week or two. Emma finds *me* irresponsible and flippant. Just think what she'd make of *you*!'

'What a foolish woman she seems,' said Roz, and went out to the kitchen. Kate heard the promising sound of glugging, as of tequila from a bottle.

'Here. See how you get on with this.' And Roz handed her daughter a misted glass of pale, pleasantly alcoholic liquid.

'Yum,' said Kate. 'I could get seriously addicted to this.'

'I'm glad you're managing to acquire a few bad habits under your mother's influence.'

'Do you realize that we've been living under the same roof for nearly three months now?'

'As long as that? And we haven't come to fisticuffs yet. We must both be growing mellower.'

'And older,' said Kate.

'Nonsense. I refuse to grow any older,' said Roz. 'And you're still far too young to do so.' Logic of the conventional variety had never been one of Roz's strong points. Her own brand of logic was incontrovertible.

Growing bolder as she drank her margarita, Kate said, 'If you could be serious for a moment, I'd like to know where you've been for the past ten years.'

'Didn't you get my postcards?'

'They weren't particularly informative. And then I'd like to know more about my father. My memories of him are from when I was a child, and quite vague. He wasn't very warm and forthcoming as I remember him. But I never knew him through an adult's eyes. What would I think of him if I met him now? How did the two of you get on? Why did you take off after he died?'

'I didn't leave immediately,' said Roz reasonably. 'I waited until I thought you were old enough to survive on your own. I didn't abandon you on the steps of an orphanage, now, did I?'

'No, but you disappeared for a few years, came back briefly –' *like you have now*, she wanted to add – 'and then went off again for another ten years. I'd like to know who you are.'

'That's the trouble with you. You know the characters in your books inside-out. You have complete control over their lives. That may be normal for a fiction writer, but it's not real life. We can never know other people the way we know characters in a book. Perhaps we can't even know ourselves that way. Knowing another person completely is an illusion, and a very seductive one. But don't confuse your fictional world with the one we both live in. Let's just get used to one another for the time being. When we get tired of that, we can move on.'

'*You* can move on. I live here,' said Kate.

'I was talking figuratively. But if you decide to stay here for ever, well, that's your choice . . .'

At this moment Susanna emerged from behind the sofa and climbed on to Roz's knees, digging her claws into the black velvet of her long skirt.

'Traitor,' said Kate.

Susanna shot her a triumphant glare through her slitted yellow eyes, then set about some serious purring.

'You'll have orange hairs all over your black skirt,' said Kate.

'They'll brush off. Now, Kate, what are you going to do about your friend Emma?' Roz was scratching Susanna behind her ears in the way the cat found particularly pleasing.

'I'm thinking of saying yes.'

'Good. I need something to stretch my brain.'

'So we're acting as a twosome, are we?'

'Of course. How else are you going to find out about me?'

Kate looked at her mother for a moment. 'You may have a point there. You think I should search for my own mother as well as Emma's?'

'That sounds a little fanciful – the sort of thing a romantic novelist might come up with. I was merely suggesting that by working together over time we might come to know one another a little better. I might even drop a few precious nuggets of information about my past into your lap from time to time. Isn't that what you were wanting?'

'Yes. Very well.' Kate frowned. 'But I'll have to find out how much money Emma's prepared to offer before I agree to take on the project.'

'That's the second time you've said that. What's up? Are you having money worries? Do you want me to lend you a fiver?'

'No, not right at this moment. But you know what the writer's life is like. I don't trust the good times. Who knows when the fickle butterfly of the reading public will flit off to sip the nectar from some new literary blossom? I'm going to drink my margarita and finish that packet of biscuits, and then wait until tomorrow morning to look at my bank statement.'

'Well, when you've finished pigging out on chocolate, I should just give Emma a ring, if I were you.'

5

Joyce

Ruth and Joyce sat companionably in their armchairs. Ruth clicked her knitting needles and Joyce finished her cup of tea. Ruth had switched on a lamp, for the morning was overcast and dark, and the light reflected off her thick lenses, giving the impression that she came from some other, alien planet.

Whatever Ruth was thinking about must have been calm and untroubling, for her expression was serene, thought Joyce. And yet she found her friend's thought processes opaque. At that moment some passing notion tugged Ruth's lips into a smile and her needles clicked faster than ever.

Joyce's own thoughts were chasing themselves around inside her head and troubling her. She would just have to open the tricky subject of her daughter with Ruth. Perhaps her friend would help her to decide what to do. But for the moment it was impossible to break through that tranquil exterior and bother her with her own problems. She picked up the tray and took it out to the kitchen. It was always easier to get on with the practical things in life than to worry about abstract questions.

'Would you like me to help with the washing-up?' called Ruth from her chair.

'It won't take me a tick,' called back Joyce. And she washed, dried and put away the cups and saucers.

When she returned to the sitting room Ruth was still concentrating on her knitting, plump hands cradling the needles, dark head bent over her work. She was chewing her lip with the effort, which distorted her face into something . . . Joyce wasn't sure what, but for the first time since they had met, she felt a qualm about leaving her home and former life so precipitately.

'While I'm out I think I'll give my daughter a ring, just to let her know I'm all right.' She spoke in a rush, as though afraid that Ruth would argue with her.

'You didn't give her the Carpenter Street address, did you?'

'No. I haven't spoken to her since I left,' said Joyce rather sadly.

'And you won't give her this address either, will you?' Ruth sounded quite sharp.

'Not if you don't want me to,' replied Joyce.

'I wouldn't like outsiders calling in until I've got the place just the way I want it.'

It seemed to Joyce that the flat was as tidy as anyone could wish, even after such a short time, but she only said, 'I'd better check that I have enough change for the call.'

'Coins won't be good enough. You'll need one of those phonecards,' said Ruth. 'We'll get you one next time we go into town.'

'Unless . . .'

'Unless what, dear?'

But Joyce felt awkward asking whether she could borrow Ruth's mobile phone. She had only noticed it by accident and perhaps Ruth hadn't mentioned it because she didn't want her to get into the habit of making calls from it. She believed that these things could be very expensive. She had overheard Ruth, only an hour or so ago, talking very animatedly into its flat grey box, telling someone, *You'd better move your . . .* she wasn't sure that she had heard the next word correctly . . . *and get the sorry* (or a word very like it) *thing off the premises by midday tomorrow. Everything is fixed for its disposal. All you have to do is bring round the pick-up and follow instructions. Hills will come with you. She'll have the new carpet and she's a great little cleaner so there's nothing to worry about in that direction. Surely it's not too much to ask, is it?*

But then she had felt guilty at eavesdropping and had scuttled back into her own room and closed the door very gently. No, she couldn't ask Ruth about her mobile phone. It would be too embarrassing.

'Yes, very well. It can wait for a day or two, certainly,' she said. The idea of phoning her daughter was fading by the minute. How would she explain why she had had to leave and what she was doing now? She couldn't possibly pile any more worries on to the poor girl's shoulders, not at the moment. And she felt ashamed at confiding in anyone. She didn't even know what words to use. She would ring later in the week, when she'd worked out what to say. Or maybe she'd send a postcard instead. She needn't put her address on a postcard, after all, and the postmark would give little away.

Ruth was taking no notice of her deliberations. All her attention was on her knitting. She had a habit which irritated Joyce, although she would never mention it, of humming between her teeth so that she produced a monotonous *zzzzzz* noise. It was difficult to tell what the tune was meant to be, but the noise could be *penetrating*. It interrupted her train of thought and made it very difficult to make any decisions at all. Joyce found the best way of stopping her was to break in with a question that required an answer.

'Don't you need a pattern for your knitting?' she asked now.

'I keep it all in my head.' Ruth was counting stitches and

tutting with irritation. 'I must have dropped one,' she said.

'How awful.' Joyce tried to sound sympathetic, paused a moment to ascertain that Ruth was humming again, then went on. 'But I was just wondering. I can't help thinking about it, Ruth, you'll have to forgive me if you think I'm making too much of this. But the other morning, in the old flat in Carpenter Street, was the landlord there when I came in?'

'What makes you think that?'

'Just a funny feeling.' Joyce spoke hesitantly. It seemed a foolish thing to say, now that she heard the words aloud.

'Oh, goodness no!' exclaimed Ruth heartily, picking up an errant loop of yarn and incorporating it into her work. 'Mr Bettony was long gone by then.'

She had at least stopped her monotonous humming, Joyce was relieved to notice.

6

Kate

November is not kind to Fridesley.

In April the straight lines of its brick houses are softened by the fuzz of new leaves on the trees. Seen through a veil of plum and cherry blossom, it is – very nearly – attractive. In June and July the eye is dazzled by the flaring orange and febrile pink of its roses. (The inhabitants of Fridesley do not, on the whole, appreciate the subtler tones of blush and cream.)

But in November the sharp winds come knifing across Port Meadow, freezing and then dispersing the hardy birdwatchers on The Postle, and scattering the dead leaves along the pavements. And then Fridesley's skeleton trees and bony shrubs reveal the yellow brick and grey rendering of its undistinguished architecture in all its ugliness. Cars sit mud-splashed and rusting along Marjorie Road. There is always, somewhere in Agatha Street, an overflowing skip, containing at least one stained mattress leaking its kapok stuffing.

Things are rather better in the southern half of Fridesley, the part that sprawls back from the main road and whose short, straight streets march towards the parish church of King James the Martyr. This nineteenth-century building, masquerading as Norman, stands squat and unlovely in its overgrown churchyard, its sagging roof beneath the unremitting rain threatening ever larger bills for its beleaguered vicar. But in this half of Fridesley there are Austrian blinds at the windows, and polished brass door-knockers on the white-painted doors, and the well-brushed dogs are not allowed to roam free and unattended as they are in Agatha Street, Doyle Terrace and Marjorie Road.

'I can't imagine why you chose to live in this part of town,' grumbles Roz, looking out at wet brickwork and weeping privet.

'It's cheap and it's close to the town centre,' says Kate concisely. She might have added that she likes its social mix, the way it thumbs its nose at Authority, the way its dogs pee against any new and shining car that dares to park in its narrow streets.

'It's dirty and crime-ridden,' says Roz.

'That is the price I pay for being close to civilization.'

'I'm off to find a decent newspaper,' says Roz, pushing aside Kate's *Guardian*.

'Why, do you want something more right-wing?'

'I want something with decent coverage of the racing,' says Roz and wraps herself in a voluminous scarlet raincoat before leaving the house. 'I shall make us both rich.' And then, as a parting shot, 'One of us has to do it.'

She crosses the main road, pointedly ignoring the pelican crossing, dodging through the continuous stream of cars, throwing her brightest smile at drivers forced to stand on their brakes. She flings wide the door of the newsagent's and advances on the racks of papers.

Mrs Clack, the owner, glares at her and barks, 'Shut the door, will you? That wind goes through me like a scalpel through butter!'

'You poor thing,' says Roz, with mock sincerity.

Since it is November, Mrs Clack has wrapped her grey curls in a checked woollen headscarf, topped with a brown woollen hat. Behind Roz, another customer enters the shop and Mrs Clack goes through the same routine.

'Like a scalpel through butter,' says Roz sympathetically, and pays for her newspaper. Mrs Clack sniffs critically at her choice.

Back in Agatha Street, Roz settles herself down with a fresh pot of coffee and a pile of toast and butter – 'just to keep the wolf from the door until lunchtime.'

'Off you go, Kate,' she calls.

'Anyone would think it was *her* house, not mine,' mutters Kate, scowling at Susanna, who looks as though she will curl up next to Roz and lick the melted butter from the top slice of toast just as soon as Kate has left the two of them in peace.

Roz reads down the lists of runners with a pencil in her hand. There's more skill to this game than there is to playing the lottery, and more chance of mending the Ivory fortunes, she thinks.

Kate edged her car out into the line of traffic in the Fridesley Road and aimed for the centre of Oxford. Emma lived in the north-eastern corner of the city, but it wasn't worth taking the bypass once the rush hour was over. The road was greasy with the morning's rain, a mist coated her windscreen with a grey film that the wipers managed to smear across her field of vision. The heater was pumping out nothing but cold air as yet, and she wished she had worn thick socks and her sensible boots. She envied Roz, curled up on the sofa with a newspaper. Emma Dolby might live in a posher part of the town, but her central heating was unlikely to be as effective as Kate's.

Emma had taken it as a matter of course that Kate would fall in with her wishes when she rang her back the previous evening.

'I'd better come over to your place for a briefing,' Kate had said.

'Whatever for?' Emma had parried. 'Can't you just go out and look for her?'

'With a placard, you think, like those people at the airport? "Emma's mother" scrawled in black felt-tip on the inside of an old cereal packet. For goodness' sake, Emma, I don't even know your mother's name, let alone what she looks like.'

'All right,' Emma had sighed. 'I suppose you'd better come tomorrow morning. Eleven-thirty.'

'Fine,' said Kate, knowing that this meant that Emma was unlikely to offer her either coffee (too late) or lunch (too early). But then, if you had all those children, a husband in hospital, a missing mother and a living to make, you might well resent the five minutes it took to make coffee for a single, childless, able-bodied person like Kate.

'And before you ring off, Emma, can I just check that you've done the obvious things.'

'What, for example?'

'Reported her as missing to the police, asked around at hospitals, that sort of thing.'

'Of course I have. At least, I've tried the hospitals. But there's no need to bring the police into it. Mummy would hate to think that people like that were prying into her affairs. And anyway, they have far too many missing husbands and teenagers to search for to worry about someone as innocuous as my mother.'

Kate didn't ask what Mummy's attitude would have been to her own prying. And it didn't seem to have occurred to Emma that there might be anything suspicious in her mother's disappearance that the police might take a legitimate interest in. But there was no point in alarming her just yet. There could well be a quite simple explanation that

Emma, in her intellectual way, hadn't noticed. Her mother had probably remembered an appointment with her own dentist and caught the next train home. And come to that, where did she live when she wasn't looking after Emma and her family?

At the pedestrian crossing she revved the engine in neutral, hoping to encourage the heater. Already the traffic was building up towards the Christmas hysteria. To the people in the Oxfordshire villages this city wasn't a centre of academic excellence, but their nearest major shopping centre. From the Fridesley Road there weren't even glimpses of spires and towers. She might have been driving through any suburb to any town in central England.

She sat and drummed her fingers on the steering wheel in one traffic jam, tried to catch the eye of an interesting-looking man in an adjacent car at the next set of lights, and wished she had remembered to return her removable radio to its slot so that she could amuse herself with some music. The traffic advanced another few yards and stopped again. Oxford's car-owners were still ignoring all pleas to leave their vehicles at home and use public transport. The shivering, miserable figures she passed at the bus stops, craning their necks to see if a bus was anywhere in sight, doubtless wished that they, too, were inching their way forward in a closed tin box with the heater belching hot air over their faces and feet.

As Kate approached the town centre, the traffic slowed again as crowds of shoppers surged across in front of the cars, in defiance of the green lights. They were all wrapped up against the cold and rain: so many thousands of dun-coloured packages with pale faces and sour expressions. On her right rose Wren's elegant gate-tower for Christ Church, dwarfing the bowler-hatted custodian who guarded the entrance. But was he keeping the crowds of ordinary people out, or rather making sure that the members of the college could never escape back into real life? At this whimsical thought a gap opened up ahead of her, a car horn blasted behind her, and she removed her foot from the clutch and bounded forward, with only the lightest clashing of gears, towards Carfax. Anglo-Saxon kings had founded Oxford in the ninth century, as a bastion against the Danes. Modern Oxford was waging a similar defensive war, but with less success, against the motor car.

Kate sang tunelessly to herself. In spite of their argument yesterday evening, it seemed to her that she and Roz were establishing a new understanding. She wondered what it had been like for that volatile, quick-witted, butterfly of a woman to be married into middle-class respectability for a dozen years or more. The word 'stultifying' came into her mind. Could she blame Roz for escaping as soon as she could? *Yes. She could have taken me with her.*

Someone behind her hooted and she noticed that a gap had again opened up in the traffic in front of her. A bicycle overtook her on the inside, then wobbled slowly down the middle of the road ahead so that she had to follow at ten miles an hour, a trail of slow-moving cars in her wake. And then, at last, Kate could drive up a hill with comparatively free-flowing traffic towards Emma's house.

7

Roz

Roz was tapping her pencil against the list of runners for the two-thirty.

Tap.

It was hopeless trying to pick a winner for a steeplechase, she thought. You never knew when one of the stupid buggers would fall over and bring down your horse as it did so.

Anyway, her heart wasn't in it.

Tap, tap, tap.

Susanna, irritated, removed herself from Roz's lap and went to find a quieter sleeping-place.

Roz was thinking about Emma Dolby's mother. Much of an age with herself. But what sort of woman would she be after a lifetime of tending other people's needs? Roz tried to picture herself in Emma's mother's place. She tried to imagine forcing herself to enjoy washing and ironing, and cooking endless shepherd's pies, and cleaning the oven every week. Impossible. She would be sullen and resentful. Probably bitchy and interfering. But no, she'd have taken off with someone else's husband long before reaching that stage.

Maybe that was what Emma's mum had done. (And why couldn't Emma refer to her mother by her given name, like any civilized person? She was getting tired of thinking of her as 'Emma's mother' all the time, as though motherhood were the only way she could be defined.)

But then, if she was the sort of woman who insisted on being called by her first name, and who walked off with someone else's husband, she wouldn't have waited until her sixties, she'd have done it years before.

Like Roz.

And when Emma's mum finally returned – if she was still alive and capable of doing so – would Emma ever forgive her, or would there always be a shadow of doubt between them? *You let me down when I needed you.*

That's what had happened to her and Kate, after all. They had been living under the same roof since early September and were apparently getting on surprisingly well. But beneath the surface were all those unanswered questions: *where have you been and what have you been doing?* Probably, too, what Kate really wanted to know was why Roz hadn't taken her with her when she went. Kate's anger with her mother exploded from time to time, usually over some unrelated, trivial matter. Was Emma as angry as that?

Tap, tap, tap.

Roz threw the pencil into the fireplace, bundled up the newspaper and went out to put it in the recycling box. On her return she rescued the pencil and put it away in a drawer. They couldn't afford to be extravagant just yet.

I don't know why I went, she wanted to say to her daughter. I only know that I had to get away. I stayed as long as I could, really I did. I thought I'd done all I could for you, and if I hadn't, then I'd like to apologize. I don't understand my feelings, so how can I ever explain them to you? And if she didn't understand herself, what hope did they have of getting inside the mind of a stranger, Emma's mother?

Maybe there was some simple explanation for her disappearance.

I'm just off to Marrakech, I'll see you in ten years' time. Simple enough for you?

8

Kate

Sam Dolby's parents had bought this house in the days when such houses were to be had for just a few thousand pounds. And then they had died, sadly but conveniently, and left it to their eldest son and his expanding family. These days it must be worth an enormous sum, but it was impossible for Emma and Sam ever to realize this family asset. They would need to turn out all the cupboards and drawers and pack the contents into tea chests. They would have to organize themselves and their family's belongings into a whole fleet of removal vans. And where would they find another house large enough to accommodate them all?

Meanwhile, they lived here in shabby splendour, with Sam looking more worried and Emma more brittle whenever such things as holidays or new clothes for the children were mentioned.

The house was tall, wide and gabled, with a few rows of yellow bricks set in a Fair Isle pattern among the smoky red ones. Kate found a space to park in the same road, only twenty yards or so away. She walked briskly through the dilapidated wrought-iron gate into the front garden. Someone, probably Sam, had decided to gravel this area, but the weeds still pushed up through the stones and no one had bothered to pull them up. In the centre of the gravel, where one might have expected a rose bush, or perhaps even a magnolia, a red-and-yellow plastic tractor lay overturned and abandoned.

Kate crunched her way across the gravel towards the front door. The roomy, cobwebbed porch was a haven for discarded wellington boots and trainers, and two or three bicycles leaned against its outside wall. Large bay windows on either side of the porch looked out at her like hooded eyes.

Kate lifted the sad-eyed dolphin knocker and let it fall, then rapped once again, firmly, so that the sound echoed through the house. There was a long wait.

Emma Dolby eventually opened the door, called, 'I'm on the phone. Make your own way into the sitting room,' and clattered back down the tiled passage.

Kate entered the large room on her right. This was on the other side of one of the hooded eyes, and was as chilly as she had feared. She wondered whether she should turn on some of the lights to relieve the gloom, but reflected that Emma might well be economizing on her electricity bill. So she removed a pile of children's clothes from one end of the sofa, picked what looked like a half-sucked toffee from the balding velvet of the arm, and settled down to read *My Big Colour Book of Disasters* until Emma should disengage herself from the telephone.

'Oh good. You're here,' said Emma, entering the room and speaking as though Kate had kept her waiting.

Kate put her book down and sat looking eager and efficient, or so she hoped.

Emma had put on weight after the last baby and most of it had settled round her waist and hips, with a little left over to round out her chin and jowls. Her skin was dry and there were flakes of dandruff on the shoulder of her sweater. She wore faded jeans which had fitted her a couple of years ago, but were now held together at the waist with a large safety pin. She needed a decent haircut, but then she'd never made her appearance much of a priority.

'Sorry I'm such a mess,' she said, pushing back a lump of sandy hair that looked as though it had come into contact with creamed carrot. The remark was less an apology, Kate felt, than a criticism of her own French Connection top and Whistles trousers, which she had thought the ideal casual dress for visiting a family home. She could see now that the colours were too pale for safe contact with the surfaces in Emma's house.

'Well, what do you need to know?' asked Emma, sweeping aside a jumble of toys and seating herself in an armchair facing Kate.

Kate took a spiral-bound notebook and pencil out of her large handbag and prepared to make notes. 'First, I should like to know your mother's name,' she said mildly.

'Joyce Fielding,' said Emma. 'Do you want me to spell that for you?'

'No.'

'Is this going to take long? I wanted to prepare some material for tonight's class before getting the lunch ready.'

Kate headed a clean page with the name 'Joyce Fielding'. 'Not long. Age?' she asked. 'Description? What about a photograph? Any known friends locally, any haunts and habits?'

Emma clicked her tongue impatiently and rattled off the answers so that Kate had to scribble down the information and just hope that she would be able to read the scrawl back afterwards.

'She must be, oh about sixty, I suppose. Maybe sixty-four. I can't remember exactly. Her hair is mostly grey and always nicely cut and waved. She's five foot four and on the plump side. She dresses in a skirt and blouse with a cardigan. Her eyes are blue and she wears glasses for reading. I suppose I have a photograph somewhere. I'll have to look it out for you. Friends? I don't think so. She was too busy looking after the house and children. She used the local shop for oddments of groceries, though I told her it was much cheaper to do a big shop at the supermarket once a week. Haunts? Habits? I don't know what you mean. You really do talk nonsense sometimes, Kate.'

'Church?' asked Kate tersely, before Emma could wander off the subject. 'Did she sing in the choir?'

'She might have gone to church occasionally, I suppose. But I don't think she mixed with the rest of the congregation, and she didn't join the choir. She didn't have time.' Emma glanced at her watch. 'Is that all you need to know?'

'And what about her husband, your father, that is?'

'He died nearly twenty years ago.'

'And she didn't remarry?'

'Of course not! They were devoted. And she stayed faithful to his memory.' Emma glared at Kate as though daring her to think otherwise.

'Oddly enough, I've found that it's the devoted ones who, when widowed, do marry again quite quickly, as though they want to repeat the experience as soon as possible. It's the unhappily married who hang back.'

'I don't know where you get these odd ideas from. Is there anything else?'

'I'd like to look at her room,' said Kate. Then she added boldly, 'And I think we should discuss my fee.'

'Tell me how many hours of actual work you put in and I'll pay you sixty per cent of the rate I get for teaching. That's fair, isn't it?' She didn't give Kate a chance to reply. 'And I'm only paying for your work. You can drink coffee and chat to your mother on your own time.'

'Yes, miss,' said Kate primly.

'What? I do wish you wouldn't make these silly jokes all the time, Kate.'

'No, miss.' But Kate spoke under her breath this time. 'One more question before we move on. To be perfectly honest, I don't understand why you want me to work for you. You don't seem very impressed with my abilities, so why did you ask me?'

'I want you to find my mother,' said Emma impatiently. 'Isn't that what I've been saying?'

'But why *me*? You keep referring to my undisciplined mind, my coffee-drinking and gossiping habits. Why don't you ask someone more suitable to find your mother for you?'

'Well . . .' Emma thought hard for an unflattering moment. 'It's true that you have an untrained mind, but I suppose you do have a certain tenacity,' she said eventually. 'Once you get an idea in your head you don't let it go. And you know your way round this town the way I never could.'

'But you've lived here for years!'

'Sam and I live in a small section of Oxford. All the people we know have stable marriages, and children who learn to play the violin, and houses full of books. I only found out yesterday that there's such a place as a greyhound stadium just a couple of miles along the bypass. And I still don't understand what line dancing is.'

'You wouldn't want to,' said Kate.

'There you are. You've probably been going to the greyhound races for years. I expect you have a diploma in line dancing. And you seem to know all those peculiar neighbours of yours in Fridesley. I wouldn't know how to begin to talk to them. They'd just laugh at me. But you can speak their language and translate their glottal stops. And then there's the way you dress. You always seem able to pick up useful men who help you out when you get in a mess.'

'I do have a certain fatal fascination for the opposite sex,' smirked Kate.

'I don't know about that,' said Emma severely. 'Come upstairs and I'll show you Mummy's room.'

As Kate followed Emma as demurely as she could manage, Emma said, 'Mind that rollerblade,' and led the way down a broad passage. 'Here,' she said, opening a door. 'It's Abigail's room, really. She'd like to move back in. She hates sharing with Amaryl, but I've told them that Granny's bound to be back soon and she'd only have to move out again. She can't stay away much longer, can she?'

Kate could hear the desperation behind the question. 'I'm sure I'll soon find her and bring her back,' she said soothingly, and walked past Emma and into Joyce Fielding's room.

'I'll go and get that photo for you,' said Emma and to Kate's relief she left her to look round on her own. 'You'll be careful with her things, won't you?' Emma's voice floated back down the passage.

'Of course. Trust me, Emma.' *Trust me, Emma: I'm a writer of historical romances with a strong sense of curiosity and no experience whatsoever of finding missing grandmothers.*

Kate closed the door behind her and looked around. In that over-stuffed, messy, noisy house, Joyce Fielding's room was a haven of order and calm. She sat down in the only easy chair. She closed her eyes. It might have been her imagination but she could smell lavender, very faintly.

Joyce Fielding was such a stereotype of a dear little old-fashioned grandmother that she found it hard to believe in her, any more than she believed in fairy godmothers or dragons. Or, to be more precise, if she was such a perfect, lavender-scented old lady, then why had she disappeared and where was she now? Why hadn't she phoned, or written? She should have sent a postcard at the very least.

Even Roz had sent a postcard, eventually.

And Roz and this woman weren't so very different in age.

Emma had been a bit vague about how old her mother was, but Kate remembered quite well that Roz was fifty-eight. Or possibly fifty-nine by now. Not more than sixty-two, certainly. Sixty-four at a push. So why were they thinking of Joyce Fielding as a white-haired old granny when she might at this very moment be dyeing her hair red, wearing a swirling velvet skirt and sipping a margarita? If Roz were suddenly abducted by aliens, you would find traces of her about the house all right, from the coating of foundation mousse in the bathroom basin to the flash of bright silks in her wardrobe and the whiff of *Gitane* and cannabis smoke in the bedroom.

Kate opened her eyes and started to look around her properly.

The walls were painted a bright hyacinth blue. Presumably Abigail's taste rather than Joyce's. The walls were bare and clean. But Kate was sure that Abigail would have covered them with posters. Teletubbies or Spice Girls. Whatever the young and female were obsessed with at the moment. So Abigail had decamped with her posters, and Joyce had cleaned all the blue-tack marks from the walls.

By the window stood a three-drawer chest, painted green. Someone had stuck glittering stars all over it, but the top had just the light coating of dust that you would expect after a few days, not the months' or even years' ration of dust and cobwebs that coated the rest of the Dolbys' house. On the chest were displayed a hairbrush, a hand mirror and a small china box. Kate walked across to it, stared at the box and then lifted the lid.

Three hairpins, two paperclips and a darning needle stared back at her.

Well, Miss Holmes, and what do you make of that?

Nothing, thought Kate gloomily. Nothing at all.

She opened the drawers in turn. Sensible old ladies' vests

and knickers in sober whites and pinks were folded in piles. Tights, thirty or forty denier, mid-brown. Thick stockings, rolled into pairs. Handkerchiefs, ironed into crisp triangles. The smell of lavender was stronger here. Vests, blouses (cream or pale blue, ironed, folded), nightdresses (pink, long-sleeved, high-necked), pullovers (pastel colours). She had never seen such unalluring, anonymous belongings. And all so practical, so serviceable. Not a frippery in sight. Perhaps Joyce had woken up one morning, realized the dullness of her possessions, and indeed of her whole life, and moved out into a new, stunning, technicolour existence. Unlikely, she had to admit.

Kate was about to start, without much enthusiasm, on the wardrobe, when Emma returned.

'What are you doing?' she asked sharply.

'Trying to make sense of your mother and her disappearance. Isn't that what you wanted me to do?' Kate looked at her watch. 'Eleven minutes,' she said.

'Really, Kate! I don't know how you can be so insensitive! And why are you poking about in Mummy's things? She wouldn't like that at all. She was very particular about her privacy.'

'When I get her back into this room she can grumble about it all she likes. Meanwhile, I have to pick up every little clue I can.'

'And what have you found?'

'Nothing so far,' admitted Kate. 'Let's have a look at the photos.'

'Will one of these do? They're not very professional, I'm afraid. Just family snapshots.'

'They're fine,' said Kate, glancing at the informal family groups. Joyce was easy to pick out. She was just as Emma had described her, and indistinguishable from a thousand other grandmothers she might bump into anywhere in the city. Kate slipped the snapshots into her notebook. 'I'll get copies made and return the originals to you in a day or two.'

'Why do you need copies? You're not going to do something awful like stick them up on lamp posts, are you?'

'Don't worry. I only do that for lost cats. But a photo could be useful if I want to ask someone if they've seen her.'

'Ask whom?' asked Emma.

Kate sighed. Trust Emma to know the difference between who and whom. 'I don't know yet *whom* I shall be asking. I haven't had a chance to find out much about your mother, and until I do, I don't know where to start.'

Emma stood by the door, looking indecisive.

'Why don't you go and get on with your lesson plan?' suggested Kate.

'Yes. What a good idea.' Emma shot one final, suspicious glare at Kate and then left.

What was wrong with the woman? She was always a bit sharp, a little lacking in the social graces, and regarded Kate as clever but unreliable, but wasn't she even edgier than usual today? Kate didn't know whether to put it all down to her worries about Sam and her concern for her mother, or whether there was something more behind it.

As she sifted her way through the grey tweed skirts (sizes sixteen and eighteen), the beige raincoat, the navy jacket, the grey cardigans, Kate grew steadily more concerned. The very ordinariness of Joyce Fielding's possessions seemed to underline the unusual way she had disappeared into the blue. The woman she saw revealed in this room would never have left without a word to anyone.

As Kate stared at the two pairs of polished, low-heeled shoes in the bottom of the wardrobe, the brown tartan slippers aligned with the foot of the bed, the blue woollen dressing-gown hanging from a hook on the back of the door, she was forced to a single conclusion. Joyce

Fielding had not left of her own free will.

She checked the cupboard on the wall opposite the window, but this was crammed with what were obviously Abigail's possessions, cleared away to make room for her grandmother. The only thing left to search now was the small table by the window with the bookshelf above it.

The table was bare except for a biro and a ruler. Kate expected to find volumes of *The Bumper Book of Fun for Girls*, or whatever the young were reading these days, on the bookshelf, but this, too, had been cleared by young Abigail and contained six or eight of Joyce's books, their spines in a straight line. Kate read some of the titles: *The Plain Person's Guide to the Scriptures, Daily Prayers for Ordinary Folk, How Can I Tell Right from Wrong?* The others were in the same style and a prayer book and a Bible stood at the end of the row. Kate wondered about leafing through *How Can I Tell Right from Wrong?* for messages or clues to Mrs Fielding's secret life, but doubted that she would ever be able to return it to quite such a straight line on the shelf.

She considered the uncommunicative table. If Joyce Fielding had received any letters while she was staying with the Dolbys she hadn't kept them. If she had paid any bills she had thrown away the receipts. It did seem odd that she could have spent several weeks in this room without acquiring any papers at all. Kate thought of her own bulging files and boxes at home in the study in Agatha Street. *I could have filled a whole manilla folder in three weeks.* Didn't the woman jot down addresses or phone numbers, or even make a shopping list? Perhaps she had a diary or notebook and kept it with her.

She was about to leave the room, when one last thing occurred to her. She checked the waste-paper basket. At least in Emma's house you could be sure that no one would have emptied it during the past week, or possibly even during the past year.

A couple of crumpled pink tissues, a bent cotton-bud, the empty cardboard pack from a tube of toothpaste. And then, something gleaming like gold, nestling amid the dross. Kate picked it out and took it to the light. It was a small brooch, made from crude yellow metal, definitely not gold. On the back there was a pin but the ring it should have slipped through to fasten the brooch to a blouse or jacket was missing. Kate turned it over and looked at the front again. It was enamelled in simple colours and showed a pink, smiling face surmounted by golden curls, flanked by small white wings and crowned with the golden ring of a halo.

Taking the brooch with her, Kate went downstairs to find Emma.

'Does this belong to Abigail?' she asked.

'Let me see. Oh, goodness no, that isn't her style at all.'

'Or one of the other children?'

'I don't think so. I've never seen it before.'

'I suppose it might have come out of a Christmas cracker.'

Emma shook her head. 'It's too large and grand for the sort of crackers we have.'

'Do you mind if I take it away with me?'

'It's broken, isn't it? Whatever do you want it for?'

'I don't know. But it's the only thing in your mother's room that doesn't fit.'

'Oh, very well.'

'And did your mother keep any of her things anywhere else in the house?'

'What sort of things? I suppose she kept her toothbrush and flannel in the bathroom. And the powder she used on her teeth, of course.'

Kate ran an exploratory tongue over her own teeth. All

her own, thank goodness. 'I was thinking of papers, letters. Bills, maybe.'

'I don't think so. She was a very practical person. She wasn't much given to collecting papers of any kind.'

'And did she take her toothbrush and flannel with her? And the powder and glue she used on her teeth?'

'Now you mention it, I haven't seen her toothbrush. It was a bright-green one and I would have noticed it, I'm sure. Her flannel might have gone, but then again, it might have found its way into the linen basket—'

The door flew open at this moment, interrupting Emma's response, and a small child, of indeterminate sex and with the pugnacious looks of a successful wrestler, erupted into the room.

'Isn't it lunchtime yet?' it demanded.

'Five past twelve. There's another twenty-five minutes to go,' said Emma soothingly.

'What's twenty-five minutes?' demanded the child.

'Look at the clock, Ammie. When the big hand ticks its way down to the bottom, then it will be time for lunch.'

'I'm hungry,' said Ammie stubbornly. 'I'm hungry *now*.'

'You'll have to wait,' said Emma patiently.

'Who's that?' Ammie pointed at Kate.

'This is my friend, Kate Ivory. And this is Amaryl.' So the wrestler was female.

Amaryl studied Kate for a disconcerting minute or two.

'Is her hair real?' she asked.

'Most of it,' replied Kate.

'Go and play with Tristan's Action Man. I'm sure he won't mind,' suggested Emma.

'Oh yes he will. I lost one of its legs last time,' said Amaryl, but she took herself off anyway.

'She's got a bit of a rash,' said Emma. 'I thought I'd better keep her at home for today.'

'I'd better be going, too,' said Kate, hoping the rash wasn't something catching. 'I'll think over what you've told me and see if I can come up with a plan.'

'Please, Kate,' said Emma. 'Please just find her for me. I'm going out of my mind trying to cope with everything.'

'I do understand what you're going through,' said Kate carefully, aware that she was about to trample all over Emma's emotional toes. 'When Roz disappeared all those years ago, I did feel very angry. I felt guilty about it at the time, but I can see now that it was a perfectly natural reaction.'

'Oh, spare me the amateur psychology!'

Kate was putting her notebook back in her handbag, checking that she had the photographs safely, and was carefully wrapping the brooch in her handkerchief when there was a ring at the front doorbell.

'Who can that be?' asked Emma and hurried out.

'George!' For once she sounded unaffectedly pleased to see someone and Kate waited with interest to see who this paragon could possibly be. When Emma returned to the sitting room with a man in tow, she thought at first that it was Sam. Then she realized that this man was younger than Sam, and thinner and less hairy about the face, and he was wearing quite respectable clothes and was altogether more fanciable than Emma's husband. He had hazel eyes and thick brown hair and a most attractive smile. Before Kate could get any further with her inspection, Emma said, 'This is George, Sam's brother. And *this* is Kate Ivory, but she's just leaving, aren't you, Kate?'

'Yes,' said Kate regretfully, scraping the dregs of her brain for a reason to stay and talk to the delectable George, but coming up with nothing suitable.

'Nice to have met you, George, even if briefly,' she said, twinkling at him in her most shameless fashion.

56

'I'm sorry you have to rush away,' he said, and sounded as if he meant it.

'I'll give you a ring, Emma,' said Kate, smiling into George's hazel eyes. Green, flecked with brown.

'Make it after five-thirty,' said Emma. 'I should have persuaded the children to sit down to a meal by then and they might be quiet enough for me to hear what you have to say.'

Kate left them in the sitting room and went outside to her car. Perhaps she could find a reason to come back and take another look at Joyce Fielding's room. She wondered whether George Dolby often came visiting his sister-in-law and her family. She did hope that he did. It would liven up this unpromising job no end if she bumped into him with any regularity.

On the drive back to Fridesley she considered the sparse information she had gleaned at Emma's house. All her musings on the charms of George Dolby faded from her mind as she considered Joyce Fielding and her unaccountable disappearance. She had very little to go on, but somehow she would have to find a way of tracing her. The more she thought about it, the more sure she was that Emma's mother was not the type to walk off without a word, and the more worried she was for Mrs Fielding's safety.

9

Emma

'I'll be with you in just a minute, George,' said Emma, leaving her brother-in-law in the sitting room, and disappearing into the cold, echoing spaces where she produced so many meals and washed so many clothes. 'Make yourself at home,' she called back down the corridor.

She sat hunched over a mug of coffee at the kitchen table, and munched on a special-offer biscuit. The grooves above her nose were more pronounced than ever, and her thick eyebrows met like two friendly caterpillars above her deep-set eyes. She sniffed, choked on biscuit crumbs, found a clean but crumpled handkerchief in the ironing pile and blew her nose. She needed to compose herself before going back to talk to lovely George, and she blamed it on Kate.

Why did Kate Ivory make her feel so dissatisfied with herself? It was partly her clothes, she admitted: those pale, clean, uncreased garments that wouldn't last five minutes in the Dolby household. 'Not one of them bought in Marks and Spencer's,' Emma muttered to herself. And then there was the way she could swan in and out of Emma's life at a moment's notice, as though she hadn't a care in the world, not a single responsibility. *I do believe she's taught that cat of hers to open its own tins of cat food.*

And another thing, she managed to get all those books published with only the skimpiest sort of education behind her, and made at least twice as much money as Emma did from her carefully pondered children's stories.

Don't be unfair, she scolded herself. Who was it who invited Kate into your house in the first place?

It was you, Emma, she replied. You phoned her, you asked her to help you find your mother. And what was wrong with Mummy for goodness' sake? What had got into the woman? What could possibly have induced her to go off like that, leaving her grandchildren to fend for themselves?

At the thought of all those helpless grandchildren alone in the wide world, Emma felt her eyes filling with tears. She looked for another clean handkerchief but failed to find one.

Oh, bugger that, she thought, I'll have red, swollen eyes as well as grubby clothes and an expanding waistline if I go on like this, and she pushed away the depleted biscuit packet and wiped her tears away with her sleeve.

Kate Ivory would never do a thing like that, she sniffled. Kate would have a clean handkerchief in her pocket, or a packet of tissues in the large and expensive leather bag that she always carried with her.

'What's up?' asked George, coming into the room.

'If I had a bag like hers it would be covered with splodges of ink (or worse) and filled with spare disposable nappies, or bottles of orange juice, a child's colouring book and a set of felt-tipped pens. Or a half-bottle of gin, more likely.'

'What are you on about? You're talking nonsense and you appear to be making yourself thoroughly miserable.'

'Kate Ivory makes me feel inadequate.'

'She does no such thing. You're making a perfectly good job of it all on your own,' George said good-humouredly.

'You know me too well, don't you?'

'I should do by now.' He ruffled her already-ruffled hair

as though she was one of the children.

'Thank you, George,' she said, beginning to feel better. 'Why are you hiding in the kitchen instead of making interesting conversation with me in the sitting room?'

'It's warmer in here. And it'll be even warmer when I turn the oven on,' said Emma, avoiding the awkward part of the question.

'Well, if you insist on sitting out here, please get cake-making or something. Anyone would feel miserable in a house as cold as this.'

Emma rubbed her cheeks with her sleeves to rid them of the last signs of self-pity and padded over to the cooker. She turned the oven on to high so that the orange light glared at her like a disapproving eye. Then she sniffed hard to stop her nose from running, and placed a bright smile on her face to fool George into seeing her as a happy, attractive woman who had no need to feel jealous of anyone, let alone Kate Ivory.

'I have a suggestion,' he said. 'Why don't you leave the oven on to warm the place up, but forget all about preparing a meal.' He raised a hand and made patting motions in the air to silence Emma's protests. 'And then, when the Dolby horde descends for lunch, I'll go and get us all a Chinese takeaway. How about that for a suggestion?'

'But it's such a waste to burn the electricity if I'm not cooking,' objected Emma.

'I'm buying lunch, and you'd be burning the electricity anyway, so nothing's wasted,' said George with a certain logic.

'I'm not sure about that,' said Emma doubtfully. 'But the big ones won't be back till four o'clock. There's only you, me and Ammie here for lunch, and little Jack.' Preparing a meal for four people was a bagatelle for Emma.

'Nevertheless, little Jack could eat something ready-prepared in a jar, and the rest of us could eat Chinese.'

'All that monosodium glutamate,' said Emma lugubriously.

'It won't do us any harm just this once.'

'Are you sure?' Emma allowed herself to be convinced. 'Thanks, George.'

'Anyone could get a bit down in your situation. It's only natural.'

'Apart from cheering me up, was there anything else you came round for?' enquired Emma.

'I thought I'd see whether you needed any help. I know I'm not as practical as Sam, and I haven't much of a clue about children, but I'm probably teachable.'

Emma found herself smiling. 'Sam's not much good at practical things, either. I've always been the one who mended fuses and put up bookshelves. But I do miss his support. I just miss *Sam*, I suppose.'

George passed over a clean handkerchief, since Emma's eyes were brimming with tears again.

'And then Mummy had to disappear and I'm all on my own,' said Emma when she'd dabbed at her face.

'Perhaps I can help to find Joyce. Tell me what you've done about finding her so far, and then I'll see if I can come up with any useful suggestions.'

'I can't imagine where she can be, and why she should have gone off like that,' said Emma dispiritedly. 'I did try the hospitals, in case she'd had an accident, but no unidentified woman answering her description had been taken in. I didn't want to contact the police.'

'I suppose you've tried her flat?'

'Yes. I didn't like to think that she'd just gone home, but I did ring her there and there was no reply.'

'Maybe she'd popped out for a pint of milk.'

'I rang lots of times. She wouldn't have been out at ten o'clock at night.'

'That's true.'

'And I have her neighbour's number, in case of an emergency, and I rang that, too. But apparently no one's seen her since she left to come to Oxford.'

'Neighbours can be mistaken.'

'But I've rung her flat every morning with no response. I thought she might find her way back there eventually, even if she didn't come here. I even got BT to check the line in case there was something wrong with it. And all I could think of in the end was ringing Kate Ivory to see if she could find her.'

'That's the woman I met as I arrived?'

'Yes. I hoped she could help.'

'Why? Is she a private detective? She didn't look much like one to me.'

'She's a novelist of sorts. She writes outlandishly inaccurate romantic historical things which seem to make enough to pay her mortgage and provide her with food and drink. But every now and then – much too often, really – she gets involved in some mystery or other, as though she were an urban Miss Marple.'

'She looked a bit young to play Miss Marple just yet,' said George mildly.

'I'm sorry. Put my acid tongue down to jealousy. I just wish I could look as good as her in a simple pair of trousers and a jacket.'

'You look lovely to me,' fibbed George. 'And I think you're going through a very tough time. I doubt whether your friend Kate Ivory could cope with all that you're doing.'

'You're right. She couldn't,' said Emma, cheering up. 'Anyway, what I've done is ask her to find Mummy for me. She knows her way around this town. And she's got the time on her hands to make enquiries.'

'I'm sure she'll soon find her. She looked quite competent to me,' said George.

'I don't know about competent, but she is an incurable nosy parker,' said Emma. 'And she never minds asking questions of complete strangers. I could never do that sort of thing, I'd be much too embarrassed. But Kate has a thick skin, so she'll manage it much better than me.'

'Haven't you any idea why your mother left?'

'No. It's completely incomprehensible,' said Emma, polysyllabic even when upset.

'Remind me. What happened exactly? She left in the afternoon?'

'She gave the two little ones their lunch, then took them for a walk in the park. I believe she let Ammie play on the swings for a bit while Jack sat in his buggy, then she came home again. Nothing unusual happened. I know, because I asked the children to tell me about it. She just settled Ammie and Tris down with a Disney video for half an hour while she dealt with the day's laundry. I'd had a good morning, getting on with some work, and was feeling really happy. The children love being with their granny so they hadn't bothered me at all. At about three o'clock, Mummy left the house. I thought she was just going out to the shops. She didn't mention how long she'd be, but I assumed she'd be gone for about twenty minutes. I went to read a story to Ammie and Tris, since their video had ended. I thought she'd be back by the time I got to the end. But she wasn't. And that's the last I saw of her.'

'Are you sure there's nothing else? Anything you remember might help us to find her.'

'I think I heard something while I was reading to the children. I can't be sure, though. My mind was on the story, not on what was happening outside the room. But it might have been a click of the door, the sound of her feet on the stairs. Maybe I'm remembering from some other occasion. But I should have called out. I should have made sure that she was all right.' Tears started to trickle down Emma's face. 'Do you think she's all right? She is all right, isn't she George? She'll be back.'

'Of course she will,' said George. 'It's just some sort of misunderstanding. And you're sure that nothing out of the ordinary happened that day, or even the day before?'

'I don't think so. But then, I was at the hospital visiting Sam that last evening, and he seemed to be progressing so slowly, and my mind wasn't really on what was happening here at home.'

'I'm sure you'd have noticed if something had been up with one of the children,' said George.

'But I wouldn't have noticed if Mummy was upset. Is that what you're saying?'

'Of course you would have noticed. She's your mother.'

'No, you were right the first time. If she'd been one of my children I'd have noticed immediately if anything was wrong. But just because she's my mother, I took no notice. Maybe she was a bit quieter than usual. Maybe I've got it all wrong. I can't even remember whether she was cheerful or not when she left the house that last time. I don't really know what she was wearing, except that it can't have been anything out of the ordinary. I'd have noticed that. How is anyone going to find her with so little to go on?'

'Perhaps your friend Kate will find out something for us. When did you say she'd be calling here again?'

'I didn't. She's going to phone me later this afternoon.'

'I suppose she has a husband or something at home.'

'Not as far as I know. She's unattached, I think. Or loosely attached, perhaps. Who knows with Kate? I believe she has her own mother staying at the moment. But don't get involved with her, George. She isn't nearly good enough for you. She doesn't know what commitment means. She leaves a trail of broken hearts behind her wherever she goes.'

'I can't believe that.'

'Men never can. That's their tragedy.'

George laughed. 'She looked a thoroughly nice person to me.'

'And men are always taken in by a woman's looks: if a woman has blonde hair she must be a warm-hearted paragon.'

'But she doesn't have to be a cold-hearted bimbo either,' said George reasonably.

'By the way, shouldn't you be at work?' asked Emma, resolutely changing the subject.

'Probably. But I've sent them all away on a field trip, so I've taken the afternoon off.'

'And you're spending it with me!' Emma was touched.

At this moment Ammie came into the kitchen.

'I'm really hungry now,' she said in her assertive voice. 'And Jack's getting hungry, too. It *must* be time for lunch by now.'

'Of course it is,' said George heartily. 'And you can come in the car with me and help choose our lunch. While we're out, Mummy will open a jar of baby food and spoon it into your little brother.'

'Are we going to get some junk food?' asked Ammie eagerly. 'Mummy doesn't let us.'

'Definitely not junk food,' said George. 'But perhaps not exactly Mummy's usual healthy fare.'

'Oh good,' said Ammie. 'Come on then, Uncle George. I like your car better than riding on the back of Mummy's bike.'

'Goodbye!' called Emma from the kitchen, in quite a cheerful voice for her. 'And don't say I didn't warn you about Kate Ivory!'

* * *

Later, at about five-thirty in fact, Emma's telephone rang.

'I'll get it,' said George, since Emma was busy arguing with her older children over their homework.

'Hello. It's Kate Ivory here.'

'This is George Dolby. We met briefly on the doorstep, as it were.' George looked for a chair to sit on while he indulged in a long conversation, but failed to find one.

'I rang to ask a few supplementary questions about Joyce Fielding.'

'Emma's rather tied up at the moment. Why don't you let me write them down, and find out the answers from Emma. Then I could ring you back.' That's clever of me, he thought. Now she'll have to give me her phone number.

'I'd better give you my phone number,' said Kate.

10

Kate

'There are two possibilities that I can see,' said Kate.

Roz wasn't listening to her. 'What on earth is that dreadful noise?' She was staring at the window in disbelief.

Kate pushed the curtain aside and looked down into Agatha Street. In the space between her own car and the lamp post sat a mud-splattered white pick-up truck. Someone had written 'CLEAN ME' in the dirt along the side. In the back were thrown an assortment of unidentifiable tools and coils of wire. A thick-set man of about thirty-five sat slumped in the cab. He had a shaved head and an unusually short neck. He was listening to the van's stereo cassette-player at such high volume that the cab itself appeared to pulsate. As she watched, he lifted a red-and-white can to his mouth and drank.

'Well?' asked Roz, an increasingly pained expression on her face.

'Oh, that's just Jason,' said Kate, letting the curtain fall back into place. 'He's been living next door with Tracey since her husband left. But now Tracey and Jason – generally referred to as "Jace", by the way – have started to fall out. You will, from time to time, hear their arguments in embarrassing detail through our shared wall. From what I've heard recently, and if her past record is anything to go on, I'd say that Tracey is about to throw Jason out for good.'

'And how does that explain the appalling racket?'

'When Tracey throws him out for the evening, he retires to the van and listens to head-banger music and drinks lager to drown his sorrows.'

The red-and-white can came hurtling through the side window of the pick-up, hit the low wall in front of the neighbouring house and rattled its way into the gutter.

'I might go and have a serious row with him myself. How long is he likely to remain there?' asked Roz.

'All night, if Tracey's feeling really narked with him. If she's in a forgiving mood, she may let him back indoors in the next hour or two.'

'Let's hope that she relents soon, or I'll go and tear his head off and then have my own argument with Tracey.'

'Actually, the Venns have been rather subdued since we returned from Gatt's Hill.'

'The Venns?'

'Well, the Toadface family if you prefer it. Tracey, Harley, Shayla, little Toadface – that's the ugly toddler with the raucous laugh and homicidal tendencies – and their mongrel dog, Dave. Harley and Dave nearly took up residence here in my house at one point. Harley showed signs of becoming the white sheep of the Toadface family. I introduced him to strange objects, like books, and another friend of mine made sure he did his maths homework. He showed talent in that direction, apparently. We were making good progress before the tragedy and I hope to take up where we left off after Christmas, but I haven't got within chatting distance of him since we returned from Gatt's Hill. I've caught sight of him inspecting you from a distance and sliding off down the road again, and Dave once came snuffling round to the back door, heard your voice, and legged it back home. So I think you're the one who's scared them away.'

'*Moi*? I wouldn't scare a mouse. I think you'll find that Harley and Dave have started to notice the existence of females of their own generation and respective species. Their defection is quite natural and has nothing to do with me.' As if to prove her point, Roz at this moment was joined by Susanna, who settled herself neatly on Roz's velvet-covered knees, tucked in her paws and closed her eyes in contentment. In case Kate hadn't got the message, she opened her yellow eyes briefly, glared scornfully at her nominal mistress for a few seconds, and then settled back to purr on Roz's knees.

'All right, Susanna,' said Kate. 'What can I say? I'm really sorry that I left you for those weeks . . . well, *months* if you're going to be picky about it.'

'What on earth are you on about?' asked Roz.

'Just getting back into apologetic mode.'

'I wish you'd get into bloody-minded mode and tell that man to turn his cassette player down.'

'I wouldn't dare,' said Kate. 'I only pick on people smaller than me. Have you seen the muscles in his neck?' But luckily, at this moment Jason changed cassettes, switched on his engine, played around with the accelerator for a while, then drove erratically away in a cloud of blue smoke. They heard the bass thumping away down the Fridesley Road until it was finally swallowed up in the traffic noise.

'Now, where had we got to?' asked Roz.

'I was telling you about my visit to Emma's place.'

'Right, well, get on with the story.'

'You don't feel like making us a margarita each to oil the narrative flow?'

Roz smiled her assent and disappeared into the kitchen from whence came the clinking of glasses, bottles and ice and other promising sounds.

'I have some rather nice little Greek olives here,' said

Kate. 'Will they go as well with the margaritas as chocolate biscuits, do you think?'

'The second law of gastronomy is that Greek olives – they are those lovely plump little black ones, flavoured with basil, aren't they? – go with absolutely everything that one would wish to eat or drink, with the possible exception of strawberry ice cream.'

'To return to Joyce Fielding,' said Kate.

'Who?'

'Emma's mother. That's her name.'

'Ok. I'm with you.' Roz reappeared with their drinks and a silver cocktail shaker in case they needed refills. 'You're running out of Cointreau, by the way.'

'I'll put it on the shopping list. Now, Joyce Fielding appears to be the most conventional member of the English middle-classes you can hope to meet.'

'I'm not sure that I do hope to meet her, then,' said Roz unsympathetically.

Kate ignored this comment. 'She has been widowed for twenty years and, according to Emma, there hasn't been another man in her life after Mr Fielding.'

'She can't have been much past forty when he died. Do you believe that about the constant, grieving widow?'

'Yes, I do. And if you'd seen her underwear drawer, not to mention the contents of her bookshelf, you'd believe it too.'

'How depressing,' said Roz, who hadn't been far short of forty herself when she was widowed, and who had certainly not spent the past twenty-something years grieving for the defunct Mr Ivory in celibate isolation. Her underwear drawer did not contain a single pair of pink or white cotton knickers, nor vests of any colour. She stretched out her slim ankles and admired her lustrous patterned black tights. 'What happened to that nice policeman friend of yours, by the way?'

'Why are you changing the subject?'

'I didn't think I was. And dear Tim. I thought he was rather keen on you.'

'Who?'

'Tim Widdows. Your friend, the vicar at Gatt's Hill.'

'That's all he was. Just a friend.'

'You could have fooled me. And there's some more of this if you'd like it.' Roz rattled the cocktail shaker enticingly.

'Yes please,' said Kate, passing across her glass.

Roz emptied her own glass, then said, 'Very well, you can carry on about the astonishingly boring Mrs Fielding now.'

'Everything in her room was so neat, in contrast with the rest of the house. She seemed to be the still centre in that maelstrom of screaming children and demanding adults.'

'Surely you're exaggerating,' said Roz.

'I'm trying for some graphic description,' said Kate, sipping appreciatively at her drink. 'I am supposed to be a writer, after all.'

'Of course you are,' agreed Roz without conviction. She was helping herself to olives and then licking the oil from her chin with her long tongue.

'There was nothing in her room that was out of character, nothing that told me anything at all about her, apart from her crushing conventionality, except for this.' And Kate rescued the angel brooch from its handkerchief nest in her handbag and showed it to her mother.

'Hideous,' said Roz. 'It proves that the woman has no taste.'

'It was in her waste-paper basket,' said Kate. 'Perhaps she agreed with you about its hideousness.'

'She threw it away because the pin's broken,' said Roz.

'What do you think it is? What does it mean?'

'I've no idea. But it does seem to be the only clue we have, so I suppose we'd better try to find out.'

'It looks like the kind of badge they give you when you join something like the Girl Guides,' said Kate after staring at it for a while.

'The Angels, perhaps? The Cherubs? The Small Fat People?' suggested Roz. 'I've never heard of any of them. Have you?'

'No. But they'd be connected with good works, don't you think? And that would fit in with the scant information we have about Joyce.'

'If you're right, there's a chance your vicar friend would know about them.'

'You ring him. He'll only think I'm encouraging him if I do it.'

'Very well. He won't be working at this time of day, will he?'

'Vicars only work on Sundays,' said Kate inaccurately.

Roz left the room and telephoned from the extension in the hall. She came back a few minutes later.

'He doesn't know. He doesn't think they're anything to do with the Church of England. But he did eventually admit that he might have seen something like our badge, only he can't quite place it at the moment. He'll ring back if he thinks of anything.'

'That's pretty useless of him.'

'Perhaps if you'd rung him yourself instead of leaving it to me, he'd have made more of an effort. I believe he did get the message that you didn't want to speak to him.'

'Oh, well, maybe I'll give him a ring in a day or two to see whether he's come up with anything.'

'Now,' said Roz, rearranging Susanna on her knees and helping herself to the last of the olives, 'let's have another look at it.'

They both stared at the brooch. The enamel blue eyes stared disingenuously back.

'It's very simple. Simplistic. Simple-minded, even. Perhaps it belonged to a child.'

'Emma reckoned that none of hers had ever had such a thing.'

'From the way you've described her, I'd have thought she wouldn't know one way or the other.'

'When it comes to her children, Emma is utterly reliable. I bet she knows what each of them eats for breakfast, which their favourite socks are, and which Disney film sends them to bed with nightmares.'

'What a strange view of parents and children you do have.'

They were getting dangerously close to their own past history.

'I suppose it could have belonged to a visiting child who discarded it when the pin broke. In which case we are no further forward,' said Kate.

'What would a visiting child have been doing in Joyce's room?'

'Good point.'

'A little earlier, before Jace interrupted us, you said there were two possibilities. What were they?'

'I don't believe Joyce Fielding is the type to run away and not inform her daughter she's safe. She knows Emma would worry herself sick. Not only that, but she must have known what problems she was making for her daughter by her absence. Either Joyce Fielding was forced to leave Emma's house by threats or through deception, or she left of her own free will and *then* was kept away, and prevented from communicating with Emma, by force. In either case, she's in danger.'

'Unless she's already dead,' said Roz.

There was an uncomfortable silence.

'No. No. I refuse to believe it. I'll find her,' said Kate,

shaking her head as though to emphasize her intention.

'There's one thing that struck me,' said Roz. 'Would you like to hear what it was?'

'Of course.'

'Emma overwhelms you with a torrent of words. I heard them pouring out of the phone when she was talking to you. Everything inside her head at a given moment seems to come spurting out, unedited. And yet she's told you very little about her mother. I know she's a friend of yours, but just how reliable is she?'

'She's not a close friend. In fact, all we have in common is our writing. She's someone to discuss sales with, or contracts. Apart from that, we have very little contact. I irritate her because I haven't settled down to marriage and motherhood. And all that messy, domestic side of her life leaves me baffled. As to how reliable she is, well, I'd have to say that I don't find her very perceptive when it comes to people. I'm sure she knows everything about children, but I think her judgement of adults is superficial.'

'So, she tells the truth as she sees it, but you don't think she sees very much.'

'Exactly. And if Joyce was going through some painful emotional experience, I wouldn't trust Emma to know what it was, or even to notice that it was happening.'

'That leaves plenty of room for speculation. But there are still some simple details that Emma could provide.

'There doesn't seem much to tell.'

'Exactly. That's the impression she's left you with. But there's a lot more that you need to know. For example, where did she live before Sam's accident? Has she a house, a flat, a room? And who's looking after it now?'

'I did ask her where Joyce lived, and she flitted off after something else.'

'Is there anything sinister in that?'

'I doubt it. She seems unable to concentrate on anything at all for longer than thirty seconds. That's what motherhood does for you.'

'Not necessarily,' said Roz tartly.

'Emma has a mind like an overflowing cupboard. She opens the door and a shower of oddments cascades on to the floor.'

'Interesting but unhelpful. And I was in the middle of a list of pertinent questions. I shall continue. What was her job before she retired? Does she keep in touch with her former colleagues? How well-off is she? And what other family members are there on the Fielding side? You mentioned meeting Sam's brother, George.'

'Only fleetingly,' said Kate wistfully.

'But what other relations does she have? Has Joyce Fielding escaped from Emma and gone to stay with another daughter, or daughter-in-law? Perhaps Emma is one of six daughters and one of them has called on Joyce with an even more pressing demand. Why hasn't Emma filled you in on this background?'

'Emma's mind was full of the baby, who was briefly sleeping, and Ammie, a female child as far as I could make out, who was demanding food, and who was afflicted with a worrying rash.'

'I do hope it wasn't catching.'

'So do I. And even Emma would have phoned round to her sisters, if she has such things, wouldn't she?'

'Not if she was feeling guilty at losing her mother in such a careless fashion. Perhaps they don't get on.'

'We're getting too far away from the facts here, and into the realms of fantasy.' Kate conveniently forgot her own habit of doing just that on so many former occasions.

'Are you going to phone Emma? I think you should pin her down to answering some of your questions, instead of allowing her to witter on about how dreadful everything is.'

'I tried her at five-thirty, as she suggested, but Samson had a homework crisis and Emma was helping him out. I'm expecting a return call at any moment.'

'*Samson?*'

'One of the brood. Perhaps he's named after his father. Maybe that's what Sam's short for.'

'Maybe they gave their children peculiar names to develop their strength of character. I'm starting to feel sorry for Emma's mother.'

'You're being unkind. I do think Emma's having a rough time at the moment.'

'Oh, all right. Waste your sympathy on her if you want to. But she is a most irritating woman.'

'You haven't met her yet!'

'I feel as though I know her only too well. I shall be surprised if she rings you back at all, never mind with any coherent account of her mother's details.'

'Actually, I spoke to Emma's brother-in-law and left a long message with him. He's the one who's going to ring me back with the answers.'

Roz lifted her eyebrows at this. 'Does this mean that you're at last showing an interest in men again?'

'Certainly not. I am interested only in my work,' said Kate loftily.

'Huh!' said Roz.

'You can't wind me up today. I'm in too good a mood. I posted my excellent manuscript to Estelle, my agent, this morning. I feel liberated, successful, full of the joys of late November. I am even looking forward to Christmas. I refuse to be irritated by anything or anyone for the rest of the day.'

Roz changed tack. 'Did you get any photographs of Joyce from Emma?'

'I'd nearly forgotten about them.' Kate delved into her

handbag and came out with the carefully wrapped package of snapshots. 'Here they are.' And she handed them to Roz, then stood behind her chair and looked at them over her mother's shoulder.

'The one with the messy hair is Emma, is it?'

'Yes. And the big hairy one is Sam, her husband. Don't ask me to identify the children, every time I get them sorted out they grow a bit more and confuse me again.'

'And this must be Joyce.'

They both stared at the face in the photo. The picture was in colour, had been taken by Sam rather than Emma, and so was in focus and well lit.

'What lovely blue eyes,' said Roz.

'You're right. I didn't notice them before. And I've always thought blue eyes were so trustworthy.'

'Unlike our own shifty-looking, multi-coloured eyeballs.'

'What do you make of her?'

'At first glance she is just what you've described: a conventional middle-class grandmother. She has hair that is mostly grey, with just a few strands of the original dark brown. She has the fair skin that often goes with dark hair and blue eyes, and the clear pink complexion, with no visible broken veins, that is the result of a life lived without much alcohol or over-indulgence in rich food. She hasn't got a smoker's squint, either.'

'A paragon of clean-living,' said Kate without enthusiasm.

'On the other hand,' continued Roz, 'she doesn't look terribly brainy, does she? I don't see the bright light of intellect shining from those candid blue eyes. I'd have thought that she doesn't like to read anything more demanding than a cosy women's magazine or a Catherine Cookson. That calm, untroubled brow, so free of the lines and wrinkles that we, with our expressive faces, will soon acquire, has stayed that way for sixty-odd years because she hasn't concerned herself with the nastier aspects of life, I would think. I doubt whether she sat brooding about The Bomb in the fifties, or demonstrated outside the American Embassy in the sixties. I doubt, too, whether she followed Barry Manilow from gig to gig in the seventies.'

'She was too busy knitting baby jackets and making sure that Emma ate up all her strained spinach,' said Kate. 'Now that you mention it, I, too, can see all that in this one snapshot!'

'At least some of what I've said is true,' insisted Roz.

'And are we any nearer to understanding why she left and where she might have gone?'

'If we crack the puzzle of why, we may be nearer to finding where,' said Roz.

'You're talking a large amount of sense this evening,' conceded Kate.

'What I do think is that we have to think sideways. *You* might have run away from your house for a few weeks because you found a dead body on the hall carpet – and who can blame you? Joyce Fielding might have felt the same horror about a dead mouse, or . . . Well, that's what we don't know.'

The phone interrupted their unusually productive discussion.

'Hello?' said Kate. 'Oh, yes. Hello, George.' She waved a hand at Roz, trying to persuade her to leave the room and give her some privacy, but Roz looked blandly on and listened shamelessly to every word.

'Just a minute, I need something to write on,' said Kate.

Roz obligingly passed her one of the notepads that her daughter kept in every room, ready for such a contingency.

Kate scribbled on the pad while listening to George, punctuating his narrative with occasional comments of, 'Yes. Yes. Fine. Yes,' which she knew would irritate Roz with their lack of information.

Finally, she said, 'Yes. That might be a good idea. We could talk it over. Maybe between us we could come up with some suggestions.'

A short pause while George spoke.

'Why don't you come here? I'm sure we could find you a meal.'

Another contribution to the conversation from George.

'You poor thing. It'll be soft-boiled eggs and Marmite fingers.'

And with that obscure remark, Kate put the phone down and turned to her mother with a satisfied smile.

'That was George. Sam's brother,' she said.

'I gathered that much. What did he have to say?'

'I've written it down.' Kate pushed the pad across to Roz, who frowned over her daughter's handwriting.

'This is worse than when you were six.'

Kate translated. 'Emma is an only child. Sam and George are the only two on their side of the family, and the Dolby brothers' parents died some years ago. George is so far unmarried and unencumbered with offspring – yes, I know, I was just satisfying my curiosity. So there are no other grandchildren demanding Joyce's attention, only Emma's. Joyce's own parents are both long dead, and she has a married sister living in Canada with whom she exchanges birthday and Christmas cards but otherwise ignores.'

'So there goes a large part of our speculation. What else?'

'I asked where she had been living. She is not, apparently, an Oxford person. She has a pension that allows her to live in modest comfort if she's careful. She has a flat – which she owns outright – the sort of small flat considered suitable for a respectable widowed lady, situated in a town in some county I've never heard of, like Leicestershire.'

'I'm sure it's an excellent county, full of excellent people,' said Roz.

'She lives within five minutes' walk of the austere, brick-built church to which she belongs. She attends services twice on Sundays, and also gets herself involved in good works – sewing skirts for immodest natives, or something.'

'You're making some of this up.'

'Possibly. But not a lot.'

'What's this squiggle here?' asked Roz, pointing to more of Kate's scrawl.

'On the day she disappeared, Joyce called in at the corner shop on her way home from the park. According to the unreliable Ammie – bribed by George with large helpings of some unhealthy, sugar-laden food – they had to wait while the woman put a postcard in the window. Then Joyce bought a pint of milk and had a few words with the woman in the shop. Ammie didn't bother to listen to them, she was too busy leaning over into the freezer cabinet and choosing herself a disgusting ice cream on a stick, which Joyce refused to buy for her.'

'This piece of evidence sounds authentic.'

'Since it's the only place I can start, and it's too late to find them open now, I'll go over to the corner shop tomorrow and see if the shopkeeper remembers her, what it was they were talking about, and whether there was anything odd about her behaviour.'

'Is that all?'

'For the moment. But George's coming round tomorrow evening at about eight-thirty for a discussion on what we're going to do.'

'Another jolly threesome,' said Roz.

Kate glared at her.

'You want me to retire to my room with a mug of cocoa and a good book?'

'You needn't bother with the cocoa.'

'No way. I'm going to be in on this. I might have some pertinent questions to ask.'

'You're sure you haven't something better you'd like to do?'

'I have a small idea of my own which I shall pursue in the morning.'

'What idea?' asked Kate suspiciously.

'We'll exchange information over lunch.'

'If I get some useful answers from the woman in the corner shop, we might have solved our mystery.'

'Hm,' said Roz.

11

Kate

The next morning Kate chose a black-and-white head-and-shoulders portrait of Joyce from the photographs that Emma had given her and walked down to the local photo-copying shop to have copies made. It was probably the oldest of the pictures, taken some five or so years previously, but she thought it would reproduce better than the snap-shots. The face looked blandly out of the picture, believing that the world – or at least her corner of it – was a wonderful place and nothing nasty ever happened there. Did anyone have that sunny a life, wondered Kate.

She sat with Roz to drink a coffee and eat a chocolate biscuit, then set off in the direction of Emma's house in a spirit of optimism.

I'll soon have this mystery cleared up.

After the usual battle with the Oxford traffic, she reached Emma's suburb and parked a couple of hundred yards from the Dolbys' house. She had passed the park with its swings and slides, where Ammie had played and the baby had dozed that last afternoon, and she had followed the route she thought Joyce would have taken back to Emma's house.

The corner shop was barely five minutes' walk away. It must be the right one, as it was the only one she could find on this side of the main road, and Kate approached the door with confidence.

It was just the sort of place she had expected, its windows filled with useful, basic groceries at prices well above those of the supermarket. To one side of the door was a glass-fronted case, full of postcards offering items for sale, or plaintively wondering whether anyone could provide five hours' housework a week in return for a pittance. On the lintel, a neatly painted statement announced that Mrs S. Prescot was licensed to sell wines and tobacco.

The bell rang in the interior as Kate pushed the door open and went in. The shop smelled of a mixture of recently delivered bread and synthetic lemon cleaning spray. She was glad to see that the place was empty of customers, and the person behind the till wasn't a teenager engrossed in its Walkman, but was instead a middle-aged woman wearing a beige overall and checking figures in an accounts book.

Kate picked up a familiar packet of chocolate biscuits and approached the counter.

She handed over an exorbitant sum, hoping that the contents weren't too far over their sell-by date. Then she smiled her most ingratiating smile and said, 'Mrs Prescot?'

'Yes?' Mrs Prescot had hair dyed a plum colour, skin so thickly powdered it looked like crumpled pink winceyette, and heavy bags under her eyes. She was wearing lipstick to match her plum hair. Making an effort to see her through Joyce Fielding's eyes rather than her own, Kate perceived that she was vulgar. Common and vulgar. That's what Joyce Fielding would have thought as she refused to buy ice creams for Ammie and the baby. So why had she come in here in the first place?

'I wonder if you could help me,' said Kate, taking one of the photos from her bag and passing it across the counter. 'Do you remember seeing this woman at all?'

'That's Mrs Fielding, isn't it? Ammie and Tristan's nan.'

'And little Jack's. It is indeed.'

'I won't let those two in my shop unless they're with their nan,' said Mrs Prescot darkly. 'She's an unfriendly woman, but at least she can keep those children under control.'

'She had Ammie and the baby in its buggy with her on the afternoon I'm interested in. At the end of last week. Do you remember?' asked Kate.

'Ammie was screaming for something her nan wouldn't let her have. I remember that all right.'

'That sounds like the Ammie I know. Do you know if anything special happened?'

'What sort of thing?'

'I don't know. Anything. Was she in a funny mood, did you notice?'

'She was a bit quiet. I did notice that, but then she was never a very outgoing person. Withdrawn, I'd call it.'

'That's interesting. Anything else?'

'Why do you want to know? What's happened to her?'

'Nothing, nothing at all,' said Kate swiftly, before Mrs Prescot could ask what she, Kate, had to do with any of it, and why she was asking these questions. 'It's just that we've lost something and we're trying to trace her movements.' No point in mentioning that the 'something' they had lost was Joyce Fielding herself.

'I haven't seen her around for a few days,' said Mrs Prescot suspiciously.

'Such nasty viruses flying around at this time of year. I'm sure she'll be out and about again soon,' said Kate breezily.

Mrs Prescot searched Kate's open and cheerful countenance as though looking for signs of untrustworthiness. Failing to find any, she added, 'And then I suppose you'd want to know about the postcard.'

Kate raised her eyebrows. 'Postcard?'

'The card in the window. She saw it as she came in with the children and then she came back to the shop a bit later, as though she'd forgotten something, and asked me about it. I got it out for her and she copied down the details.'

At this interesting point in their conversation the door behind Kate opened, the bell pealed and Mrs Prescot abandoned her for a discussion of the relative merits of various over-priced jams. Mrs Prescot was maintaining the superiority of Real Chunky Apricot at two pounds thirty-five, but the customer escaped from the shop with Economy Mixed Fruits at ninety-three pence. Kate studied the covers of Mrs Prescot's women's magazines for several minutes before she could return to the subject of Joyce Fielding.

'Have you any idea what it was for?'

'Of course I have. It was advertising a room to let. They never stay up long if the rent's reasonable. She was lucky to find it. Though I had thought she was staying with Mrs Dolby for as long as Mr Dolby was in hospital.' She looked sharply at Kate.

'Yes, we all thought that. I don't suppose you have the address?'

'Why do you want to know?'

This seemed a reasonable question and Kate hoped her rapidly invented reply would satisfy the woman. 'Mrs Dolby has mislaid her mother's new address and obviously she wants to get in touch with her. We hoped that you would still have a note of it.'

'Funny that Mrs Fielding hasn't written to her daughter, or phoned her up. You'd have thought a sensible woman like her would do that.'

'I expect she's busy. Or still in bed with the virus. Or else she did and Mrs Dolby forgot to write the address down. Or mislaid it again. The poor woman is so worried about her husband that she doesn't know whether she's coming or going.'

'Never had much sense of direction at the best of times, that one.'

'She does her best,' said Kate loyally. 'But tidiness isn't her strong point, I'm afraid.'

Mrs Prescot pursed her plum lips to indicate that she was thinking, then pulled out another hardbacked notebook and checked an entry. She found a blank postcard and copied the details for Kate on to the card.

'Here you are,' she said, handing it across to her. 'This is what it said. Was there anything else you were wanting?'

'I'd better have a newspaper,' said Kate, realizing that she was supposed to spend more money, but not wishing to trust any of the perishable goods around her. She handed over the coins and left the shop, Joyce's new address clutched firmly in her hand.

'You've forgotten your newspaper!' called Mrs Prescot.

Kate took the unwanted paper and retired to her car to read what Mrs Prescot had written.

Room to let. Quiet professional female preferred. Non-smoker. Use of kitchen. The rent was modest and there was a telephone number at the bottom of the card. Kate took out her mobile phone and rang the number. She heard the ringing tone and waited for a while until it became quite obvious that no one was going to answer.

Bother.

She left the car and returned to the shop. Mrs Prescot was still alone. There was no great rush of customers at this time in the morning, apparently. Kate picked up a jar of instant coffee from the shelf, shuddered at the price, and presented herself at the counter.

'You again?'

'I forgot the coffee,' said Kate.

'Three pound seventy,' said Mrs Prescot.

'And I was wondering whether you possibly had an

address to go with this phone number,' said Kate, fishing the money out of her bag.

'I might of,' said Mrs Prescot, and pulled out the notebook again. She leafed slowly through the pages.

'And I'd better have a pint of semi-skimmed milk,' said Kate resignedly.

'Forty-eight pee,' said Mrs Prescot. 'We sell a selection of wines, too.'

'No,' said Kate firmly. 'My mother and I are strictly teetotal. But I'll take one of your lemons.'

'Another forty-five pee,' said Mrs Prescot triumphantly. 'And here's the address you wanted.'

'Thank you,' said Kate and stuffed her latest unnecessary purchases into her bag. She reckoned that she'd been overcharged by about two pounds for information she would have been willing to pay a fiver for.

Back in the car she looked at the address written in Mrs Prescot's tidy and legible hand. Carpenter Street. It wasn't so far from where she was: down Headington Hill and into the network of narrow streets behind the Cowley Road. She could be there in ten minutes. She could reunite Joyce with her loving daughter in half an hour.

12

Roz

It was such a simple idea that she couldn't imagine why one of those needle-brained friends of her daughter's hadn't thought of it before.

Roz wrapped herself in a warm coat and wound a long velvet scarf round her neck before venturing into the cold Fridesley wind. Of course, none of them knew their way around the world like she did, she told herself smugly. What you needed was common sense, not the theoretical stuff you found in books.

She wouldn't bother to wait for a bus – there was probably a clutch of five of the things somewhere in the stationary traffic further down the Fridesley Road. And a walk would add a glow to her cheeks and a sparkle to her eyes. Roz did not despise such vanities. She set off with a stride that allowed her to overtake all the other pedestrians in her path, and she was soon in the centre of the city.

She found the newspaper office tucked away in a side street and went inside, glad to be out of the wind. She took the prepared sheet of A4 from her bag, checked the wording – simple but effective, she considered – and handed it, together with the fee, over to the woman behind the counter.

'Three insertions, in the Personal column,' she said.

This would probably bring a result far quicker than all the soul-searching that Kate was going in for. Who cared *why* the woman had walked out? All that mattered was to get her back again as soon as possible so that the dreadful, voluble Emma would stop harassing them over the telephone.

She left the newspaper office and headed back towards the centre of town.

And another thing, just think how pleased with herself she would feel when she had outsmarted her daughter and her daughter's friend.

She wandered through the aisles of the covered market, bought some unusual bread, another pound of olives, a couple of bottles of decent Rioja and one of Cointreau. Kate's new friend George would probably need a drink after spending the first part of the evening with Emma and her children.

Finally, heading home with her purchases, she noticed a particularly delectable scarf – finely pleated silk, marvellously subtle colours – and bought that, too.

A thoroughly satisfactory morning's work, she considered.

13

Kate

Kate stood for a moment in front of Emma's door before she lifted the tarnished brass door-knocker and let it fall. She hoped that no one would hear it. She hoped that Emma was out. She should have gone home to recuperate before coming round to the Dolbys'.

'Hello,' said Emma. 'I wasn't expecting you.'

'Can I come in?' asked Kate.

'If you like. I was just going to ring you, anyway. You needn't stay long.'

'Thank you.'

'What? No, I mean that everything's going to be fine.'

'It is? What's happened? Has your mother come back home?' Kate welcomed the delay in telling her own story.

'Not exactly. But I've had a postcard from her. She says that she's well and happy, and she's sorry if I was worried, and she'll be in touch again soon.' Emma hadn't moved from the doorway and Kate still stood on the doormat, the light rain hazing her hair and face.

'Does she say why she left?'

'No, not exactly.'

'And does she mention where she's staying?'

'Not really.'

'Can I see the postcard?'

'What for?'

90

'I'll tell you in a minute.'

'I suppose you'd better come in, then.'

Emma at last moved aside to allow Kate into the house. Kate shook the rain droplets from her hair like a small dog and followed her in.

Emma said, 'Shall we go into the kitchen?'

'Thanks.' Kate guessed that the kitchen, though chilly by her standards, would be warmer than the rest of the house.

They sat in Emma's Windsor chairs at one end of the large pine table. Someone had been working on their school project at the other end, and someone else had been eating a chocolate yoghurt and a packet of nuts and raisins somewhere in the middle. Emma was wearing a pair of blue dungarees that were popular in the seventies with liberated women, but they made her look shapeless and depressed rather than liberated.

'Here you are,' said Emma, handing Kate a postcard.

'A very fine black cat,' said Kate, looking at the picture on the front. 'That doesn't tell us much, does it?' She thought it was a pity Joyce hadn't chosen a local view. Most people did, so why couldn't she? She turned the card over to look at the message.

'You're right. Joyce is well and happy and sorry if you're worried.' That was all. No mention of why she had left, or where she was now. Kate turned the card round and examined it from all angles.

'What are you expecting to find?' asked Emma, irritated.

'I was hoping to see the postmark,' said Kate.

'Well?'

'No luck. There's only a small smudge here, and I can't read it at all. I can't even see when it was posted.'

'I think they do that on purpose so that you can't tell how long they've taken to deliver it to you.'

'So young, so cynical!'

'Anyway, that means that everything's all right now and you can stop looking for her. Let me know how many hours you've spent so far, and I'll send you a cheque. I'm not paying for any of your ridiculous expenses, by the way. I know how creative a romantic novelist can be with an expense claim.' Emma stood up to indicate that Kate's visit was at an end.

'Sit down a minute, Emma. I've got something to tell you.'

'What's wrong?'

'Nothing, probably. Not as far as you're concerned. But I have to tell you what I've found.' Kate stopped again.

'Go on.' Emma's face had fallen back into its habitual worried lines and she was trying to pick up all the shards of nut that one of the children had scattered on the table.

'I managed to follow your mother's trail after she left here quite easily. You told George that she went to the corner shop on the day she disappeared, so I called in there and asked about her. They remembered her very well, because she had asked for the details of a card in the window.' Kate discreetly omitted all references to the unruly Dolby children.

'What sort of card?'

'One advertising a room to let.'

'Why on earth should she enquire about that?'

'I don't know. But if she left here, then it makes sense that she'd need another place to stay.' Kate ignored Emma's indignant stare. 'And luckily the woman in the shop—'

'Mrs Prescot. A frightful woman. I hope you checked your change if you bought anything from her.'

'Yes. Mrs Prescot remembered the card your mother asked for. She had the details in her book, and she looked them up for me. She gave me the address.'

'And you went round? You found my mother?'

'I went round, but I didn't find your mother. I'm afraid that I found something else.' Kate paused again. She had been hoping that by spinning out her story she would manage to calm Emma down. If she was like this before she broke the news, what would she be like afterwards? How much should she tell her?

'*What?*' Emma sounded impatient.

Kate had been afraid that she'd cause Emma unnecessary worry, but it struck her that whatever Emma was worried about, it didn't appear to be her mother's safety. She wasn't showing nearly enough concern for Joyce, even if she had received a postcard from her.

'I found a dead body,' she said in a rush.

'What!'

'It wasn't very nice.'

'Did you call an ambulance?'

'There wasn't much point. It was very dead.'

'The police, then?'

'No.'

'Honestly! You are *impossible!* I can't trust you to do anything responsible!'

'Stop for a minute and think, Emma. Don't you want to know who's dead?'

'Why? Why should I be interested? It's nothing to do with me . . .', Her voice trailed off. 'Was it?' she queried.

'No. It wasn't your mother, if that's what you're asking. It was a man.' Emma looked as though she was about to break in again, so Kate carried on forcefully, 'You know your mother, Emma. You must know what she is and isn't capable of. Is it possible, could it possibly happen under extreme circumstances, that she could kill someone?'

'This is absurd! You're wondering whether Mummy killed this unknown man!'

'Perhaps he wasn't unknown to your mother.' Kate

instinctively flinched at the expression on Emma's face, as though expecting a blow.

'You're inventing things as usual. I never know when to believe you.'

'I only invent things for my books. I don't waste good ideas on real life,' said Kate drily.

'You shouldn't judge *my* mother by *your* standards,' snapped back Emma. 'Just because you and that mother of yours go off with some unsuitable man at every opportunity, don't think my mother could ever behave like that. She's lived an exemplary life since my father died. She lives only for me and the children.'

How do you know? How can you be so sure? But Kate said only, 'I had to make certain. I didn't want to call the police before I'd spoken to you.'

Emma drooped over the table and a wash of pink stained her pallid face.

'You know the police better than I do, don't you? You think they'll assume that my mother is implicated somehow in this sordid killing.'

'It had occurred to me, yes.'

'And you think so, too. I can tell by your face.'

'I'm sure she couldn't be responsible,' Kate began. *Well, maybe I'm not quite as sure as you are.* 'But we don't know what she's been doing for the past few days. She sounds innocent enough to have got mixed up in something without understanding exactly what it was.' She spoke carefully, trying not to infect Emma with her own doubts. The woman had enough to worry about already.

'And the police will think that she was involved with this awful man. They'll assume that she and he were . . . lovers.'

'Not necessarily,' said Kate, remembering the placid, unexciting face that had smiled out from the photographs. 'He was a fair bit younger than her.'

'What should we do?' asked Emma plaintively. 'You're the practical one. Tell me what we should do.'

'I think I should ring the police and tell them what I found. I don't have to tell them who I am. I could do it anonymously.'

'Is that wise? It sounds a bit shifty to me. If you're going to phone, do it from here and get it over with.'

'I was thinking of you. I need to do this in a way that doesn't associate what I found with you and your mother.'

'But you'd better call them immediately. They'll want to know why you took so long about it.' Emma's voice was rising again.

It must be the effect of childbirth, thought Kate. It made women liable to hysteria, apparently. 'They might want to know why I came round here to your house before calling them,' she said.

'Well? *Do* something!'

'I'll ring from my mobile phone. They can trace the number, but I don't think they'll know exactly where I am.'

Kate brought the mobile phone out from her capacious handbag. 'Can you find me the number of the local police station in the directory? I don't want to ring nine-nine-nine, it's too melodramatic.'

Emma found the number and Kate dialled. She declined to give her name and address and merely gave the information that there might, possibly, be a dead person in a ground-floor room at seventeen Carpenter Street. From the tone of the policeman's response, she thought he suspected her of making a hoax call.

'I don't think he believed me,' she said to Emma when she had disconnected the call. 'But they should send someone round to look. Eventually.'

'It'll be in the paper, I suppose,' said Emma.

'Or on the local news.'

Emma sagged suddenly, as though someone had dropped the strings that were holding her up. 'You do think it has got something to do with Mummy, don't you?'

'I don't know. But it has to be a possibility, doesn't it? And we still don't know where she is. Aren't you worried about her?'

'Of course I am! I'm worried sick. But I haven't got the time or the energy to indulge myself. I have to convince myself she's all right. It's the only way I can cope. She *is* all right, Kate, isn't she?'

'I can't be sure about that,' said Kate reluctantly.

'You think you should go on looking for her?'

'I would if it were my mother, yes.' For a moment, Kate imagined that it was Roz that had disappeared into the blue. What would she feel? Panic. Loss. Grief. She'd be rushing round the town, searching everywhere until she found her. She remembered back to when Roz *had* disappeared. Did she carry on her life as usual? No. She raged and cried and then got into all sorts of scrapes, as though proving to the absent Roz that she wasn't capable of surviving on her own. And she at least had been prepared – after a fashion. She might have worried about Roz – and she did, in the darkness of the night – but she didn't have to imagine that she had been abducted or injured. Roz had had the decency to say a proper goodbye before taking the taxi to the station. But Emma was different. Perhaps it was because her first responsibility was to Sam and the children. Perhaps it was because Emma was a cold fish.

'The police will investigate the man's death. If there is a connection with Joyce I'm sure they'll find it sooner or later, whatever we do. But let me continue with the search,' said Kate. Emma looked at her, and she had the feeling that she was expected to volunteer her services without any pay. She resisted the appeal on Emma's face.

'Very well. I suppose you'd better,' said Emma reluctantly. 'Though you haven't done much so far, have you?'

Kate stopped herself from remarking that she'd done more than Emma herself. The woman was right: she was under dreadful pressure and she didn't need Kate to add to her worries.

'Can I take the postcard with me?'

'Postcard?'

'The one that Joyce sent you,' explained Kate patiently.

'Whatever for? It won't tell you anything more.' Emma was holding on to the card so tightly that there was a crease across the cat's cheerful face. Kate thought of the cards – birthday, Christmas, exotic beaches – that had arrived from time to time from Roz, just when she might have thought her mother was dead, or lost. Just when she might have allowed herself to forget that she had ever had such a thing as a mother.

She picked up her bag and walked to the kitchen door. Emma stayed where she was, staring at a coffee stain on the surface of the table.

'I'll ring you as soon as I have some news,' Kate said.

'Thanks,' said Emma listlessly.

Kate fought the urge to shake her into animation. 'I'll see myself out. Don't bother to get up.'

Emma didn't reply.

14

Joyce

I don't suppose I'd have done it unless I'd been really upset. It's not as if I'm usually what you'd call an impulsive person. Sudden impulses make me feel nervous, as a rule.

But I was upset after what I'd seen. After what had happened.

I left the house all in a rush, just running down the road. I still had the thing in my hand and I pushed it deep into the builders's skip at the end of the road. I suppose I had in the back of my mind that I'd seen a postcard in Mrs Prescot's window. A room to let. I wasn't thinking of running away, but I just wanted somewhere else to go, just for the time being, so that I could think. There never seems to be the time or the peace and quiet in Emma's house to do much thinking.

Anyway, I went back into the shop on the corner. I don't like that Mrs Prescot much, but when you're worried you don't think about things like that. She got the postcard out of the window for me and I copied down the details into my notebook. It's funny how you never forget to take your handbag with you, whatever state you're in. She said she'd keep it out of the window for the rest of the afternoon, and I know she wanted to know what I wanted it for, but I didn't tell her. I just phoned the number on the card from the phone box on the corner and arranged to go round to see the room straight away. I could tell that Ruth and I would get on, just from talking to her on the telephone.

'Take a taxi and come straight round,' she said. 'There'll be a number to ring somewhere in the phone box. And don't you worry about the fare; let me treat you to it.'

And so I was there, just ten minutes later.

She asked me in, she showed me the room, and then we sat down to a chat over a cup of tea. She made proper leaf tea, and used the strainer, and we drank it from china cups and saucers. I could see that we were the same type, that we came from the same respectable background.

She must just have got home from work, because she was wearing her pink overall with the Sunshine Angel badge on it, and I asked her all about it. I suppose I was just looking to make polite conversation, but she told me all about them. She said how important it was to have the right type of lady, since they went into hospitals and clinics and met some very well-off people, as well as the ordinary patients.

'Maybe you could join us one day,' said Ruth, and she took the brooch off her own overall and pinned it on my blouse, as a sort of joke. 'There you are! Doesn't that look nice!'

I didn't notice at the time that the catch was faulty. It's a funny thing, but I've never been able to stand things that aren't quite perfect. I've been like that since I was a child.

And somehow, over the next twenty minutes, I managed to tell Ruth just a little of what had happened, and she seemed to understand completely. I must stay there with her, she said. I must never go back. But I told her I had to go and fetch a few of my things.

'Just your toothbrush, then, if you insist,' she said. 'I'll come with you. We'll take a taxi and I'll wait outside for you.'

So that's what we did. 'Don't you go speaking to anyone,'

ordered Ruth. So I crept upstairs and just pushed a few things into my handbag and filled a plastic carrier I happened to have in my room. You must have a couple of changes of underwear, I always think. It was when I was checking how I looked in the mirror that I saw the catch on the brooch was broken. I threw it away in the waste-paper bin, and hoped that Ruth wouldn't notice. Then I crept back downstairs and out into the taxi with Ruth. No one noticed. I could hear Emma reading to the children and I felt a bit guilty at leaving without a word. But what could I say? I couldn't tell Emma about it. I wouldn't know how.

15

Kate

'I need your help. I realize that now,' Kate was saying. 'I'd been thinking that Joyce Fielding and Emma, or maybe Joyce and one of Emma's children, had had a trivial row and Joyce had flounced off in a huff for a few days. Either I'd find her, collect my fee and all would be well, or else she'd come down off her high horse and wander back through Emma's front door, ready to take up the household reins again. I know I'd worked it all up into a big mystery, but underneath, that's what I believed.'

'And now you don't.' Roz was unusually thoughtful as she listened to her daughter.

'How can I? Joyce has disappeared, and when I follow her to her rented room – easy-peasy, aren't I clever? – I find a dead body.'

'Which may have nothing to do with Joyce.'

'Is that a pig flying past our window? No!'

'How old was the man you found?'

'I don't know. Fortyish, I suppose.'

'So he didn't die of old age.'

'Even if he'd been ninety he wouldn't have died of old age. Not with his head bashed in and his brains lying on the carpet.'

'You're getting hysterical. Have another cup of sweet tea.'

'I hate sweet tea. And you'd be upset if you had to

talk about . . . that thing on the carpet.'

'When do you think it happened?'

'There were no flies buzzing around, but then, it is November. There was a bit of a smell, but it was pretty cold in that flat.'

'So, a couple of days, do you think?'

'It could have been. About that. I really don't know. I'm not an expert.'

'Go over it again for me.'

'Stop sounding like the police!'

'Just be glad I'm not the police. Come on, tell me again.'

'I went to the corner shop, spoke to Mrs Prescot, the owner, and found the address of the room to let quite easily. Carpenter Street is only short, a row of terraced houses in east Oxford, built around the turn of the century. It took me less than ten minutes to find it, even though I had to drive round that vicious one-way system. Number seventeen didn't look as though it was let out by the room, more as though it belonged to someone who was letting a spare bedroom. The other houses in the area looked as though they were let to students. There were a fair number of bikes chained to gates or lying in front gardens, but none in front of the house I was looking for.'

'Good,' said Roz. 'That's more than you told me before.'

'It doesn't help us, though, does it?'

'We won't know till you've told me it all. Go on.'

'I rang the bell, but there was no reply. I lifted the flap of the letter box, but I couldn't see anything.'

'Were you wearing gloves?'

'It's a cold day. Of course I was.'

'Thank goodness for that.'

'You're thinking of fingerprints?'

'Yes. If the police ask your Prescot woman any questions, she'll tell them that you asked her for that address just a few minutes before they received an anonymous phone call about a dead body at the same place.'

'Why should they ask her? The shop isn't near Carpenter Street.'

'The report of the murder will be all over the front page of the local paper tomorrow morning. There will be a large photograph of seventeen Carpenter Street. She'll remember about it then and go running round to the police.'

'What could she tell them? She doesn't know my name. She probably doesn't even remember what I look like.'

'I bet she does. And she knows you're connected with the Dolbys.'

'True. But she may not be very friendly with the police.'

'I shouldn't rely on it if I were you. She didn't sound as though she liked the Dolbys. She'd be pleased to shop one of their friends, especially a smart-alecky one like you. Perhaps you should go and see the police before they come to see you. Isn't it your duty to help?'

'I walk into a house I've never visited before and I find a dead body. I don't recognize the man. I have no idea who killed him. I don't even know whether he's the owner of the house or whether it belongs to someone else. What information can I give them? I'd just waste their time as well as mine if I went to see them. I'd rather keep out of it, and I bet that's how Mrs Prescot thinks, too.'

'I hope you're right. And by the way, how *did* you get into the house? You'd just got to the bit where no one answered the bell, so you peered through the letter box.'

'I tried to look through the front windows, but the curtains were drawn nearly shut and it was too dark in the room to see inside properly. There was a door to a side passage, which no one had bolted, so I went round to the back of the house to see if anyone was in the garden.'

'In November? Sunbathing, I suppose.'

'I'm not that stupid. They might have been pruning. Mulching. Sweeping up leaves. I don't know what people do in their gardens, do I?'

'Ignore my interruptions. Carry on.'

'There was no one in the garden, as you so rightly guessed. It was full of overgrown shrubs and oversized trees, so the neighbours couldn't have seen much of what was going on there.'

'You're about to tell me that you tried the back door handle.'

'I tried the back door handle, and it was locked. But someone had left a small sash window just a couple of inches open. I tried pushing it up, and it rattled all the way up to the top, leaving plenty of room for a slightly built woman to climb through.'

'I'm praying now that you left no footprints or other evidence behind you.'

'I'm a well-brought-up person, as you should know. Of course I left no signs of my presence. I was standing in a small utility room. There was a mop leaning against the wall, so I used it to make sure I'd left no footprints. Satisfied? The room was clean and had nothing odd about it, so I opened the door into the kitchen. The door on the opposite side, the one leading into the downstairs hall, was open, too. And the first thing I noticed was a bit of a smell. I thought it might be drains, or cat food left out in a bowl for too long. I called out, but there was no reply, and then I pushed open a door or two – yes, still wearing my gloves. It was freezing cold, as though the heating had been off all day, or maybe longer.'

'Why didn't you just leave again straight away?'

'I was looking for Joyce. I was determined to find her and prove my intelligence and competence to the doubting Emma. This address was the only lead I had, remember. I thought, even if she wasn't there, I might find some clue to her whereabouts. I might even find out if she was staying in the house, but had popped out to the shops for an hour.'

'I suppose I'd have done the same,' said Roz reluctantly.

'The house, although narrow, was very deep, much bigger than it looked from the front. There was a hallway running the length of it, from the front door down to the kitchen. I forget how many rooms led off it, but three, maybe four, anyway. The body was in the one furthest from the front door, next to the kitchen. It looked as though it had been used as a sitting room: there was a rather nasty red sofa and a table with an orange veneer surface, and a picture over the fireplace of boats sailing into the sunset. That's all I noticed, because on the floor, on the garishly patterned carpet, between the table and the sofa, there was a man lying in a mess of blood and . . . stuff. And he was dead. Very dead. Maybe I should have taken notes, but all I could think of was getting out of there as soon as I could.'

'Should I get you another cup of strong, sweet tea?'

'No thanks. I'm all right now.'

'And you'd never seen this man before?'

'I doubt it. He didn't strike me as familiar, but I didn't turn on the lights or peer into what was left of his face.'

'At least it wasn't Joyce Fielding.'

'No. Thank God for that. I'd have had to break it to Emma.'

'What did you do then?'

'I made sure that the window I'd used was shut, and that I'd left no traces of my presence. Then I let myself out, very quietly, through the front door, and walked, unsteadily I have to say, back to the car.

'I thought about calling the police from my mobile. I'd parked the car twenty yards or so down the road, and I sat there, watching the trembling of my hands and wondering what I'd let myself in for, taking on a simple "missing granny" case. In the end, I went straight round to Emma's. I drove very sedately, so that no one would remember me, but ended up going twice round the one-way system because my mind wasn't on it. At one point I thought I would be driving round those streets for ever, I was in such a state of shock. And I got a bit of a fright when I was waiting to turn right into the Cowley Road: a white pick-up pulled up beside me, apparently wanting to turn left, and I thought for a minute it was Jace. It had the same head-banger music blaring from its speakers, and the same assortment of ladders and gas cylinders and unidentified rolls of stuff in the back, and I couldn't see the driver's face because his arm was in the way. But then I noticed that the truck was spotlessly clean, so it couldn't possibly have been Jace, and when he pulled forward I saw there was a woman sitting in the front who definitely wasn't Tracey. It was just guilt on my part, I suppose. I was sure that someone would see me, would know what I'd been doing. Anyway, I finally got to Emma's without hitting any other road-user and I told her what I'd found. She persuaded me to report it to the police, so I used my mobile phone, just told them I thought they might find a very sick, or possibly even dead, man at seventeen Carpenter Street, and didn't give my name and address.'

'Why on earth did you go to Emma's?'

'I wanted to let her know that her mother might have been involved in something dangerous.'

'Is that likely? You still don't know that there is any connection between Joyce and Carpenter Street. She might have taken down the address in the corner shop and then changed her mind.'

'If she'd changed her mind, she'd still be at Emma's.'

'She might have found another place to rent, either in

the local paper or in another shop window. She's probably sitting in a comfortable flat, getting on with her knitting, at this very moment.'

'But there's another possibility, isn't there? Suppose, just suppose, that it was Joyce who killed the man on the carpet.'

They were both silent for a moment as they thought about it.

'She wouldn't,' said Roz, but she didn't sound completely convinced.

'What do we know about Joyce Fielding, when it comes down to it?' said Kate.

'We know she's a dull, respectable, middle-aged woman,' said Roz firmly.

'We know what Emma wants us to know,' said Kate. 'Joyce might be an absolute fiend. And if Emma isn't as worried about her mother's safety as I think she should be, maybe it's because she knows her mother's more than capable of looking after herself.'

'A fiend in a knitted twinset?'

'Those are the clothes she left behind. Maybe she took the scarlet feather boa and the slinky black satin number away with her.'

'Is that what you really think?'

'I don't know. I think we have to find out more about her, and not necessarily from Emma.'

'How?'

'Joyce left Emma's place for some reason I don't understand. Emma is covering the problem up with a torrent of words which tell me nothing and obscure the truth. I need to approach it from a different direction.'

'There's something about the way you're looking at me that makes me think you expect the next move to be mine.'

Kate chose her most conciliatory tone.

'When you said you wanted to help Emma and me find

Joyce Fielding, you pointed out that you were the one who understood a woman of her generation. Well, I have to admit that I don't understand her at all. At least, I thought I understood a woman who was interested only in making a home for her husband and children, and then helping out with her grandchildren. A woman who enjoyed knitting and baking, and who smelled of baby powder and Pears' soap. But I don't. I can't imagine why she walked out of that house and into the blue. I know why *I* would have done so. But then I wouldn't have been there at Emma's beck and call in the first place. And what would turn a dull mouse into a murderer if it comes to that? Or at the very least the witness to a murder? So I'm asking you: tell me about Joyce Fielding. What do *you* understand about the way she behaved?'

Roz took a moment to think before she replied.

'You're asking me to tell you why *I* walked away after your father died, when you were only seventeen.'

'I thought I was asking you about Joyce Fielding.'

'I'm not sure I understand her any better than you do. There must be as many reasons for disappearing as there are women who leave. I'd have thought they divided into two main categories: the ones who were bored and needed a bit more excitement, and the ones who found there was too much pressure at home and opted for peace and quiet. At first glance, Joyce falls into the second category rather than the first. But if you're right and she is somehow involved in this death . . .'

'Murder.'

'If she's involved in this *murder*, then, and goodness knows what else, then she might be the sort who was looking for adventure.'

'Exactly. So how about getting stuck into the story of your life? I shall lie back on the sofa and listen to it in a mellow mood of acceptance and tolerance.'

'You'd better have the cat to stroke. It's supposed to help with reducing stress levels. I don't want you running off into the blue, just when life was getting interesting.'

But Susanna wasn't having any of it. She lifted her tail high and howled to be let out of the room, leaving Kate and Roz on their own.

16

Roz

Are you sure you want to hear this? You really think it will help you to understand someone like Joyce Fielding? I can't believe that this is going to get you any further in finding out what's happened to the woman. She and I may be about the same age, but I think that's all we have in common. No, I'm not trying to weasel out of it. Oh, very well then. But I shall edit the story as I see fit and you're not to argue with me.

How far back would you like me to go? What do you mean, I can start as far back as I like, since I've never told you anything? What mother tells her daughter all about her own upbringing? I like to think that you and I have a certain reticence in our relationship, that we respect one another's privacy.

That's just the way you argued when you were fourteen and wanted to stay out late on a Saturday evening: *everybody* else does it. All your friends were allowed to stay out till one in the morning and I was the only mean, strict mother. Well, I didn't believe you then and I don't believe you now. But if you insist on hearing the story of my life, I shall give you the whole boring shooting match.

I was born in Brockley. I don't suppose you've even heard of it. It was one of those featureless suburbs for the upwardly mobile who had reached their social ceiling. Instead of looking around them and thinking, *God, how awful!* they smugly congratulated themselves on travelling so far up in the world and then sat down to conform to all the other dreary people around them. No, really, I'm not exaggerating. That's just the way it was. You'd have hated the place, just as I did, once I was old enough to notice my surroundings.

You want me to be more specific? My whole life was clogged with details that other people thought were important.

According to my earliest memories, we lived in a semi-detached villa in a chestnut-lined street. The houses were new at the time, I suppose, and typical of the nineteen-thirties. In the autumn the pavements were heaped with fallen leaves like large brown gloves, and in spring we sneezed at the pollen from the pink candlestick flowerheads. In the front gardens the favourite trees were ornamental cherries and almonds, the sort that had little bunches of fluffy pink blossoms and made you believe that the world was a beautiful, fluffy pink place. I wore clean white socks in summer, with well-polished brown leather sandals. My dresses were neat flower-printed pastel cotton, with Peter Pan collars and puffed sleeves. In winter my black lace-ups were Start-Rite and I wore a grey pleated skirt and a freshly laundered and ironed white blouse with a maroon tie. My party dress was of deep-blue velvet with embroidery on the collar. Is this trivial enough for you? Have you been wretched all these years because I didn't tell you about it sooner?

Where were we? Oh yes. Early childhood. I envy people who have instant recall of everything that ever happened to them. My own memories are like tiny little currants in a great doughy bun. The war arrived while I was still too young to realize what it was all about. My mother and I moved into the country for a couple of years for safety, then back to Brockley towards the end of the war. It's no good asking me intelligent questions about that time: I remember very little and, anyway, I accepted whatever happened to me as normal, the way all children do.

My parents never stopped bemoaning the changes that they saw in the country after the war had ended, but it looked all right to me. I went to tea parties where the sandwiches had the crusts removed and were cut into triangles. I started piano lessons. (I expect you've noticed that I have no musical talent. It must have been agony for my teacher. I suppose she needed the money.) I'm afraid I can tell you no stories about smoking filched cigarettes behind the garden shed or drinking illicit ginger beer in the greenhouse. My friends were hand-picked by my mother and were goody-goodies every one.

I'm so glad that you call me by my name. I had to call my mother 'Mummy' for her whole life. I've always found there is something just a little odd about people who are supposed to be adults who still do that, haven't you? What does Emma Dolby call her mother? Mummy. Yes, I might have known it.

To continue. At six, I went to school. First I went to a nice little private establishment run by Miss Robinson. And when I say 'little', I mean tiny. There were about thirty of us. I learned to read and write and to do quite a lot of sums. I enjoyed myself. Once I got used to the place I could boss the other girls around.

What do you mean, move it along a bit faster? I thought you wanted to hear all about my background. And no, I'm not getting aggressive. I'm *much* more frightening than this when I get aggressive.

Very well then, at eleven I progressed to the high school. A short journey by train, and this time a *blue* pleated skirt with a *yellow* shirt and a navy-and-gold striped tie. Hair neatly tied in plaits, surmounted by a black pudding-basin hat which had to be worn at all times when outside school – presumably to deter any male who might be interested in young females. Over my shoulder I carried a leather satchel with a mess of sweet papers and pencil sharpenings swilling about at the bottom, and, eventually, after years of being good, I wore on my pullovered bosom an enamelled prefect's shield. No, it was nothing like that horrid little angel, so don't look for clues *there*.

My parents? Your grandparents. I'm sorry you never met them, but then again you didn't miss much. You could sum my father up in one word: grey. And if I'm thinking in terms of colour, my mother was a light-absorbing olive green. Anything with any liveliness or laughter about it was swallowed up by that dour personality and nothing was given back. Am I being unfair? Probably.

They had married when they were both well into their thirties and I was born when my mother was forty-two. Poor things. They didn't live long enough to see the reality of their own offspring, of what they had brought into the world. For, Kate, I did conform in those days. I wanted to please my parents. I took my exams – O-levels, very newfangled – and then I went to a local secretarial college to learn how to do shorthand-typing and earn my living in an office. This was the extent of my parents' ambition for me, and I have to admit that I thought no further than an office job myself. I didn't see any point in staying on at school, and university seemed an extension of lessons and homework and people in authority telling you what to do. I didn't fancy mixing with those bescarfed and duffle-coated youths, and student women looked so dreadfully dowdy.

What would I have liked to do, to be, if someone had ever given me the choice? Something creative, I suppose, but this didn't enter our field of vision. The things I wanted from life were *out there*, unknowable and lacking neat labels.

How can you know what you want if you can't put a name to it?

Don't be too hard on us all. Did you do so much better when it came to your turn?

Are you wondering how I got away from it? I have to admit that it was my shorthand and typing skills, such as they were, that took me into a job in central London. After a year at a local solicitor's office, irritating everyone with my bad spelling and inaccurate typing, I found a job in an advertising agency, and I can tell you that it was a very glamorous place indeed for a girl from the sticks. In a matter of a few weeks I learned to despise my parents and everything they stood for. I met a man. As a matter of fact, I met lots of men. I learned how to dress and talk, how to drink gin and tonic and smoke cigarettes.

But I didn't marry one of the exciting young men, or even one of the older ones on the look-out for a second, younger wife to replace the discarded earlier model. I might have done. I had enough opportunities. After a while the gloss was wearing off my life at the advertising agency: however much of a buzz there was in the place, I was never going to be more than a shorthand-typist. I looked around me again and decided that the only route out was through marriage. Don't look like that. It was a perfectly acceptable option for a young woman at the time. Women's liberation wasn't due to appear on the scene for another ten years. So, I changed my image again, back to something wholesome and near-virginal, I went to the tennis club and to subscription concerts, and I snaffled your father.

What was he like? It's hard to look back and see him clearly. He was just a man in a suit. A very nice, dark-grey suit with a thin white stripe to it. He wore white poplin shirts and dark-blue silk ties. He was polite, and well educated, and knew how to talk to my parents. He owned a small car. What more could one ask for? Perhaps I wouldn't get a second chance. Looking back on it, I suppose I was suffering from a form of depression. It all seems quite ludicrous now. Why on earth didn't I take a risk or two, or get myself some useful qualifications, and grab my chances? Ah, well.

So, John and I were married. It seemed a good idea at the time. I blame all that pink cherry blossom in the suburban streets. Every spring it reminded me of marriage, or if not of marriage, of a wedding. White dress, pink flowers. A bridesmaid in pink tulle. You don't believe me? No, you're right. Even for my parents' sake I wouldn't go through that. I wore a striking little silk twill suit, a wide-brimmed scarlet hat and lots of lipstick. There are some photographs somewhere, with me looking triumphant and John looking bemused. What more can I say? I'm sorry. I expect I was very unfair to the man.

It was all fine at the beginning. I went on working. I found a job close to East Dulwich where we were living. I shopped in my lunch hour. I cooked in the evening. I did the laundry and cleaned the house at the weekend. I didn't know that life could be so tiring. But we saved enough money for the deposit on a house, and carpets, and furniture. And eventually we bought a nice little semi in a town in north Kent. And a year or so later you turned up.

I was a good mother to you when you were little, wasn't I, Kate? I did love you, you know. I doted on you. Maybe I got a bit bored from time to time, but that's only normal. All mothers get bored sometimes, even when they're devoted to their children. And John. Yes. Dear, good, dreary John.

When you were born and I left work, we used to talk about you after supper. He wanted to know every detail of your day. He followed your progress through creamed carrot to minced spinach, and from crawling across the carpet to drawing on the dining-room wallpaper. I think you were the only thing we had in common. Certainly, I can't remember any other topic of conversation when we were on our own. It was a year or two before I started to notice how impoverished our lives were, and then—

There! That's the front doorbell. You sit there. I'll get it.

Do come in and sit down. I'll go and make us all a nice cup of tea. Kate, this is Constable Hutt, who says he's come to see you.

17

Kate

Kate was expecting Constable Hutt to be very young and rather bashful. It was the assumption you made about a man with a name like Hutt and a title like Constable. He should be holding his helmet under his arm and wondering where to hide his large black boots.

In fact, someone nearer forty than thirty walked into the room, who looked as though he had a loving wife at home who fed him frequent and nourishing meals. He wore perfectly normal black lace-ups and Kate was disappointed to see that he didn't have a helmet with him at all. In an uncertain world it was reassuring when people conformed to their stereotypes.

'How can I help you?' she asked when he had settled himself in an armchair and Roz had been banished, under protest, to the kitchen. Now that she saw him properly, she could tell that Constable Hutt looked quite at home against the pale-green linen. He looked full of common sense and a modicum of intelligence. He even looked as though he might manage to eat a digestive biscuit without dropping crumbs down his clean navy pullover, but she thought it might be a bit forward of her to offer him something to eat before she found out what he wanted. She waited politely for him to speak.

'I believe you telephoned East Oxford police earlier today

and reported the existence of a potentially deceased person in a house in Carpenter Street,' he began. He took a black notebook from his pocket, as though prepared to make a note of her reply.

'Oh! Are you quite sure it was me?' She wondered whether she was getting away with her wide-eyed and innocent act.

'Quite sure. We traced your call back to your mobile phone, and since the call was recorded at the station switchboard, and I have listened to the recording, I have heard your voice before and I can confirm that you were the informant. It is quite a distinctive voice,' he said.

Kate switched to her most helpful mode. 'Well, what can I tell you? I'm sure I gave all the information at my disposal to your excellent tape recorder,' she said.

'Did you? Are you absolutely certain?' He didn't sound as though he believed her.

'Why shouldn't I tell you all I knew?' countered Kate.

'Well, you see, when we entered the house a couple of hours after you rang, we didn't find a body, dead or otherwise.'

There was a silence while Kate digested this information.

'Are you sure? There was definitely one there earlier.'

'How do you earn your living, Miss Ivory?' Constable Hutt looked around the cosy room, as though assessing how much it had cost her to furnish it.

'I'm a writer.' She was sure he knew the answer to his question before he asked it.

'Non-fiction?' he enquired solemnly. A pause. 'Or fiction, possibly?'

'Fiction,' she answered shortly. 'Romantic historical fiction, to be precise,' she added defiantly, seeing the patronizing expression on his face.

'The sort of thing my elderly mother-in-law enjoys

reading,' said Constable Hutt, confirming Kate's opinion of him. 'And I'm sure it takes plenty of imagination to think up those exciting stories of yours, doesn't it?'

'Could we cut the clod-hopping humour and get to the point? You're telling me that your colleagues couldn't find a large dead body in the lounge of seventeen Carpenter Street after I had given them the relevant information, so now you're accusing me of making it up. Either that, or you believe I have such a vivid imagination that when I walked into an empty house I *imagined* I saw an overweight forty-year-old man with his head bashed in, sprawled on the hideous patterned carpet?'

'It's one possibility, don't you think?'

'And then, just for fun, because I'm that sort of irresponsible person, I rang up the police and told them what I'd invented. Why? As a joke?'

'It's known as wasting police time,' said Constable Hutt. 'Some people do find it an amusing thing to do.'

'I don't.'

'And what were you doing at seventeen Carpenter Street?'

'I was looking for someone.'

'Mr Bettony.'

'Who?'

'Mr Bettony. The owner.'

'No. I was looking for a woman.'

'Does she have a name?' Constable Hutt seemed to possess unlimited patience.

'Joyce Fielding. I thought she had rented a room at number seventeen, but I must have been mistaken.'

'You didn't find her?'

'No. And instead of wasting *my* time with your nasty little insinuations, why don't you go out and find Mrs Fielding for us? You could save us a lot of time, not to mention worry and grief, if you could do that.' She heard, as though it belonged to a separate person, her voice rising unattractively high and shrill.

'I don't believe I know about Mrs Fielding's disappearance,' said Constable Hutt, smugly in control. 'Would you care to tell me about her?'

'No. She's not *my* mother. And I'm not sure her daughter wants to have anything to do with the police.'

They sat glaring at one another for a moment, then the door opened and Roz – who looked remarkably like someone who had been successfully eavesdropping – entered with a big, peace-making smile and asked brightly, 'Tea, anyone?'

'No, thank you very much,' said Constable Hutt, rising in one smooth movement to his feet. 'I'd better be getting back to some real work.'

'And what did Mr Bettony say about the body on his sitting-room floor?' asked Roz.

'We haven't spoken to him yet,' said Constable Hutt.

'I think you should,' said Roz. 'He sounds a much more suspicious character than my daughter.'

'I'll see you out,' said Kate, as though she expected him to depart with her silver spoons in his pocket if left to his own devices.

As soon as he had passed through the front door she closed it with a decisive click behind him.

'Well?' asked Roz.

'The body's gone.'

'And you're sure it was there this morning.'

'It's not the sort of thing I'm likely to imagine, is it? You're sounding like Constable Hutt. You know how upset I was. I saw a dead man with his brains on the carpet.'

'And when the police arrived – several hours later, by the sound of it – the body was gone.'

'So someone must have removed it.'

'Presumably the same person who committed the murder.'

Kate thought for a moment. 'If I'd been there earlier I might have seen the murder happening, and if I'd been just a little later, I might have interrupted the removal of the body. I think I've been lucky.'

'They wouldn't have wanted witnesses,' agreed Roz.

'Could Joyce have been a witness?' wondered Kate.

'I should have thought that if she was, there would have been two dead bodies in the house rather than just one.'

'You do believe me, then. There *was* a dead body?'

'Yes. I do.'

'Did Joyce kill him?'

'No, I shouldn't think so,' said Roz. 'But we'd better find her before the police do. If it is Bettony who's been killed, they'll have her down as his murderer.'

'My first response is to think, Oh no! No one could think that dear little granny is a murderer.'

'But we're back to the fact that we know so little about her, except for what Emma's told us.'

'When I looked at her room in the Dolbys' house, I got a strong impression that she wasn't there,' Kate began.

'That's why Emma asked for your help,' said Roz drily.

'What I mean is, that she had been there for several weeks, she had tidied everything up, but there was nothing of *her* in the room. Hardly a beige shadow on the carpet, a dun-coloured ghost sitting on the chair. She kept everything she was strictly under wraps. I think it's possible that Emma's told us so little because she genuinely doesn't know anything about her. We need to speak to someone who does.' Kate looked at Roz as though asking for inspiration.

'George Dolby,' said Roz suddenly. 'He's coming this

evening. Perhaps he's noticed more about Joyce than Emma has.'

'I'd forgotten about him.'

'You surprise me. Now we've got rid of Constable Hatt—'

'Hutt,' corrected Kate.

'Whatever. Now he's gone, we can start preparing for the arrival of the delightful George,' said Roz.

'We don't have to cook for him, do we?'

'No. But we can put a few flowers in a bowl, and plump up a cushion or two. Then we can choose what we're going to wear and spend a little time making our faces look fabulous.'

'I only hope he appreciates the effort,' said Kate.

'It's not necessarily his appreciation we need, it's the low-down on the saintly Joyce.'

'It might be a good idea to keep my adventure in Carpenter Street a secret just for now, don't you think?'

'Yes, I do. We don't want George to come to the conclusion that we're a family of housebreakers and wasters of police time.'

'Certainly not. We're serious investigators, you and I.'

'If you say so.'

18

Roz

Up in her room, as she looked through her wardrobe, deciding what to wear, Roz thought about what she had overheard of Kate's conversation with Constable Hutt.

Hutt might have been a dull-witted policeman who had written Kate off as a time-waster whose over-developed imagination had led her to invent a dead body in a house in Carpenter Street, but Roz knew her daughter better than that. If Kate said so, there must have been a body on the carpet. And from her description, it wasn't someone who had fainted, come round again after Kate left, and then carried on their normal life. It had been a man with his head bashed in, according to Kate.

So, the question remained: why had there been no dead body there when the police arrived? Answer: someone must have removed it. And who was that? The murderer (or murderers). And where did Joyce Fielding fit into any of this? Roz had to admit that she had no idea. Though if she was as good at tidying and cleaning as Kate had described, then she might well have had a hand in the removal of the body and the mopping-up, even if she hadn't wielded the blunt instrument. Was that what they called 'accessory after the fact'? If Joyce was that deep in trouble, she might be too frightened to come home.

And then, as she brushed her hair, Roz remembered the

advertisement she had placed in the local paper.

**JOYCE FIELDING. Please contact me in confidence.
We need to know that you are safe and well.
Telephone me on—**

and here she had given Kate's number. Maybe she'd get a
response and all her questions would be answered to her
satisfaction. Still, it was only this morning that she had gone
into the newspaper office, so the ad wouldn't have gone in
until this afternoon's late edition. She had paid for three
insertions. The first she might ignore, the second would
prick her conscience, the third would surely force her to
pick up the telephone. If she couldn't face her daughter,
she might at least contact a stranger.

Roz pulled an emerald-green skirt from its hanger and
looked at it critically. She had to admit that she had made
some assumptions. She was assuming that Joyce bought the
local paper every day, that she looked at the small ads, and
that she still had a conscience.

Suppose she was involved in something illegal.

Suppose she was already dead.

Roz put the skirt back in the wardrobe. They said green
was an unlucky colour and she wasn't taking any chances.

She chose another garment. Red and black should be
safe enough.

19

Kate

George arrived at the house in Agatha Street just five minutes after eight-thirty. Roz answered his ring at the door and showed him into the sitting room, which was looking its best, now that they had tidied away Roz's *Sporting Life*, Kate's sheaves of notes, and assorted toys belonging to the cat.

'We're drinking red wine,' said Kate. 'Would you like a glass of the same thing, or do you prefer something more exotic?'

'I'd enjoy a glass of red wine,' said George. 'Especially since I haven't brought the car with me.'

He was wearing a jacket and shirt in very dark grey, and a peacock-blue silk tie. Now that Kate could look at him properly she could see that he wasn't really like Sam at all, apart from the superficial resemblance of one brother to another. He was quite a bit younger than Sam, for a start. Or maybe Sam looked so much older because he had been worn down by the cares of marriage and fatherhood. George looked as though he had spent many of those same years on a ski slope, or lying on a tropical beach, and playing regular games of squash. If there was one thing Kate liked, it was a man in good physical nick.

'Any news from Emma?' Kate asked, crossing her fingers.

'Nothing new,' said George. 'I spent an hour sorting out

Samson's maths homework for him. I hardly spoke to Emma at all.'

While Roz was pouring the wine, George asked, 'What's up?'

'What do you mean?' countered Kate.

'There's a feeling of tension in the air, as though you are about to reveal some horrid secret.'

'No, really,' said Roz, since Kate seemed unusually silent. 'There's nothing like that. It's just that we've had an exciting day, one way and another, haven't we, Kate?'

'It had its moments,' said Kate. 'But now I'm quite sure that nothing unexpected is going to happen for the rest of the evening, and since this is our favourite Australian red, it seems a good moment for us all to relax.'

George gave her an enquiring look, which Kate ignored. She wasn't about to speak of dead bodies and visiting policemen. She didn't want to send George screaming from the house before they had even begun to get to know one another.

'You'll have to forgive her,' said Roz. 'She's accustomed to the uneventful existence of a writer. Any upset to the quiet routine of her life and she gets confused, poor girl.'

Kate scowled. 'There's no need to exaggerate,' she said.

'Here you are,' said Roz, handing round glasses of wine. 'Why don't you sit over here, George, and tell us all about yourself.'

George said modestly, 'I'm really very dull. I just do a bit of teaching.'

But to Kate's eyes he looked more like an artist or a musician than a teacher. She could imagine him at the Symphony Hall in Birmingham, drawing thunderous music from a piano. Or a cello, perhaps. He would rise to his feet, flick that long, dark lock of hair from his forehead and smile at the ecstatic audience. Or then again she could see him at a *vernissage* (though she wasn't entirely sure what that was), answering deep and intelligent questions about his paintings.

'Why don't you pass round the olives?' Roz interrupted her fantasy. And, much later, George told Kate that he was so bad at drawing that, when he was a child, even his doting parents hesitated before sellotaping his infant pictures to their kitchen wall.

'Now,' said George, chewing on a green olive, 'aren't we gathered together to pool our ideas on how to find Joyce Fielding and return her to the bosom of her family?'

'Succinctly put,' said Roz. 'I'm sad to report that Kate and I have really not got very far at all,' she added airily, conveniently forgetting Kate's expedition to the house in Carpenter Street. 'And we hoped that you could tell us more about her to give us some idea of where to start looking.'

'We need the unexpurgated version,' put in Kate. 'Emma hasn't told me much, and what she has said is so bland that I wouldn't recognize her mother if I bumped into her on the street.'

'Joyce *is* bland,' said George. 'Or at least that's the way she struck me. What can I tell you about her? As far as I know, she is a deeply conventional woman, the sort who goes to church on Sundays, who polishes her shoes and irons her blouses, and joins in with the hymns on the morning service on Radio 4. She was never unfaithful to her husband, she hasn't looked at another man since he died, and she lives only for her daughter and her grand-children.'

'That's more or less what Emma told me,' said Kate. 'Isn't there anything else? No secret vices? No disreputable friends? What about her missionary work with the fallen women of Summertown?'

'I wish!' said George. 'The only thing I can think of – and

it's only a faint possibility – that might upset her enough to make her give up her dutiful behaviour . . . ' He paused.

'What's that?' prompted Roz, since George seemed disinclined to continue.

'It's just that I'm not sure how she would react if any of her family disagreed too strongly with her own well-defined ideas. I think she is out of touch with much of modern life.'

'And yet she's about the same age as me,' said Roz.

'At least a generation older, if not two,' said George.

'Thank you. But we've learned nothing new yet, have we?' said Roz. 'More wine?'

'Thanks. But if you think that wine will make me indiscreet on the subject of Joyce, then I'm afraid I'll have to disappoint you. I can't think of anything scandalous to say about her.'

'Then perhaps we should approach the problem from a different angle,' said Kate thoughtfully. 'If Joyce is so conventional, then how would she react to some scandal in the Dolby household? Suppose she found out that Emma's eldest was pregnant. Or one of them was on drugs. Or Emma was having an affair with the milkman.'

'Emma's eldest is a boy, and eleven years old,' said George. 'They're all a bit young for drugs, even in this day and age. I certainly haven't noticed any symptoms, anyway – and I do come across that sort of thing as a teacher. And Emma . . . well, I'd say that Emma isn't the sort to go looking for sex outside her marriage.'

And from the tone of his voice, Kate wondered how keen Emma was on sex even inside marriage. But then, who knew about married couples? They were certainly a closed book to her.

'No teeny Emma-style orgies?' queried Roz. 'No drunken evenings on the fireside rug with a sexy novel? No fuzzy afternoons with a joint and her favourite CDs?'

'I'm sorry to disappoint you, but no. Emma, if anything, takes after her mother. She believes in hard work and cared-for children. I can't think of anything likely to happen in that household that would shock Joyce into leaving.'

'Apart from the tedium,' said Kate.

'Joyce enjoys tedium,' said George. 'It is her natural environment.'

'And she arrived while Sam was already in hospital, I assume, so we can't blame him for upsetting her.'

'Sam hasn't even had the pleasure of a visit from Joyce. She would always babysit the children while Emma went to the hospital to visit him.'

'This is getting us no further,' said Kate.

'Just a minute,' said Roz. 'Are you telling us that Sam and Joyce don't get on?'

'I wouldn't put it quite like that. But Sam and I come from a different background. Our parents were liberal-minded academics. They grew up in the post-war period, I suppose, and couldn't wait to throw off the constraints of their parents' generation. Sam and I were brought up in a very tolerant family. It was intellectually challenging, of course – something else that Joyce didn't appreciate about Sam – but demanded nothing of us in terms of conventional religion and strict morals. Sam's changed over the years, and I suppose he and Emma have come to a compromise, but I don't think that Joyce has ever trusted him completely. She can't trust a man who doesn't believe firmly in a paternalistic god and who doesn't take his large family to church every Sunday. The only book is the Good Book, in Joyce's vocabulary.'

'But they haven't come to blows?' Roz sounded as though she would like to hear of fisticuffs in the Dolby household.

'They are always polite to one another. And anyway, they

only meet a couple of times a year, so it is no great strain on either of them.'

'And Joyce came to help Emma after Sam went into hospital,' said Kate.

'That's right. I don't suppose they'd seen one another for six months before that. You can't blame Sam for Joyce's disappearance. The poor bugger's been out of it for weeks, and I don't think he's strong enough yet to mount an attack on Joyce's religious beliefs, even if he wanted to.'

'We might have to give up,' said Kate. 'We're not getting anywhere, are we?'

'We're not giving up yet. What's wrong with you, Kate? And there is just one more thing,' said Roz. 'Why don't you show Sam the brooch?'

'Good thinking. I'd forgotten about it. I'll go and fetch it.'

Kate was gone only a few moments. 'Here it is,' she said, and handed over the cheap yellow metal badge with the grinning angel and the broken catch.

'Oh yes,' said George. 'I've seen one of these before.'

'You have?' Kate sounded elated. At last there might be a breakthrough in the case.

'Let me think. Yes. I saw one just this afternoon. I went to visit Sam in the nursing home, and while I was there a woman came round with a trolley laden with newspapers and magazines and all the things you might have forgotten to bring into hospital with you. She was a big woman with a dour expression and beefy forearms, not at all the sort you associate with good works and mopping brows in hospital wards. But she was wearing a pink cotton overall thing, and on the lapel she had a brooch like this one. I think it was fixed to a name badge, though I have no idea what she was called, and there was the title of her organization, too, in curly lettering.'

'Can you remember what that was?' asked Roz.

'Something sweet and syrupy,' said George. 'What was it, now? Angels of Mercy? No. Helpful Cherubs? No, Sunshine Angels. That was it.'

'Now we're getting somewhere,' said Kate. 'We'll find out who these Sunshine people are and then we'll get them to tell us where Joyce is.'

'You're making rather a lot of assumptions there,' said Roz doubtfully. 'You're jumping to the conclusion that Joyce is a Sunshine Angel because she has one of their broken badges in her waste-paper bin.'

'It's the most likely explanation,' insisted Kate. 'Tomorrow morning I'll go to the nursing home. What did you say it was called, George? And whereabouts is it?'

George gave her the address of the Maxwell Clinic. 'Would you like me to come with you?' he asked.

But unfortunately for Kate, she couldn't think of any good reason why he should. 'Really, I can manage on my own,' she said.

'As it happens, I'm not teaching tomorrow morning,' he said. 'And I think it would be much easier if a close relative of one of their patients were with you, don't you?'

'Very well,' said Kate, persuaded to do what she really wanted.

'I'll pick you up at ten,' said George. 'That'll give them time to clear away breakfast and make sure that everyone's lying tidily in their beds.'

'And now that that's agreed, I think we should all have another glass of wine,' said Roz.

20

George and Kate

It was an unusually lovely day for late November. The sky was blue, the sun was shining and there was even a hint of warmth in the air. Kate dressed in a golden-yellow shirt and dark-grey trousers, adding a light pullover as an afterthought. It might have been April, she thought, humming to herself as she went to answer the ring at the doorbell.

It was just ten o'clock, and there was George. If there was one thing Kate appreciated, it was a man who arrived on time.

He had parked his car outside Kate's house, but they decided to go on foot to the Maxwell Clinic, to take advantage of the unseasonable weather.

'We can walk across Port Meadow and then up through north Oxford,' said George, who had dressed more casually this morning than the previous evening.

Kate picked up her jacket and gloves. There was no need to change her footwear, since she always wore the sort of boots that enabled her to stride forcefully through Oxford's mean streets.

'Let's go,' she said, leaving the house and rapidly closing the door behind her, before Roz could decide that she needed to accompany them.

There were still single roses shining in the front gardens of Fridesley, as if they were refusing to believe that winter

132

had arrived, though the trees thrust bare black branches into the blue sky. George and Kate turned their backs on the Fridesley Road and its rumbling traffic and made their way down Waverley Lane, walking towards the river. It was so peaceful that they might have been deep in the country.

'So, tell me about yourself,' said George eventually, after they had walked for a few minutes in companionable silence.

'Hasn't Emma filled you in?'

'I don't believe everything that Emma tells me.'

'I'm sure that Emma never tells a lie.'

'You're right. But her judgement of people isn't always accurate. In fact, I'd go so far as to say that Emma's judgement of people is usually wrong.'

'That's interesting,' said Kate. 'But surely she'd know about her own mother.'

'Let's forget about Joyce for the next twenty minutes,' said George. 'I'm much more interested in you.'

And if there was one thing that Kate liked in a man, it was his willingness to be interested in *her*.

Kate considered for a moment how much she could get away with. Should she tell him about the life she would have liked to have lived, instead of the one that actually belonged to her? But then, did she really want to fool George? You could invent a past for yourself, invent a personality perhaps, edit out the boring bits of your life, but only for a short time. She wouldn't be able to keep it up. And it was possible that she might want this relationship to last.

'Start at the beginning,' said George into the silence.

They were swinging along, stride for stride now, approaching Port Meadow and the river.

'I think I'll miss out some of the boring early stuff,' said Kate. 'Why don't I start with my career as a successful novelist?' Then she remembered that this was going to be the honest version of her life story. 'My career as a mildly successful novelist,' she amended.

'Lurid. That's the way Emma described your books.'

'But we've agreed that we won't believe a word that Emma says about me.'

'True.'

'I write historical novels. Romantic historical novels,' she said. 'Not at all the sort of thing that is described as "literary". I do a lot of research into the historical bits, then try to forget much of what I've learned and concentrate on the romantic angle. I'm afraid that it's the romantic parts that sell the books.'

'But you manage to earn a living? That's quite an achievement, isn't it? I thought there weren't many writers who could do that.'

'Mostly I manage to earn a living at it. I scrape by.' Then, because this morning she was attempting to tell the whole truth, she added, 'Quite often I have to take a job for a month or two to make up the shortfall. I don't mind doing it really. It makes a change from crouching over a word processor in my cellar.'

They had reached the river now and could see the trees and towers of north Oxford in the distance. A few hardy ponies cropped the grass in the meadow on the farther bank. George and Kate picked their way through a herd of black-and-white cows, aiming for the stile and the bridge beyond it.

'And don't you find time for a man in your life?' asked George, balanced for a moment on top of the stile.

There was a short silence while Kate wondered how much to tell him. George landed lightly at her side and they were standing close together. George was a lot taller than she was, and her eyes were on a level with his open collar. His shirt was hyacinth blue today.

'There has been time for a man or two. Just occasionally. But I've usually picked the wrong man,' she added.

'Emma mentioned something about a policeman,' said George. The noise of their feet drumming on the wooden slats of the bridge drowned out any reply that Kate might make.

Kate looked up at the sky, as though expecting small clouds to block out the sun, but it still shone down with its oblique blue November light.

'There was a policeman in my life for quite a while,' she said. Then she laughed. 'It sounds ridiculous, doesn't it? Not at all my style. Hardly stylish at all. But a really nice man, in spite of his job. Dependable, kind, honest. Most of the time. You shouldn't expect more than that.'

'You sound as though you're writing him a reference.'

'Am I making him sound like a nanny?'

'Just a bit.'

'He'd have made a very good nanny. In the end, I found him just a bit stifling. I felt that really he disapproved of my lifestyle and wished I'd get myself a proper job, instead of wasting my time writing all those unimportant books. It all came to a head a few months back, when I really needed someone to lean on, and he opted out.'

'What happened?'

'A friend of mine died in terrible circumstances. Paul was away on a course, or so he said, and I tried to contact him at the number he'd given me, but they hadn't heard of him. He wasn't there, and they weren't expecting him. I was too concerned about my friend to pin him down at the time, but it niggled.'

'What was it, another woman?'

'No. That's the stupid part. It was nothing like that. He was on a course, of sorts. One of those community-relations exercises where they make nice, narrow-minded policemen go off and get acquainted with some minority – gays, blacks, women. You know the sort of thing.'

'It sounds most praiseworthy,' said George, straightfaced.

'Possibly. But he was ashamed of what he'd been doing. He didn't want to tell me about it. He had to pretend he was off on a management course. And he couldn't understand why I got so angry about it.'

'Probably not the right man for you,' said George judiciously.

'And he and Roz didn't take to one another, either. I watched them being painfully polite to one another.'

'Really? I find your mother great fun.'

'She is. But she doesn't conform to Paul's ideas of respectable behaviour for a middle-aged woman. Or even a young one. He wanted me to get married, and settle down, and have children, and learn to iron shirts.'

'And what about you? What did you want?'

'I wanted the time and space to think and to write. I still do. I'd like a man around – of course I would – but not one who has such definite ideas on what I should be.'

She felt a twinge of guilt at being so dismissive of Paul. He had been in her life for quite a long time and was more reliable than most men. She wondered how *he* would have described *her*. But Paul didn't go in for analysing people. He described such conversations as gossip.

A flock of beige and grey geese crowded down by the river's edge, honking with what sounded very much like derision.

'It sounds like the ideal we're all looking for. Someone who'll be there when we need them, but then disappears when we want to get on with the other bits of our life,' George said after a while.

'Exactly. It's not an impossible quest, is it?'

'I've always found it so.'

Behind them, on the towpath, a man with a megaphone was cycling slowly along, shouting instructions to a tired-looking rowing eight on the water.

'What about you?' asked Kate. 'Why haven't you followed Sam's lead and settled down with a wife and twelve children?'

'Have they really got that many? I thought it was only five or six. Seven at the most.'

They both giggled, and it was a minute or so before Kate noticed that he had evaded her question. They had crossed Port Meadow and were coming out into one of the back streets of Jericho, in north Oxford.

'We turn right along here somewhere,' said George.

The narrow streets were packed with parked cars along both kerbs. An occasional bicycle passed them, but there were few other pedestrians.

'I think we're the only two people who still enjoy walking in this town,' said George.

Kate nodded. She liked a man who kept the same rapid pace that she did.

'The other thing I wanted to ask you about was Roz,' said George.

'I thought we were looking for Joyce Fielding,' said Kate crisply.

'We will be in about five minutes. But first you have to tell me why such an independent-minded woman lives with her mother.'

'Another long story,' said Kate. She paused, wondering whether she could change the subject, but she guessed that George was as single-minded and obstinate as she was herself when he wanted to know something. 'She doesn't really live with me. It's just that she's been staying for a while, and she'll be staying with me as long as we're both happy with the arrangement. We hadn't seen one another for about ten years, and really we'd lost touch for most of the ten years before that. It seemed a good idea to get to know one another again after all this time.'

'Now your search for Joyce is starting to make sense,' said George, nodding.

'It sounds to me as though you're reading too much into it.'

'Perhaps. But I doubt it.'

If there was one thing Kate hated it was a man who thought he understood her.

'It has nothing to do with my past history. Well, not much, anyway. Emma asked me to find her mother for her. I'm doing it as a favour to her.'

'I thought she was paying you a fee.'

'That, too. The money comes in useful,' admitted Kate.

'So this is one of those times when you need help to make ends meet?'

'The Maxwell Clinic's just round this next corner,' said Kate, who felt she had given quite enough away already. 'I think you should get your attention back to Joyce, not my affairs. At least I know where my mother is at this moment, even if I did lose sight of her for a year or two a while back.'

21

Roz

While her daughter was out, Roz undertook a little light housework. She didn't like to be caught by anyone she knew with a Hoover in her hand, or wielding a dishmop, since it ruined her reputation for irresponsibility and raffishness. However, it was also true that she liked a clean and ordered setting in which to pursue her Bohemian life.

This tidy streak had been the cause of the end of several promising relationships in the past, she admitted to herself occasionally. Perhaps she was still a suburban housewife at heart, for she hated overflowing ashtrays and cleaning up after people who had had far too much to drink and had forgotten where the bathroom was.

She had washed up the breakfast things and had put them away and was just wiping down the tiles surrounding the kitchen sink when the phone rang. For a moment, she thought she'd let Kate's answering machine pick up, but then she wondered whether it wasn't Kate herself ringing in with some news.

'Hello?'

'You put an ad in the paper.'

An answer to her ad! This was quicker than she'd expected. On the other hand, although the voice at the other end of the phone was female, it didn't sound the way she imagined Joyce Fielding sounded. Joyce would have a genteel, well-modulated, slightly elderly voice, Roz considered. This one was sharp, aggressive, of indeterminate age, and had the rough undertones of someone who smoked a lot.

Roz found herself saying, 'Ad? In the paper? I might have done. Is this about the armchair for sale? Who wants to know?' Why was she being so melodramatic? She felt that she had to protect herself from the person on the other end of the phone. She was being ridiculous: she must have been watching too much television since she'd been back in England.

The other voice was saying, 'Stop farting about. I have your ad here. I've just rung the number you gave. Now, what do you want with Joyce Fielding?'

'I was hoping she was well,' said Roz. 'We haven't heard from her for a while. We were getting a little worried.'

'Are you her daughter?'

'No, I'm not. But—'

'Some other relation?'

'Not exactly.'

'So you're just some interfering old cow.'

'I wouldn't put it quite like that,' replied Roz, stung by the 'old'.

'I would. What is your name, anyway?'

'Why should I tell you?' countered Roz.

'Because you want to know about Joyce, don't you?'

'True.' Roz thought about producing a pseudonym.

'It's no good making something up. I'll check in the phone book.' The bloody woman could read her mind, apparently.

'This is Mrs Ivory,' said Roz, with as much dignity as she could muster. 'Now, tell me about Joyce.'

'I'll tell you this, Mrs Ivory.' The voice was full of venom. 'You can take it from me, you can just leave Joyce alone.

She wants nothing to do with you or anyone else from her past life.'

'Now, I'm not sure you can know that,' Roz began. 'And what happened to our agreement?'

'We had no agreement. And I'm off now.'

'Just a minute! Why don't you put Joyce on the phone and let her speak for herself? I'd like to talk to her.'

'She's not talking to you, and if you know what's good for you, you'll leave her alone, like I said the first time. I don't want to see any more of those ads in the paper. And I don't like repeating myself. Understand?'

Roz was about to explain that she had paid for three insertions, but the phone was replaced with a decisive click at the other end of the line.

And what was all that about? Was that Joyce's minder? Or was it someone who knew nothing about her, but had seen the ad and just wanted to make trouble? Roz suddenly remembered something that Kate had told her, and quickly dialled 1471. She might have known it wouldn't work: 'The caller withheld their number.'

She returned to her cleaning. There was nothing like a little brisk housework for making you forget that you'd just made a fool of yourself, she found. She swept the crumbs from the kitchen floor and then went into the sitting room to straighten the cushions on the sofa. If her anonymous caller really did know Joyce, and knew where she was, then Joyce Fielding had got herself involved with some very odd people. Perhaps it was one of these religious cults, where they cut their followers off from friends and family. Wasn't Joyce a little old for that sort of thing? And she had a perfectly serviceable religion already, as far as Roz could make out.

The doorbell rang.

Was this Kate and George back again already, or had

Joyce's minder called round to follow up her verbal instructions with something a little more physical? No, she was getting too fanciful. It was probably someone canvassing her vote, or asking for the milk money.

She opened the door. She recognized the man who stood there.

'Constable Hatt,' she said, pleased that she had remembered his name.

'Hutt. May I come in?'

'If you must.'

She showed him into the sitting room. He chose the sofa with the newly plumped cushions.

'Is your daughter in, Mrs Ivory?'

'I'm afraid not. Can I help you at all?'

'When are you expecting her back?'

'In an hour or two, I should think. I don't ask her to clock in and out, you know.'

'Then, if you don't mind, I'll wait for her to come back.'

'Really? Can't you go away and return later? It can't be a very serious matter, surely?'

Constable Hutt leaned back against a cushion. She would have to plump it up again when he had left.

'We've found a dead body,' he said. 'And I'd like to ask Miss Ivory a few questions.'

22

Ruth

It was as she had thought: the ad had been inserted by
some interfering old cow. It was a good thing that Joyce
didn't bother with the local paper. ('It's full of nothing but
gossip. Just as bad as those dreadful tabloids.')

Of course, she'd dialled 141 before the telephone number,
so that she – *Mrs Ivory* she'd called herself – wouldn't be
able to find out where she'd rung from. But she'd seen the
woman off, stupid cow that she was, talking at her with her
mouthful of plums. She'd check the paper again tomorrow,
just to make sure there were no more appeals for Joyce to
contact someone from her old life. If the Ivory woman
interfered again, she'd see that she regretted it. She might
lose her temper like she had with that fool, Bettony.

She'd have to talk to Joyce again, very severely. Sadly, but
still severely. She couldn't have her running off to her old
friends and family just when she thought she would. She
thought she'd already made it plain that Joyce's old life was
evil and must be ruthlessly left behind. If Joyce wanted to
live the clean, pure life that Ruth had described to her, she
would have to stop speaking to sinners like her daughter
and this Mrs Ivory.

Away from Joyce for the time being, Ruth lit a cigarette.
She pulled in the smoke and let it out again in a slow,
sensuous stream. It was murder pretending to be a non-

smoker all the time Joyce was around. She waved the smoke away with her free hand. She'd have to open a window before Joyce was due back. *And* squirt some more Gold Spot into her mouth.

Then Ruth pulled the telephone directory out and turned to the private numbers at the back. Ivory. Ivory, K. Yes, there it was, with the phone number from the newspaper listed against it.

And Ruth carefully copied down the address in Agatha Street. You never knew when it might come in handy.

She took out a packet of strong mints and popped one into her mouth. She didn't want Joyce suspecting she'd smoked a cigarette while she was out.

23

Kate

'This is very classy,' said Kate, as they turned into the drive of the Maxwell Clinic.

Since the question 'And how can Sam afford it?' hung in the air between them, George said, 'Medical insurance. It seems to be the one perk of Sam's job.'

'Thank goodness for that,' said Kate. 'I was worried for a moment that Emma and the children would have to go around barefoot and hungry to pay the bill.'

The clinic, built in mellow grey stone, porticoed and balustraded, looked like one of the newer Oxford colleges – one that had been heavily endowed by a beneficent patron who had made a lot of money in some unglamorous trade and had wanted his name to be remembered for something other than bathroom fittings or cold cures.

'Can you fill me in on the background?' asked Kate.

'It was a private house until the nineteen-twenties,' said George. 'It was bought by a charitable trust, who then quietly bought up the surrounding property, added a discreet wing or two and turned the inside into a modern clinic. And all without frightening the neighbours too much.'

'Who do they cater for?' asked Kate, whose experience didn't run to private medical care.

'A few like Sam, who still need nursing and physiotherapy, and who are being paid for by an insurance company. Then there is a small obstetric unit for women who want to spend the maximum on their babies from the very beginning. I suppose they do the usual "women's surgery", and replace a worn-out joint or two; they can strip out varicose veins and reduce unsightly bulges. And it's probably the most discreet place to send your errant teenage daughter to have an abortion, your alcoholic uncle to dry out, and your stockbroker son to get free of his expensive cocaine habit.'

'Is this set of prejudices based on known fact, or are you guessing?'

'Guesswork, mostly. But it's largely true, I should think, give or take a little exaggeration here and there. Depression and exhaustion are two other ills afflicting all ages that are treated with great sensitivity in the Maxwell Clinic.'

'You've been reading their PR handouts,' said Kate. 'You shouldn't believe everything they say.'

'It's doing good things for Sam. He's cheered up no end in the few days he's been here.'

'You'd better lead the way in,' said Kate. 'Do you think you should have worn a suit and tie? Will they allow us in looking this casual?'

But the atmosphere inside was perfectly friendly, and a pleasant-looking receptionist smiled at George, looked Kate over and then smiled at her, too, and wished them both a good morning. 'I expect you know where to go by now,' she said to George.

'You were right,' said Kate. 'It's easier getting in with you than it would have been on my own.'

And Kate appreciated a man who refrained from saying, 'I told you so.'

'How are we going to play this?' she asked belatedly, as they ignored the lift and walked up broad stone stairs towards the second floor.

'I suppose I'd better chat to my brother for ten minutes,'

said George. 'It might look a little odd if I didn't. What had you in mind? I'm not sure what this detecting lark of yours entails.'

'Don't worry, I'm not going to throw one of the nurses against the wall, twist her ear off and demand information. But I thought I'd go looking for a pink-overalled cherub. Give me a second or two and I'll think of a reason to be wandering around the corridors.'

'Sam likes to read the *Guardian*. Why don't you go in search of a copy?'

'Good idea.' George was shaping up well as her sidekick, though she hadn't yet told him that this was the role she had in mind for him.

They had reached the second floor and George was about to turn left through double glass doors.

'How well do you know Sam?' asked George.

'Not very well at all. I've met him two or three times, spoken on the phone a couple more. And I don't think he likes me much,' said Kate honestly.

'In that case, I'll go in to Sam on my own, and you go off on your sleuthing.'

'Detecting. Or "investigating" would be better,' corrected Kate. 'And you'd better give me fifteen minutes. I'll need all of that.'

'This is the King George Wing. Sam's in Silvester Ward, through the doors and a couple of doors down on the right. If you're not back in fifteen minutes I'll come looking for you.'

'Just a minute! How is this place organized? Do they segregate men and women, or are they mixed wards? What will I find on the upper and lower floors?'

'They have small wards of two or four beds. Each ward is single-sex, but there are male and female wards in each wing. King George seems to be full of people getting over nasty accidents. I think you'll find Queen Adelaide is full of women with small babies. The rest you'll have to find out for yourself, I'm afraid. I haven't explored the whole building myself.'

When George had disappeared in the direction of Silvester Ward, Kate stood thinking for a minute. It occurred to her that she had two alternatives. Either she could find someone in authority and give them an inventive story about needing to do research for her new book (very effective as long as they didn't know she wrote historical novels), or she could explore on her own, nosing into places that looked interesting.

The first alternative was inviting, since she would be issued with an identity badge and not challenged by the security staff, but she had to set against this the fact that she would probably be saddled with an official helper and would find it more difficult to stop and ask searching questions of anyone who caught her fancy.

So, she would take up George's idea of looking for a copy of the *Guardian*. Putting a bright and innocent smile on her face, she pushed her way through the double doors facing King George. She was apparently now in Henrietta Wing.

'Yes? Are you looking for someone?' She was immediately confronted by an efficient-looking woman in a nurse's uniform. Auburn hair, parted in the middle, and waving in two wings around some sort of white cap, did nothing for her long face and straight, thin lips. Kate was too ignorant to know whether she should address her as 'matron', or something less exalted.

'Hello!' she said brightly. 'I was looking to buy a newspaper for my friend Sam.'

'The nearest newsagent is a few hundred yards north of here,' was the reply, given in a strained voice. 'Out of the front door and turn left. You'll soon see it.'

'Thanks,' said Kate, defeated in record time, even for her. 'And what about toothpaste?' she tried. 'Don't you have a shop for your patients?'

'I'm afraid not. There's a volunteers' trolley that comes round every morning and afternoon. Perhaps your friend could wait to clean his teeth until it next appears.'

'Why don't I go and find one of the trolleys now? I could find some toothpaste for my friend, leave the correct money and bother no one,' said Kate.

'The trolleys are kept in the basement,' said the nurse. And as Kate opened her mouth to argue, she added, 'And the basement is out of bounds to members of the public.' She gave a wintry smile that contained an assumption that Kate would now leave.

And she waited until Kate had walked out through the double doors again. No chance of getting past that one, thought Kate, and hoped that they were less vigilant on one of the other floors.

When the nurse had disappeared again she looked around her. She didn't want to go in search of George and Sam just yet, it might look too much like failure, so she wouldn't go in through King George. Henrietta had drawn a blank, so now she could choose up or down and an encounter with one of the other deceased crowned heads. There was a lift facing her, but she decided on the stairs. She didn't want to spend time shut in a lift with another one like the frosty sister.

She went up the stairs two at a time. The floor above had the same square hall, the same double glass doors to right and left. It was a choice between Prince Albert (left) and Queen Victoria (right). She wasn't sure which Royal was the less intimidating, and opted for Albert as having had a shorter time to practise than his consort. She pushed through the glass doors.

She was immediately aware of a different atmosphere. On the floor below, patients were in transit, as it were, between illness and recovery. Here, on the third floor, it felt as if the journey was more likely to be towards death. There was a hush, a sense of lowered voices, of muffled footsteps. It was an odd reaction to dying, thought Kate. Why should people who were soon to know nothing but silence and rest need to be shielded from the noise and bustle of continuing life?

And yet there *were* voices. They had that odd sound, rather theatrical, of an altercation carried on in lowered tones, as though the fighting couple didn't want to awaken a third person. Kate stepped softly down the corridor and stopped outside a grey door with a glass panel. 'Perpetua Ward' said the plastic nameplate. Kate stood slightly to one side, so that she could squint in through the window without being seen by the people inside. Of course, if someone came along the corridor she would have to change her position to something a little more relaxed, or they might think she was eavesdropping.

Kate had a skewed view of the ward, but she could see that it was one of the larger ones: four beds, but only two patients at present. One of them was turned towards the wall, unmoving, taking no notice of what was going on a few feet away from her. The other was a very old woman, with skin nearly as pale as her pillowcase, wispy white hair, and a very stubborn expression on her face.

A stocky young nurse was bending over the bed. She had large, muscular buttocks and well-developed calves. Her solid ankles disappeared into sensible black shoes. Kate could make out little else except a lot of curly dark hair kept in check by one of the official-looking white caps.

'Here, Annie love,' she chirped brightly. 'Let's have no more fuss. You know it's time for your tablets.'

'I don't believe I've invited you to call me by my christian name. And nobody *ever* abbreviates it.' The faint voice was surprisingly authoritative and carried quite clearly through the glass.

'What's that, love? You *are* in an uppity mood today, aren't you? Come along then, madam. I'll help you to sit up and you can take a sip of water.' The nurse held a plastic beaker of water up to the sunken lips. 'That's the way. Now, just another one for Jackie.'

Kate felt she was invading the woman's privacy and moved away from the window for a few seconds.

The nurse said, 'Has it all gone? Quite sure? There's a good girl, Annie.'

'You are not to call me Annie. My name is Mrs Bassett.' But Kate could tell that the protest this time was a formality. Mrs Bassett knew that the dreadful nurse would continue to assume an intimacy that didn't exist.

By the time she was lying back against the pillows, Mrs Bassett was too weak to argue with the nurse, but the blue eyes blazed hostile messages.

'I'll see you again before teatime,' said the nurse in her ruthlessly cheerful voice, and she clumped out of the room. Kate had moved rapidly backwards a few paces and gave her a brilliant smile before knocking gently on the door and sailing inside. She heard the heavy footsteps hesitate for a second before continuing back down the corridor. Then the only sounds were the metallic clanking noises that seem inseparable from work in a hospital.

Kate waited a moment or two for Mrs Bassett to recover, then she started to speak quietly, hoping that she would join in the conversation when she was ready.

'Good morning, Mrs Bassett. My name is Kate Ivory, and I'm a novelist and occasional amateur-investigator. At the moment, I'm looking for the mother of one of my friends, who seems to have disappeared, and I was hoping that you'd be able to help me.'

She could see that the brilliant blue eyes were alert and that Mrs Bassett was listening to everything she said.

'Why? Do you think that the nurses here have kidnapped her? I wouldn't put it past them, except that they're all so stupid they wouldn't know where to start.'

'Not so much the nurses,' Kate began. 'It was more—'

But at this moment she was interrupted by a skirling and ringing sound from her large handbag.

'Phone,' she said apologetically, and hauled it out of the depths of her bag. 'Hello?'

'Kate, it's Roz here. And I have a Constable Hatt sitting on the sofa, waiting for your return. Do you think you could get back as soon as possible?'

Thank you, Mother, thought Kate. Just as I'd found someone who might be able to help me. 'Yes, of course I can. No problem.' She cut the connection and put the phone back in her bag. 'I do apologize for that,' she said to Mrs Bassett.

'Don't let the staff catch you with one of those things in this place. They interfere with their equipment, I believe,' said Mrs Bassett, looking not at all worried by this thought.

'I'll have to go,' said Kate. 'My mother needs me.'

'But you'll come back and see me again, won't you? I don't get a lot of visitors.'

'I'll be back. Just as soon as I can get here,' said Kate. And she tried not to think how she might be exploiting Mrs Bassett.

She left the ward, ran down the stairs to the second floor, and tapped on the door of Silvester Ward. Not only was it healthily noisier down here, it even seemed lighter.

'Hello, Sam. How are you doing? Sorry to interrupt you, George, but I have to go.'

George followed her out of the ward, and Sam looked quite relieved to see him go.

When they reached the forecourt, Kate said, 'If Roz has called for my return, it must be something serious. I'd better get a taxi back to Fridesley.'

She strode off towards the centre of Oxford, leaving George looking bemused in the middle of the pavement.

24

Kate

Roz was standing just behind the door when Kate paid off the taxi and let herself into the house. She must have been listening out for the sound of the taxi door slamming and Kate's boots on the step.

'I saw the police car a couple of doors down the road. Your call sounded urgent. What's up?' asked Kate.

'I'm not supposed to tell you.'

Kate merely lifted her eyebrows.

'They've found another dead body,' whispered Roz.

Well, I had nothing to do with it, said Kate to herself as she went into the sitting room. They can't blame me for this one. I have nothing to worry about.

'Hello, Constable Hatt. Please don't get up,' she added unnecessarily.

'Hutt.' The name was expelled through gritted teeth.

Kate sat down facing him. 'And I gather from my mother that you want to talk to me. I was visiting a friend in hospital, but I left as soon as I got your message and got here just as soon as I could. How can I help you?' That degree of co-operation ought to put the man off his stride.

'We've found the body of a man,' he said heavily. 'And we were hoping that you could answer a few questions.'

'Look, Constable Hutt, you can't blame this one on me. I reported what I thought was a dead body yesterday, and you convinced me that I was mistaken, I was seeing things, but that doesn't mean that you can start blaming me for every corpse that turns up anywhere in Oxfordshire.'

'I'm asking you about this one because he has been identified as Keith Bettony, the owner of seventeen Carpenter Street.'

'Oh.' That stopped her in her tracks. 'Where did he turn up?' She wished she'd rephrased that. It sounded rather flippant.

'In Witney. They're building a new car park on the eastern side of the town. When the contractors arrived on the site this morning, they noticed that the newly laid concrete appeared to have been disturbed. After a cursory examination of the disturbance, they called us.'

'You've been quick,' said Kate, glancing at her watch.

Hutt didn't look as though he'd been splashing in the mud of a building site that morning. He was as clean and spruce as if he'd just that moment stepped from the shower. His wife must be a paragon.

'The contractors were on the site at seven-thirty this morning,' he said.

'Very commendable. What made you think it was Mr Bettony?'

'He was recognized by one of our men.'

So Mr Bettony was known to the police. She wondered in what capacity. Was it as a law-abiding, co-operative citizen, or perhaps as something less salubrious? From the closed expression on Hutt's face, she thought it was probably the latter.

'I should like you to accompany me to the morgue and ascertain that this is the same man that you saw lying on the floor of seventeen Carpenter Street.'

'I thought we'd established that I was mistaken,' said Kate, who didn't relish the thought of looking at a dead body. The one she had seen the previous day was quite enough for the year, if not the decade, she considered.

'But you reported finding someone at Mr Bettony's address,' insisted Constable Hutt. 'It's necessary for us to know whether this is the same person.'

'How long had he been in the cement?' asked Kate queasily.

'Not long. Less than twenty-four hours.'

But he would have deteriorated since she had seen him the previous morning, and that had been quite enough for her. She looked to see if there was any benevolence in Hutt's expression. There was none.

'I really have no choice, have I?'

'No.'

'Will you drive, or shall I?'

'I will.'

Kate didn't even bother to argue.

It was surprising to Kate just how smooth the journey to the police station was. Hutt was unmoved by traffic jams, by the pedestrians busy with their Christmas shopping in the town centre, by the bad temper shown by other drivers. She wished that they could stay snarled up in the traffic by the railway station, but Hutt moved into the correct lane, indicated his intention to turn right, and moved off towards Oxpens in the time it would have taken Kate to decide which way she was going.

She would have kept her mind off the coming ordeal by light chatter, but Hutt presented an impassive, unresponsive profile, and she didn't feel she could start on any lightweight topic of conversation.

'St Aldate's,' he said, unnecessarily, as he pulled into the car park of the police station.

'The morgue is downstairs, at the back,' he said, leading

the way at a brisk pace. Kate wanted to ask him to slow down, tell him that she needed to adjust to the forthcoming ordeal. 'There's a separate entrance, over here,' he said, and she didn't have the chance.

She thought of running for it, but she would be brought back, made to face her responsibilities.

'I don't have to view the actual body, do I?' she asked, as they reached the door. 'There will be some sort of CCTV, surely?'

'I doubt it,' said Hutt. He didn't sound at all sympathetic.

To the nightmare of sights, Kate mentally added smells. Did Hutt and his colleagues have it in for her? Were they trying to impress on her just what an interfering amateur she was? She was beginning to think that was the case. Not that she'd looked for any involvement in Bettony's death – if it *was* Bettony. For a moment, she considered the unpleasant thought that they had dragged her down here to look at a body that wasn't the one she'd seen yesterday. Painting nightmare pictures in her head for no good reason. No, it couldn't be. That was the sort of thing that only happened in books.

But she was certainly getting the cold treatment from Hutt. Just because she'd happened to find her way into the house in Carpenter Street, and then stumbled upon a body there, you couldn't blame her, could you? Certainly in future, she would make sure that she had nothing to do with any crime of any size or type whatsoever. Catch her trying to help the police ever again!

'Are you ready?' asked Hutt.

They had arrived.

Kate was hardly aware of her surroundings, though the smell did impinge on her consciousness and remind her of the biology lab at school, only worse.

'Just a minute,' she said.

'Yes?'

'I'm not sure I'm going to be able to help you after all. I don't think I'd recognize him again.'

'What do you mean?'

'I mean he was . . . badly damaged. I'm not sure I even looked very carefully at his face, anyway. And if he's been set in concrete since then, surely he'll have been disfigured even further.' She could hear the note of desperation in her voice.

Hutt said calmly, 'We've removed most of the traces of concrete from his face, but otherwise I believe the body is in more or less the same state as it would have been before it was deposited in the car park.'

'I was hoping you'd have cleaned him up a bit.'

'But then it would have been very difficult for you to say whether it was the same person.'

'I'm not at all sure I can help you,' repeated Kate. If she said it often enough they'd have to believe her and let her go.

'Here,' said Hutt, who had come to a halt next to a trolley. 'Take a look at this and tell me whether you've seen him before.' He pulled back the covering from the head.

There followed several seconds' silence.

'Yes,' said Kate. 'I can't be absolutely sure, but I think it's the same man.'

'Let's go upstairs,' said Hutt. 'I expect you'd like a cup of tea.'

Some time later, after two cups of tea and a plain biscuit, Kate was still trying to put the sight of Bettony's head out of her mind. She sat in an interview room, talking to Constable Hutt.

The room wasn't as bad as she'd expected. It was impersonal, furnished in shades of grey that she found unappealing, but the chairs were comfortable enough. Her empty cup and saucer stood on the table in front of her and Hutt pushed them to one side.

'First, a brief statement,' said Hutt. 'I want you to say that you have been shown a body and that you recognize it as the one you saw yesterday morning in a house in Carpenter Street.'

'Yes,' said Kate, taking paper and ballpoint from Hutt. 'I'll write the words myself, if you don't mind.'

'Very well.' Hutt sounded disapproving, as though the words she would choose would not be the permitted, official ones, but Kate was past caring whether he disapproved or not. Writing her brief statement would at least keep her mind occupied. She didn't like the pictures that crowded in on her when she had nothing else to think about.

'There,' she said, after a few minutes, handing back the page. 'You want me to sign and date it?'

'If you would.'

Kate signed, thought for a moment about the date, then added that.

'Thank you, Miss Ivory,' said Hutt, 'I won't keep you more than a minute or two,' and he left the room, presumably to pass her statement on to someone who would be interested in it, or who would file it, or perhaps even lose it.

Kate wished that she smoked. It would pass the few minutes before Hutt returned. There was a ritual to smoking that emptied the mind and occupied the hands. But it was no good, she hated the smell of tobacco smoke. She wondered about asking for a third cup of tea, but she didn't think she could face another one, even if she could find someone to fetch it for her.

She thought about getting up and walking out of the interview room, down through the police station and out into the street. It was an appealing thought, and she was about to put it into action when Hutt reappeared through the door.

'Right. Now, if you wouldn't mind answering a few questions,' he said.

'Do I have any choice?'

'I had the impression that you wanted to be as helpful as possible to the police in their enquiries into Mr Bettony's death,' said Hutt blandly.

There seemed little point in arguing.

'What is it you want to know?' she answered dutifully.

'If you could just take me through the events of yesterday morning,' said Hutt.

'But I've already done that,' she objected. 'They weren't very pleasant, and today's have been rather worse. I'd prefer to put them all out of my head.'

Hutt said, as though she hadn't spoken, 'But now I'd like you to take me through it just one more time.'

Kate passed her hand over her forehead, as though she was having difficulty with remembering the details, but she was thinking rapidly. Hutt sounded relaxed to the point of boredom, but she knew that he was noting everything she said, and she had to stay alert if she wasn't going to land Emma and Joyce in trouble. She decided to begin with some tedious, accurate detail.

'I rang the bell at seventeen Carpenter Street and I got no reply, so I knocked on the door as well. Still no reply.'

'What time was this?'

'In the morning,' said Kate vaguely.

'Can you be more precise?'

'Sometime after eleven, I think. Perhaps eleven-thirty.'

'And why were you knocking and ringing at the door of number seventeen?'

'Well, obviously because I wanted to see the occupant.'

'Mr Bettony.'

'I thought we'd agreed that Mr Bettony was dead. Wasn't that the point of my visit to the mortuary?'

Perhaps Hutt heard the edge of hysteria in her voice, for he replied in a calm, featureless voice, as though trying to bring the emotional temperature down to normal. 'Mr Bettony was the man who lived there. He was the owner of seventeen Carpenter Street. I assume that you were knocking on the door because you wanted to speak to him.'

Constable Hutt could be just as tedious as she could, thought Kate. But she had regained her composure and answered in the same bored tones. 'Was he? Well, in that case, I must have had the wrong address. I was looking for a woman.'

There was a long pause, during which Kate and Constable Hutt smiled blandly at one another and waited for the other to speak first.

'Remind me of the name of this woman?' Hutt broke first.

'Her name is Joyce Fielding.' Constable Hutt wrote it down. 'And I thought she had rented a room at number seventeen. I must have got it wrong.'

'Why did you think she was living there?'

'Why all the questions? I didn't find her there. There was no indication that she had ever been there. I must have been mistaken about it.'

'You did break into the house, I understand.'

'Not really. I just happened to find a door open.'

'I thought it was a window.'

'Window. Door. What's the difference? I was looking for Joyce Fielding and I was afraid she might be lying on the floor, ill or unconscious or something. She's an old woman,' Kate added earnestly, hoping that Roz would never come to hear sixty-something described as 'old' by her own daughter.

'I didn't find Mrs Fielding, but I did see the body of a man. I now know that it was Mr Bettony. But I had never seen him before, so I don't know how I can help you.'

'What time was this?'

'I've already told you. It was during the morning. I can't remember the exact time.'

'Try.'

'Oh, I don't know. About half past eleven, I suppose. Maybe twelve o'clock.'

'A woman answering your description was seen at the door of number seventeen at approximately ten-fifty.'

'How can whoever saw me be sure?'

'You interrupted *The Vanessa Show*, apparently, which had been on for some time and which ended five or ten minutes later. I'm giving you the benefit of the ten minutes, you notice.'

'It might have been ten to eleven, I suppose. I wasn't looking at my watch.'

'So why did you wait until twelve-seventeen to telephone the police?'

'Are you sure?'

'Quite sure. You phoned from a mobile phone and failed to leave your name and address.'

'But you tracked me down, nevertheless.'

'It wasn't difficult. Tell me more about Mrs Joyce Fielding.'

'She's a very ordinary grandmother. She was looking after her grandchildren while her son-in-law was recovering from a bad accident, and then she walked out one afternoon last week and no one has seen her since then.'

Kate found, to her exasperation, that she was about to burst into tears. The whole story seemed so sad, so hopeless. She pulled herself together.

'I don't suppose there's really anything sinister in her

disappearance. She probably needed a break from all those dreadful children, or she remembered that she'd left the kettle on in her own flat. Who knows? I'm sure we'll find her soon. And she couldn't possibly be mixed up in the death of Mr Bettony. She's far too respectable.'

She had gabbled her way through this explanation and she looked at Hutt to see what effect it was having on him. He was as impassive as ever.

'Can you give me a description of Mrs Fielding?'

'I've never met her,' replied Kate. 'From her daughter's description she looks exactly like everyone else's granny.'

Constable Hutt made a note on his pad, and she had the feeling that he would be returning to this subject before she was allowed to go home.

'Now, to return to seventeen Carpenter Street,' said Hutt. 'Give me an exact description of what you found when you went into the room where you saw the body.'

'Do you want me to draw you a picture?' asked Kate sarcastically.

'That would be very useful. Use the pad in front of you,' said Hutt.

So Kate drew a rough square for the room, and marked the door she had entered by. She indicated the position of the window, and the fireplace with its gas fire. It was surprising how much she could remember when she put her mind to it. Then she closed her eyes for a moment, so that she could remember the furniture, and where it was placed, and exactly where the body lay in relation to it all.

'It was like this,' she said eventually, passing over the drawing.

Hutt took it and examined it. 'Very good,' he said grudgingly. 'Now, tell me any other details you can remember.'

'The curtains were drawn, and the light in the room was

dim, so I pulled them open,' she began.

'You didn't tell me that before.'

'I've only just remembered it. You were right,' she conceded. 'It has helped my memory to make a drawing.'

Hutt smiled. 'Go on,' he said.

'The room was quite cold, and it gave the impression that the fire hadn't been on at all that day,' she said slowly. 'The light from the window wasn't brilliant, but all the colours in the room jumped out at me. The curtains were deep blue. There were a couple of ornaments on the mantelpiece: china cows, I think. The sofa and chairs were red, rather worn, but quite clean. Everything was very clean, now I come to think about it. The floor was covered in some neutral cord carpet, beige or green or something like that, but someone had added a couple of brilliant rugs. They were in one of those fussy, swirling patterns that make your eyes go funny. Yellow and orange and brown.' She was recalling all these details as though she never wanted to reach the object in the centre of the room. If she went on describing the objects around him she might never have to get to Mr Bettony.

'And then there was Mr Bettony,' said Hutt gently. 'The sight of that body must have been quite a shock.'

'Yes. But there had been a faint smell when I first entered the house. Nothing too disgusting, just a sort of background whiff, as though the drains were giving trouble, or someone had forgotten to rinse out the dishcloths.'

'You've marked the position on your sketch. Is that correct?'

Kate checked the drawing. 'Yes, that's right. One of the rugs covered all the central portion of the room, and the body was *here*, with the head resting in the middle of the rug.' She pointed with her pen.

'That's very interesting. Are you sure?'

'Yes. I'm sure.'

'Because there was no rug such as you describe in the room. And the carpet, a beige Berber twist, made from some synthetic material, was newly laid. It was the thing that struck me when I walked into that room the first time, the smell of air freshener and new carpet. It was quite overpowering. I certainly didn't smell any decaying body.'

'But you're agreeing with me that I did see it. You wouldn't believe me yesterday, you thought I was making it up. I saw it, and then someone came and removed the body and the rug and the carpet, in case they'd left any evidence.'

'You obviously watch a lot of television,' said Hutt drily.

'But you believe me now?'

'I believe that what you've told me is probably the truth as far as you understand it,' said Hutt guardedly.

'All you have to do now,' said Kate brightly, 'is find out who bought the fake Berber twist.'

'We're looking into it, but I doubt whether they were stupid enough to buy it locally. And it is a very popular line. And if they paid cash there would be no record of their name or address. Now, carry on with your description of what you did next.'

'I left the house as quickly as I could,' said Kate. 'I could see he was long dead, so there was no point in trying any first aid. I got in my car and I drove . . .' She was about to say that she drove home, but she hadn't. She'd driven to Emma's house. 'I drove home,' she said. That was one layer of explanations she could get out of.

'Did you see anyone in the street? Did you notice anything unusual, anything at all, in fact?' He hadn't noticed her hesitation, apparently.

'No. I don't remember seeing anyone, but I suppose one or two people saw *me*.' She stopped. 'Yes, there was one thing, but I'm sure it means nothing. I drove round the block a couple of times because I got confused by the one-way streets, and there was a white pick-up truck that pulled up next to me. I noticed it because it was playing head-banger music and I thought it belonged to the man who lives next door to me in Agatha Street. But it wasn't the same one. A man and a woman were in the cab and I didn't know them.' You're rambling, she told herself. 'I'm sorry. You remember the oddest things. I'm sure it had nothing at all to do with the case. Why should it?'

Hutt had listened patiently. 'Probably not,' he said. 'Did you note its registration number?'

'No.'

'I don't suppose it's important.'

'I drove home,' said Kate again, eager to get to the end of her story. 'And then I telephoned the police.'

'Why didn't you do this before?'

'I don't know. I just wanted to get back to my own place. I'm sorry. I suppose it's some kind of instinct.'

'You used your mobile phone.'

'Yes.'

'If you'd reached your own house, why didn't you use your ordinary land-line?'

Kate reached for an explanation. 'My mother was at home. I didn't want to worry her.'

'She's a delicate type?'

'Yes, she is, rather.' Kate hoped her mother would forgive her.

'She didn't strike me that way.'

'But you don't know her as well as I do.'

They stared at one another. Stalemate. But he knows I'm lying, Kate thought.

'Why don't I get you another cup of tea, and a sandwich, perhaps?' said Hutt.

'Thank you. But I can eat at home,' said Kate.

'I'll get you the tea,' said Hutt equably. 'And then we'll go through your morning once again. There is still some time you haven't accounted for.'

25

Roz

When Kate and Constable Hutt had left for the police station, Roz made herself a fresh pot of coffee and sat down with a pencil and one of the pads of scrap paper that Kate kept in every room. Her daughter was ready at any moment to scribble down anything that occurred to her when inspiration struck, Roz thought, and she wished that inspiration would strike her, too.

She hadn't told Kate about her ad in the paper, and she was feeling just a little guilty about it. She had been so sure that it would bring in an immediate response from Joyce and would solve all their problems. Look! she wanted to say to Kate. I've solved it! She had wanted to surprise them all: Kate, Emma, George and Sam. She could have shown them just how clever she was. But it hadn't happened like that.

She had laughed at Kate's idea that she should understand Joyce because she was the same age, and because in the past she had walked out of Kate's life. But, even so, hadn't she been trying to prove something? I can make it up to you for the years when I was away – that's what she'd been trying to tell Kate. I'll produce the missing granny for you. You can depend on me. *This time* you can depend on me.

She had put in the ad and she had received just the one reply, not from Joyce, but from someone who had appeared to know her. Roz had tried to convince herself that the whole thing had been an unpleasant joke, but she didn't really believe that. Someone who knew Joyce, who knew her present whereabouts, had phoned.

She wished now that she had given a box number. At least then she would have had a sheet of paper and an envelope to go on. As it was, she had only her memory – getting fuzzier by the hour – of a harsh female voice and a menacing tone.

And now there was another dead body – or perhaps the same dead body that Kate had seen the previous day. Not the sort of thing you could ignore, or pretend hadn't really happened. Not the sort of thing you could convince yourself was just a nasty joke.

Kate had followed Joyce's trail to Carpenter Street and had found a body. Some new friend of Joyce's had phoned and now knew Roz and Kate's phone number. She knew Roz's name, too, since she had meekly given it to her. Why couldn't she have invented a name? Because, she was forced to admit, the harsh-voiced woman would have heard the lie in her voice as soon as she spoke.

Roz found the telephone directory and leafed through it, hoping against hope that Kate had suddenly decided to go ex-directory. No such luck. There she was, one of only four Ivorys in the book, easy to find. And there was the phone number Roz had given in the ad, just in case the woman wondered which of the four she was.

Roz jotted three items down on her scrap pad:

1. Joyce is missing.
2. Someone has been murdered.
3. The murderer probably knows who and where we are.

Instead of solving the problem, she had only made it worse.

She had put herself and Kate, and who knew how many others, in danger. She should go straight upstairs and pack her things and walk out of her daughter's life again. She brought nothing but peril and destruction with her. Kate would be far better off without her. As soon as Kate got back from the police station, she would confess her mistake with the newspaper ad and tell her she was leaving.

No, she mustn't exaggerate, even to herself. She remembered why Kate was at the police station. She had to be here when Kate returned and she had to be ready to be a rock of dependability, a shoulder to cry on. It was a pity she hadn't practised such solid virtues over the past twenty years: she wasn't sure how good she'd be in this role.

She looked again at the third line. She was making a large assumption there, wasn't she?

But the sinking feeling in the pit of her stomach told her that her assumption was all too likely to be true.

26

Kate

The phone was ringing.

'Bother,' said Kate. 'I don't want to speak to anyone at the moment. And I don't suppose it's important, anyway.'

'It went out of my head,' said Roz. 'But someone's been trying to ring you all the time you were out. You have to give them points for perseverance.'

'Man? Woman?' asked Kate, reaching for the phone.

'Woman.'

'Hello. Kate Ivory,' said Kate.

'Kate, darling, where have you *been* all day?'

'Hello, Estelle. How are you?' She mouthed, 'It's my agent,' at Roz, who grimaced sympathetically and then moved out of earshot.

'I'm fine,' gushed Estelle. 'How are *you*, darling? And I'm just ringing to say that I've received your lovely manuscript quite safely. I'll be reading it this weekend, and I'm so looking forward to it.'

'It's kind of you to say so,' said Kate, waiting for the 'but'. With Estelle Livingstone there always was a 'but'.

'But,' said Estelle delicately, 'Kate darling, I've just glanced through it, just skimmed it, you might say, and I have noticed one tiny thing.'

'Yes?' asked Kate. The day had started badly and

171

continued worse. It sounded as though Estelle was going to make it a hat trick.

'Do forgive me if I'm wrong, but it does look rather like a historical again, Kate darling.'

Kate could imagine Estelle at the other end of the phone, sitting in her chaotic office, manuscripts in drunken heaps on every available surface, large, furry tabby cat ensconced on the visitors' chair, so that the next visitor to Estelle's office would leave with cat hairs all over their smart black suit. Estelle would have a mug of cheap instant coffee by her right hand. She always did. And her curly black hair would be standing out from her head, moussed and gelled to perfection by her expensive hairdresser.

'Are you still there?' Estelle asked.

'Yes,' said Kate. 'I was just thinking about what you said. You see, Estelle,' she explained, as though to an idiot, 'that's what I am. A historical novelist. A writer of historical romances. When I send you a manuscript, it tends to be yet another historical romance.'

'Well, I know that that's what you've been producing for the past few years, darling. And they've all been quite lovely. You haven't huge sales, or sold any translation rights yet, but they've been steady sellers. Not brilliant, but steady. And I expect you've made a respectable sum from your PLR.'

'Thank you, Estelle.'

'But you see, darling, you have to be flexible in today's climate.' Estelle was sounding brisk and inspirational. It was a speciality of hers. 'Historicals aren't doing very well, are they? You see them remaindered all over the place.'

It was true that Kate had noticed rather a lot of gaudy colours and heaving bosoms on dust jackets in the discount bookstore recently. She hated to think Estelle was right, but it was a possibility. 'Flexible?' she queried.

'I know you can be flexible if you try,' encouraged Estelle. There was the sound of slurping. She must have ingested another few grammes of cut-price caffeine.

'Flexible in which direction?'

'You're thirty-something, aren't you?'

'I suppose so. What's that got to do with it?'

'It's what they're all looking for these days. Racy, pacy novels for the thirty-something market. Take the lid off your frantic, sexy lifestyle and shock us all. Get it down on paper. Share it with your contemporaries.'

'Are you sure they'll be buying books? Won't they be out there, living their own frantic, sexy lives?'

'You're sounding a tiny bit negative this afternoon, Kate darling. Is everything all right?'

'Everything's fine.'

'I hope you're relaxing, taking things easy after your great efforts on the new book. You should have a holiday, then you can come back with a whole host of new ideas.'

'Beach parties?' enquired Kate gloomily. 'The holiday romance?'

'I think they've been done already. You need to come up with something more original. Well, think about it. See if you can write me an exciting proposal, hmm? And meanwhile, I'm really looking forward to reading ... umm ... this weekend.'

'I'll see what I can do,' said Kate, noticing that Estelle had already forgotten the title of her latest book, but determined not to be labelled 'negative' again.

When she had put the phone down, she wondered which bits of this particular day of her life she could share with other thirty-somethings. Inspecting a days-old corpse? Sexy? Not really. More like stomach-churning.

'Roz!' she called. 'How are we doing for red wine? Don't you think it's time we poured ourselves a drink?'

27

Kate

Once the sun sank below the suburban rooftops, the temperature dipped and reminded them that the year was entering December. No hint of April in the weather now. There was a chill wind coming down from the north, threatening them with ice and sleet.

Kate stared moodily into her glass of wine. The only thing that would take her mind off the events of the day was her work, but she didn't really have anything she could immerse herself in at the moment. She had just posted off one manuscript and she would like to take a few days' break before she started the next one. And now, according to Estelle, she had to leave the haven of the past, where anything might happen, and think up some new characters who were placed firmly in the last years of the twentieth century. Estelle might irritate her, but she had to trust her judgement.

Light-hearted, fun-loving characters, Estelle had said. But all she could see was Bettony's head, with the dried, blackened blood and the distorted features. She would never again be able to write a light-hearted novel. That image of Bettony would always intrude between her and the page of her notebook.

It was odd, too, how every bad new experience somehow attached itself to those of the past, so that their effect was magnified. When she saw Bettony's head, it reminded her of her friend Andrew, and all the emotions surrounding his death came flooding back, adding themselves to the horror of this new one.

Was there no escape? Roz had been wonderfully support-ive, producing tea – which only reminded her of the police station – and a light, nourishing meal. Kate had appreciated the effort her mother was making, but still couldn't be distracted from her own thoughts.

Luckily for her sanity, there was a ring at the front door. She heard Roz running down the stairs to answer it. She just hoped it was no more bad news. She just couldn't face any more at that moment.

It was George. Lovely, normal, cheerful George, with his head quite unmarked by a maniac's bludgeon, and an expression of concern on his face.

'I should have rung first. I'm sorry,' he began.

'Don't be sorry,' said Kate. 'Just come inside and share the wine. It's red again. It seems to be our favourite.' She pushed aside the thought that the red wine reminded her of bloodstains. She would have a word with Roz and they would buy a few bottles of Sauvignon next time they were in the supermarket. They might buy some air freshener, too, and bunches of scented flowers to get the smell of death out of her nostrils.

'I was worried about you,' said George, sitting in the same chair that Constable Hutt had filled so unpleasantly earlier in the day. 'You had to rush off in such a hurry. I was afraid that something dreadful had happened.' He glanced at Roz, as though assuring himself that she was still there and in one piece. Of course, his first assumption would have been that something had happened to *her*, when Kate went rushing off that morning.

'It's been a pig of a day,' blurted out Kate. 'The dead

body turned up again, buried in concrete, and the police insisted that I should come and look at it.'

George looked blank. 'Dead body? What dead body?' Then, remembering the disappearance of Emma's mother, he asked, 'Not Joyce? You don't mean they've found Joyce's body?'

'It's all right,' said Roz. 'It's the body of a man in his forties, apparently. Definitely not Joyce. And no one that any of us knows.'

George relaxed back into his chair. 'So why did they ask Kate to look at it?'

'She didn't tell you about her investigations yesterday, then?'

'No, I didn't,' said Kate.

'You'd better tell him,' said Roz, and while Kate did so, she sat wondering whether she could find the right moment to tell both of them about her own telephone adventure with Joyce's friend. But as she watched Kate's face as she went through her story once again, she decided that this wasn't the time. She would save it for tomorrow, or even the day after. Kate had had two horrible experiences two days running, and she was still patently affected by them. If she hadn't been so emotionally restrained, she might be weeping or shouting by now. It was a pity she didn't: it might make her feel better. Only the tension in her jaw and the haunted look in her eyes gave her away. But Roz, watching the subtly changing expressions on her face, reckoned that the constant repetition was finally doing its healing work on Kate. She was upset, yes, but she wasn't as distraught as she had been when she first arrived home from the police station that afternoon.

George was listening carefully, Roz was pleased to see. He didn't interrupt, and when Kate had reached the end of her story, he spoke quietly and calmly. He was sympathetic, but he didn't over-dramatize – a failing that she and Kate often fell into, she had to admit.

'It looks bad,' he said, eventually. 'But we needn't jump to conclusions. We don't have to believe that this Bettony man's murder has anything at all to do with Joyce, do we? Maybe it has, but I don't think we should worry too much about it until we have more definite evidence that there's a connection.'

They drank their wine and talked of other things for a while. Kate put a CD on the player to help the mood along.

Eventually, George said, 'I nearly forgot. There was another reason I came round this evening. If you remember, when you rushed off this morning, I'd been talking to Sam.'

'Of course,' said Kate. 'It seems a lifetime ago. You must have thought I was so rude, just running off like that.'

'I thought you were worried,' said George. 'But while I was talking to Sam, I asked him about the brooch. You remember, the one with the nasty little cherub.'

'The Sunshine Angel,' said Kate.

'He said that there were some of these Sunshine women around in the clinic, but of course he'd have recognized Joyce if she'd been one of them.'

'We should have thought of that. It's obvious, isn't it?' said Kate.

'Perhaps. But they operate all over the place, apparently. Not in the main Oxford hospitals, more in private clinics.'

'Hordes of them,' said Kate gloomily. 'All with their pink overalls and cheery smiles. It would be enough to send you straight into a relapse.'

George smiled. 'The other thing that Sam pointed out was that the Maxwell Clinic is much bigger than it appears at first. The place developed like a rabbit warren as they bought up adjacent property and incorporated it into the original.'

'And since Sam isn't mobile,' said Roz slowly, 'he can't have walked all round the place. He can hardly have made his way up and down all the staircases and explored the distant wings. There might be flocks of Angels all over the place, only Sam would never have seen them. Joyce might be there, just a corridor or two away, and Sam wouldn't know it.'

They looked at each other. 'We'll go back there tomorrow,' said Kate.

'I'm teaching all day,' said George regretfully.

'I'll come with you,' said Roz with alacrity. 'You need your mother with you at a time like this.'

'Huh!' was Kate's reply.

Oh good, thought Roz. She's feeling better.

'And there's another thing,' said Kate.

'Yes?'

'Has anyone been back to Joyce's flat? Maybe she's at home.'

'Why should she be?' asked Roz.

'She's lost her memory,' said Kate.

'Then she wouldn't have found her way home.'

'It's just her recent memory she's lost. Looking after all of Emma's children brought it on.'

'You're being ridiculous.'

George had been listening to this argument between mother and daughter. Now he interrupted. 'Emma has rung loads of times. There's never any reply. And she's phoned the neighbours, too.'

'I still think we should check again. It's easy enough to turn the ringing tone off by mistake. It's days before you notice that it's happened.'

George looked doubtful. 'If you say so,' he said.

'Kate and I will explore the clinic tomorrow,' said Roz. 'You and Kate can look at Joyce's flat the day after.'

'Aren't you teaching?' asked Kate.

'Not on a Saturday,' replied George. 'And I'll get hold of a key to Joyce's flat. Emma should have one.'

'Don't tell her about Bettony's body reappearing,' said Kate. 'It probably has nothing to do with Joyce.'

'I'm sure you're right. I won't say a word.'

'That's sorted, then,' said Roz. 'I'll just finish my glass of wine, and I think I'll retire to my room.'

'It's only half past nine,' said Kate, surprised.

'I'm very tired,' said Roz, yawning obtrusively. 'This exciting life takes it out of a woman of my age.'

Kate would have made a very rude reply if George hadn't been present.

'You have a good rest,' she said. 'Would you like me to bring you up a cup of cocoa a little later?'

'What a thoughtful girl!' said Roz sweetly. 'Goodnight, George.'

28

Joyce

I wonder whether I could take a look at the local paper, Ruth dear. Well, no, not if you haven't finished with it. Yes, of course it is a bit of a rag, a terrible waste of time and really no better than one of those dreadful tabloids. Nothing but gossip and scandal. But I like to know what's happening in the local community and sometimes there's a nice article about gardening or wildlife. Not that there's much wildlife about at this time of year, you're right, of course. And I don't suppose people are very busy in their gardens, either. No, it was stupid of me to think there'd be anything that would interest me, I can see that.

Yes, of course I'll go and get on with the ironing. Idle hands, as they say. And I'll give it a dash of starch, too. I do like the tablecloth to look really fresh for our supper.

Oh dear! What on earth have I done! How awful! And it's made such a dreadful mess!

Was that my fault? Silly old me, I didn't think I was anywhere near the teapot. I'm so sorry, dear. I just didn't see it there, I'm afraid. I thought I'd put it over there on the table. I must be getting forgetful in my old age. No, no, you sit down. I'll go and get a cloth. It hasn't splashed on the carpet, has it? Or on your nice frock? No. Just on the newspaper. I can see that. What a shame! It's quite ruined. Oh, I am sorry, Ruth. Would you like me to go and buy you another copy? No, I suppose it is only full of rubbish. Gossip and scandal, as you said.

There now, it's all cleared away. I've put the newspaper in the bin, and made us another pot of tea. I'll have to watch what I'm doing with this one, won't I?

You're going out? Surely you've got time to drink your tea first.

No, I'm afraid I'm not very good at finding my way round the Oxford suburbs. Agatha Street? Now that does ring a bell. Such a funny name for a street, don't you think? I can't recall ever going there myself, but then I hardly go anywhere. I'm more of a home person, you see. But perhaps Emma mentioned it, or one of the children.

Ivory. Ivory. Yes, again, I do believe I've heard that name before, but I just can't remember where. I'm sorry I'm not being very much help to you. Yes, I expect it would be a good idea to take a taxi if you don't know the way. No, don't you worry about me, dear. I'll have all the ironing done for you by the time you get back.

29

Kate

'Whatever time is it?'

Kate fought her way up through treacle, fathoms deep.

'I thought I'd let you sleep. I've been creeping round the house, trying not to wake you. Would you like some coffee?' Roz sounded concerned.

'About two gallons. Strong and black.'

'And I'll make some toast, too. With marmalade?'

'Actually, I don't feel very hungry. What's brought on this maternal attack?'

Then they were both silent for a moment, for neither wished to mention the name of Bettony.

'Shall I bring the coffee up here, or do you want to come downstairs?'

'I'll come down.'

Kate found it more difficult than she had expected to crawl out of bed. Her head hurt. Her legs felt weak. She ignored both facts, wrapped herself in a dressing-gown and stumbled downstairs.

'Don't say it,' she said to Roz.

'What?'

'I look awful.'

'You'll feel better when you've eaten something, drunk a gallon of coffee and had a bath.'

'If you say so.'

'Actually, you're looking rather flushed. How are you feeling, really?'

'I'll let you know when I've finished the coffee. I don't suppose we have any fruit juice, have we?'

'Orange or apple?'

'Orange, please.'

The orange juice was more welcome than the coffee, and Kate pushed her mug away. The headache was getting worse and her back was beginning to ache.

'I think I've got flu,' she said.

'I think you're right,' said Roz.

'I'm going back to bed,' said Kate, unable to make any sensible conversation.

'Plenty of rest and fluids,' muttered Roz to herself, starting to make a shopping list of items suitable for an invalid.

'George called round,' she said later. 'I told him you were ill. He sends fond get-well messages.'

'Mmph,' said Kate from under the duvet. It was difficult to care about anything, even George, when she was feeling this awful.

'George called round again. He's brought you these flowers,' said Roz the next day. 'I have thanked him,' she added.

'You're not going round to the clinic, asking questions, are you?' asked Kate anxiously.

'No, of course not. We're waiting for you to get better,' said Roz.

'Mmph,' said Kate, and went back to sleep.

It was five days before she could sit up in bed for longer than an hour. Roz knew she must be on the mend when she greeted her with, 'We have to get on with finding Joyce

Fielding,' when she brought up her morning glass of orange juice.

'Are you feeling better this morning?'

'Yes. And I'm going to get out of this bed. I can't stand it any longer.'

Roz managed not to tell her to take it easy. 'I'll see you downstairs, then,' she said.

Kate arrived downstairs looking pale and wan. She had washed her hair, and it still hung in damp rats' tails over her forehead.

'I need my hairdresser,' she said, sinking into a chair. She closed her eyes. 'But maybe not today,' she said.

'Give yourself another couple of days before you venture outside,' said Roz.

'Why? What's happening?'

'It's winter. There's a lot of cold rain, and occasional sleet. In the mornings, the grass is covered in frost and the pavement is icy. I'd rather you didn't add pneumonia, or a broken ankle, to the unpleasant virus you've already been suffering from.'

'You haven't caught it?' enquired Kate.

'No, thank goodness. I seem to have acquired many useful immunities on my travels.'

Kate tried to smile, but her head still hurt. The only good thing about having the flu seemed to be that she had forgotten about Bettony, even if only for five days.

'What do you suggest I do?' she asked. She wanted to say that she was bored, but it sounded too childish.

'What do you want to do? Shall I find you a book to read? Music to listen to? A colouring book or jigsaw puzzle?'

'An undemanding book would be nice.' It was lovely to be looked after, Kate decided.

Roz returned in a few minutes. 'Try this one,' she said,

handing over a paperback. 'Everyone says it's great fun, and it's been on the bestseller list for months. I bought it to read during my long, lonely evenings, but I haven't actually started it yet.'

Kate took it and looked at the cover. The latest sexy bestseller written by and for thirty-somethings, she saw.

The following evening, just when Kate was feeling listless and rather irritable with her mother, George called round.

'Thank goodness you're better,' he said. 'I was getting worried about you.'

That was nice to hear. She tried to ignore the fact that she was wearing a baggy pair of grey jogging bottoms and a faded red sweatshirt, and no make-up. Luckily, George didn't seem to mind.

Roz disappeared into her room for a while. She's being discreet, thought Kate. But after half an hour of desultory conversation, she thought it was time to bring her back.

'Roz!' she called. 'We need your contribution. We're just going to start to discuss Joyce Fielding again.'

'Are we?' asked George, sounding surprised.

'I've done nothing for a week. I must start looking for her again.'

When Roz had joined them again, George said, 'I have done one or two things while you were ill. I've spoken to Sam when I've been visiting. I didn't want to say too much, I don't want to worry him unnecessarily.'

'Emma would kill you if you did,' said Kate.

'I must meet this woman,' said Roz. 'I'm sure she and I would have so much in common.'

'What did you find out from Sam?' asked Kate, ignoring her.

'I asked him about the Sunshine Angels again. Sam couldn't see that they were anything other than kind old ladies. Definitely not the sort to go kidnapping his mother-in-law. Not that I suggested they were, of course, but for some reason, he assumed that that's what you were implying, Kate.'

'Did you manage to waylay one of these Angels and ask it some awkward questions?' asked Kate.

'I did, as a matter of fact. Two of them, to be precise. The first was younger, darker and wider than I had been expecting, and possibly not as middle-aged as she at first appeared. She frowned when I asked about Joyce. "Joyce?" she repeated quite sharply. And she stared at me. She was tall, about five foot eight or nine, with slightly raised heels, so she was staring at me nearly on a level. It's an odd thing to say about someone, but she had no expression in her eyes. She had a slablike face, putty-coloured, with flat, dark eyes that just stared at me from behind round spectacles. It was as though I existed, but I wasn't human. If I did something she didn't like, she'd just squash me like a bluebottle.'

'That's a lot to read into one pair of eyes,' said Roz. 'I've never been that good at first impressions, myself.'

'You don't believe me. I can't blame you. It does sound fanciful now I'm telling you about it, and perhaps I'm making more of it than it warrants.'

'What did she say?' asked Kate, impatient, as ever, to get to the part that interested her.

'She said "Joyce" again, as though turning the name over in her mind. "No, I don't think there's a Joyce. In fact, I'm sure there's never been a Joyce." And then she was silent again and staring at me, as though she just wanted me to disappear.'

'Did you believe her?'

'I did. But it doesn't mean she was telling the truth. She had a very forceful personality. It was as though she was daring me to *disbelieve* her. It was easier to agree that Joyce had never worked there.'

'I can understand that she might know that there's no Joyce in the clinic right at this moment, but how can she possibly be so sure that no Joyce, in any department, ever worked there?' said Roz.

'Well, after I'd spent half an hour or so with Sam, I went looking for another rose-pink overall and her trolley-load of goodies. And I found one, just leaving the bedside of an accident victim, where she had been taking down a list of his simpler needs.'

'You grabbed her,' suggested Kate. 'You sat her down in a basket-weave chair and grilled her.'

'I did my utmost to be charming,' corrected George. 'I painted myself as a person in need of help. I thought this was most likely to get a helpful response.'

'Good thinking,' said Roz.

'She was a sweet, white-haired, blue-eyed old thing, rather like the Queen Mother. I told her how distraught I was at losing touch with my dear friend Joyce Fielding, and did she know her, had she ever met her. She said no, she didn't think so.'

'Was this one telling the truth?' asked Roz.

'I don't believe she was capable of telling the tiniest lie,' said George. 'So I urged her to think again. Perhaps this was someone who had merely enquired about becoming a Sunshine Angel, who had never actually been received into the sisterhood. And then her brow ruffled just the tiniest bit, and she said, "Maybe I did meet someone called Joyce, though I'm not sure whether her surname was Fielding or not." And yes, she had appeared in Henrietta Wing briefly, being taken on a tour of the clinic, perhaps, but if she had joined the Sunshine Angels, she had been assigned to a different wing, perhaps a different section of the clinic altogether.'

'This isn't getting us very far,' said Roz.

'I persevered,' continued George. 'I suggested that being an Angel was a job for the few, for those who had special gifts of empathy and concern for others. She agreed with me, and then said that she had heard some gossip about one of the Angels, and it might well have been Joyce.'

'Gossip? What gossip?' asked Kate.

'This Joyce, and there's no guarantee it was *our* Joyce, apparently didn't get on with being a Sunshine Angel. It hurt her poor legs, apparently. And as she was unable to concentrate on doing good for the patients, she got herself a nice part-time job somewhere else.'

'Where?' Roz and Kate spoke together.

'She couldn't remember.'

'Bother!' Again they spoke in concert, only perhaps Roz hadn't used quite so mild an expletive.

'I insisted,' said George. 'I told her what a marvellous memory she had, and how surprised I was that she had been able to recall so much. And she said she thought Joyce had gone to work in one of those high-class delicatessens that also sell sandwiches.'

'I know the sort,' said Kate. 'None of your cheese and pickle. She must be filling ciabatta rolls with mortadella and rocket.'

'That would suit Joyce,' said George. 'Though I can't imagine why she'd want to do that, rather than look after Emma and Sam's children.'

'Regular food?' suggested Roz. 'A wage at the end of her week's work.'

'Did she say whereabouts?' asked Kate eagerly. 'In the city centre?'

'She didn't know. It took quite a lot of perseverance to get this much out of her.'

'You did brilliantly,' said Roz. 'Thank you George.'

'Oh yes, of course. Thank you, George,' said Kate belatedly, wondering whether George's Angel was really so believable.

'There was just one other odd thing. It's just that as we ended our conversation, an expression of relief came over her face. I know I said she was a sweet little old thing who couldn't tell a lie, but it was as if she was relieved that I'd listened to her, and surprised that I'd believed her. But why shouldn't I? Why on earth should she be lying? And then she watched me as I walked back down the corridor. I know, because when I reached the end, I turned and looked back, and she was still watching me.'

'But there has been a Joyce around, even if she hasn't left to work in a sandwich shop,' said Kate. 'We'll get out there and look for her tomorrow.'

'We're building a lot on the chance that it's our Joyce. It might not be,' cautioned Roz. 'We don't know her surname.'

'The Angels don't seem to go in for surnames. The names on their badges are all first names.'

'What about the one with the menacing eyes?' asked Kate. 'Did you notice her name?'

'I don't think she was wearing a badge,' said George.

'Perhaps she didn't want you to know her name,' said Kate. 'You, or anyone else.'

'I think we're letting our imaginations run away with us,' said Roz.

'Very well, then. We'll do something practical. We'll go back to the clinic, the way we planned last week, in case she's hidden there somewhere, or someone knows more about her. And we'll look through all the posh sandwich shops, to see if she's buttering rolls instead of looking after her grandchildren.'

'And we can check out her flat,' added George. 'We were

going to do that, too, weren't we? We'd feel pretty silly if she was sitting there all this while.'

'There,' said Kate. 'We'll find her in time for Christmas.'

'Wine, anyone?' asked Roz.

30

Kate

'Are you feeling well enough to come with me to the Maxwell Clinic?'

'You mean you're thinking of going on your own?'

'I thought you might need a little more rest,' said Roz solicitously.

'I'm not having you finding Joyce without me.'

'Very well,' said Roz demurely. 'What time do you want to leave?'

'I've no idea what time it is at the moment, but give me about an hour.'

'Of course, dear. I'll just have a little light lunch while you're in the bath.'

Kate groaned. She hadn't realized it was *that* late. She'd thought she was back to normal this morning.

'What do you think: shall we drive, walk or take the bus?' asked Kate, who was by now a lot brighter than she had been when she first woke up.

'Let's take the car,' said Roz, whose liking for physical exercise wasn't as well developed as Kate's.

'Would you like to drive?' asked Kate.

'Fine. We'll take the VW.'

Kate could hardly grumble, even if she felt that Roz's egg-yolk yellow Beetle made a style statement that wasn't quite as elegant as her own.

They had both dressed respectably, and in quite understated clothes. They didn't want to be noticed as they explored the clinic. Kate had lent Roz a less exuberant coat than the one she usually wore, and Roz had pointed out that Kate's boots were too memorable.

'I could wear a woolly hat, if you insist,' said Kate.

'No need to exaggerate,' said Roz. 'Though I have to admit that the car heater isn't quite as reliable as it might be.'

'I've got my gloves,' said Kate, settling herself into the passenger seat. 'And I've wrapped my scarf round my ears. I expect I'll survive. By the way, why aren't we starting with the sandwich shops?'

'I thought that tramping the city streets in freezing temperatures wouldn't do you any good. Better to leave it for another day.'

'We could do it this afternoon,' said Kate optimistically.

'And anyway, there are too many strands ending up at the clinic for me to believe it's a coincidence.'

Roz drove sedately towards the Maxwell Clinic, and even managed to find a parking space within a couple of hundred yards of its entrance.

'What's our cover story?' she asked as they approached the gate.

'What?'

'Are we supposed to be visiting Sam, or what?'

'That would be the easiest. I do remember my way to his ward.'

The receptionist was as well groomed and as smiling as she had been on Kate's last visit.

'We've come to see Sam Dolby,' said Kate, starting to walk towards the stairs.

'I'm afraid he already has visitors with him,' said the

receptionist. 'Do you want to wait until they've left?'

'Can't he cope with two more?' asked Roz.

'House rules,' said the receptionist.

'We'll pop in to see Mrs Bassett while we're waiting,' said Kate, inspired. 'You remember her, don't you, Mother?' she added to Roz.

'How could I forget her?' Roz was adept at following her lead.

They both flashed winning smiles at the receptionist, pushed their way through the glass doors, and were halfway up to the first floor before she could think of anything to say in reply.

'Round one to us,' said Roz. 'Who's Mrs Bassett?'

Kate didn't have time to reply. As they arrived at the second-floor landing, they nearly bumped into an anxious-looking woman with a baby strapped into a pouch and a couple of thuggish toddlers trailing along at knee level.

'Hello, Emma,' said Kate.

'Kate? What are you doing here?'

'We're visiting my dear friend Adelaide Bassett,' announced Roz. 'And I don't think we've met. I'm Kate's mother, Roz.'

Emma had met her match. She said, 'How do you do?' the way her own mother had taught her.

One of the toddlers whined, 'I'm hungry,' and scowled at Kate, who beamed back at it as though contemplating a particularly fine joint of roast lamb. Then Roz smiled at Emma in a grand way, and she and Kate went up another flight of stairs, then pushed their way through the swing doors.

'*Adelaide?*' queried Kate.

'It was the best I could come up with on the spur of the moment. Now, where is it we're going, really?'

'Along here,' said Kate, leading the way. 'There really is a

Mrs Bassett, and I promised I'd come back to visit her. I don't think she gets many other people coming to see her. And I did actually mention that I thought Joyce had been kidnapped and was being held at gunpoint by one of the Sunshine Angels.'

'Why on earth did you tell her that?'

'I thought she needed cheering up.'

When they first walked into the small ward, Kate thought it was empty. The occupants of the three other beds must have escaped to the smoking room, but surely Anne Bassett wasn't up to such a journey? The place smelled of the vaguely medicinal and disinfectant scents of a hospital, with an overlay of cheap cleaning spray. Underneath them she caught the slight scent of *L'Air du Temps* that she associated with Mrs Bassett. Then she saw a movement in the bed by the window. Only a small movement, of a head turning on the pillow. White skin against white cotton. White hair waving back from the parchment forehead.

'So you've come back,' said Mrs Bassett. 'I've been waiting for you.' The face was still colourless, but the eyes had opened and blazed as blue as before across the room.

'Come over here and sit down,' she ordered. Her voice rasped like nutmeg against a grater. On her bedside cabinet stood one or two get-well cards, and Kate recognized them as the same ones that were there last time. There, too, stood her bottle of Ribena and her water jug, a small decorative box of tissues and a carved wooden cat. There were just a couple of photographs. Old ones, these, in posed black and white, one of two young women with shingled hair and tweed skirts; the other a group photograph of more young women, probably her fellow college students. No husband, thought Kate. Perhaps he had died young. Or maybe he hadn't, but she'd long ago grown tired of him.

Roz followed Kate over to the bed, and pulled up a second visitor's chair.

'Who's this?' asked Mrs Bassett.

'This is my mother, Roz,' said Kate. She had nearly been overcome by formality and introduced her as Mrs Ivory, or even as Rosemary, which would have been even worse in Roz's eyes.

'She looks rather fast,' said Mrs Bassett. But it sounded as though 'fast' was a term of approbation. 'And you look peaky.'

'I am. Very peaky. I've had flu, but I'm over it now.'

'People make a lot of fuss about nothing these days,' was Mrs Bassett's comment on this.

Kate sat down in a basket-weave chair, with her back to the window, near the head of the bed. The rasping voice would find it hard to project any further. Roz was sitting on the other side, out of Mrs Bassett's view, and she was apparently going to keep quiet, Kate was relieved to see.

Under the stabbing glare of those blue eyes, she didn't waste time asking how Mrs Bassett was, or offer any platitudes about the weather. Nor did she offer banal hopes for her recovery. She knew they would not be welcome.

'Well, what was it you wanted?'

'I was hoping you could help me find someone who's missing.'

'You said something about it last time you were here. The mother of a friend of yours, you said.'

'That's the one. Joyce Fielding.'

While Mrs Bassett watched her without speaking, Kate took the Sunshine Angel brooch out of her handbag and held it where Mrs Bassett could see without moving her head.

The round pink face, topped by golden curls, enfolded in white wings and surmounted by a halo, smiled inanely down into the intelligent eyes of the old woman.

'Nasty, vulgar little thing,' said Mrs Bassett.

Before Kate could ask whether she knew what it was, and who had worn it, the old lady started to cough, and her face suffused with a purplish colour. Kate passed her a glass of water. She drank a mouthful or two and the colour subsided again.

Kate waited a moment or two for Mrs Bassett to recover, then she started to speak quietly, hoping that she would join in the conversation when she was ready.

'The Sunshine Angels. They are, as far as I can tell, nice, middle-class, middle-aged, charitably inclined women who each spend a day or two every week in this and other hospitals, pushing round a trolley with magazines and newspapers, and all the little things that a person might need when she is confined to a hospital bed: tissues and hand cream; toothpaste and postage stamps. They specialize in merry smiles and uplifting chat. A jolly word here, a soothing hand there, even a comforting prayer when it seems appropriate. Am I right?'

There was faint colour at last in Mrs Bassett's cheeks. 'Just so,' she said. 'And they wear pink cotton overalls with a brooch like this one pinned to the bosom.' She paused for a minute, then continued, 'The yellow signifies the sunshine, the design reminds us that they are veritable angels.'

'I think my friend's mother may have joined the Angels, or at least have made friends with one of them. She's a very ordinary grandmother, and closely resembles all the others, as far as I can tell. I believe she has worked here in the past. She may still do so.'

But Mrs Bassett's eyelids had drifted closed after her effort, and her breathing was so feeble that Kate wondered whether she would ever return to the world. But then the eyes flashed open again.

'What's her name again?'

'Joyce Fielding.'

There was a long silence. She was looking at the brooch.

'And underneath each vulgar little brooch is a name badge,' she said.

'Do you remember any of these names?'

'Oh yes.'

Another of the long, long pauses, while Mrs Bassett gathered her remaining strength to speak. Kate was sure that her memory was as sharp as ever, however.

'Ruth,' Mrs Bassett managed eventually. 'She's the one I dislike the most. I've never trusted her. A smile on her lips and a cold look in her eyes. She is a bit younger than the others, though she makes herself look matronly.'

Ruth? wondered Kate. Wasn't that the one that George had met?

'Any others?' she asked.

'Janet. Margaret,' whispered Mrs Bassett. 'Grey-haired, good-natured, stupid. And yes, then there's Joyce. No different from any of the others, as you said. I've only seen her once or twice.'

At last!

'You're a star, Mrs Bassett!' Kate said, and she saw the pale lips lift in the shadow of a smile.

The wispy hand reached out to Kate's. The touch was like that of a small bird's wing.

'You think it's the same Joyce? Joyce Fielding did you say?'

'Oh, yes. I think it could be. And I think she may still be here.'

'It's big place. Bigger than it looks. You want to go travelling. You might find more than you bargained for.' The phrases came out in staccato bursts.

'We'll look. We'll find her.'

'You'll come back and let me know what happens?' the old lady whispered.

'I will. You hang in there, Mrs Bassett.' I'll be back just as soon as I can, and I want to find you here, still in the land of the living.

Mrs Bassett looked as though she had read the unspoken command. The dry fingers fluttered against Kate's.

They were interrupted by the arrival of one of the other occupants of the ward. She was in late middle-age, wore a blue housecoat and grubby pink slippers, and brought with her a strong smell of stale tobacco smoke. Her breathing was loud and nasal and sounded as if she snored at night. She settled on to her bed with much sighing and wheezing and then sat staring at Kate, Roz and Mrs Bassett while she chewed her dentures.

'You don't often get visitors, do you, love?' she volunteered.

'Time for me to go,' said Kate, not enjoying the examination.

'What you got there?' demanded the other woman. She had a strong local accent and a voice pickled in tea and cigarette smoke. 'Looks like one of them brooches the Angels wear.'

'I believe it is,' said Kate, not wanting to get drawn into a conversation with the woman.

'Where'd you get it?' she asked belligerently. The label at the foot of her bed said she was called Mattock.

'I picked it up, Mrs Mattock,' said Kate succinctly. 'Why? Do you know whom it belongs to?' Emma would be proud of her for that 'whom', she thought. (Though Emma would have managed 'to whom it belongs'.)

'Give it here,' said Mrs Mattock. 'Let's look at it then.'

She turned the brooch over, then gave it back to Kate. 'It's lost its name badge,' she said. 'Could belong to any on 'em.'

'And do you know any of the Angels?' asked Kate, not expecting a positive reply.

'I might,' said Mrs Mattock. 'But it's no business of yours what I do with my money.'

'True enough,' agreed Kate. 'But if you find out who's lost this brooch, perhaps you'd tell Mrs Bassett.'

'If Madam Bassett will bother to listen to the likes of me,' said Mrs Mattock, and descended into a coughing fit. 'You may have persuaded the snobby old faggot to talk to you, but she won't give the rest of us the time of day.' She scratched at a plump thigh under her blue nylon nightdress.

'I'm not the slightest bit surprised!' muttered Kate.

'What was that?' she glared suspiciously at Kate, then went off into a serious fit of coughing. 'I'd better get myself another fag,' she said, and hauled herself off the bed again. Kate listened to the slippers shuffling down the polished tiles to the smoking room.

'Well, we really must be going now,' she said.

Mrs Bassett's blue eyes softened and there was a lift of humour in the mouth. 'Goodbye, Kate. Come back soon.'

'Goodbye, Mrs Bassett.'

'And bring your mother with you. She's a very restful companion.'

'Goodbye,' said Roz.

'If you come again, I'll have a present for you.'

'There's no need,' said Kate, embarrassed.

'Oh, nothing expensive. But a privilege, you might say. I think you might enjoy it.'

On the way out, Kate called in at the sister's office.

'How is she really?' she asked.

'It's not a good day,' the sister said in a matter-of-fact voice. 'But she's got a lot of spirit. You never know, she may rally and be right as ninepence for a week or two. We can hope.'

'And then, one day, she'll have a bad day and she won't rally,' said Kate.

'True enough. But Mrs Bassett is bloody-minded enough to last for a while yet. If that nurse of mine keeps calling her "Annie" and treating her like an infant, I imagine she'll be angry enough to survive for several months.'

'Can you keep me informed?' Kate said on impulse. 'In case, you know, she gets worse.'

'Leave me your name and telephone number. Mrs Bassett is more or less alone in the world. We like to have a contact number, especially if it's someone local. And don't worry, we'll be in touch if we need you.'

Kate felt cheered by this, but when she looked back through the open door at the bed which held Mrs Bassett, she saw such a flat wafer of a body under the covers that she wondered how life could survive for any time at all in such a frail container. In her imagination she could see another, stronger, younger Anne Bassett rise from the covers and hover above the bed.

'She really would like it if you came back to see her again,' said the sister. 'It would be a kindness if you did.'

'I will,' said Kate, and meant it.

Roz was waiting for her outside the ward-sister's office.

'You were very subdued and quiet,' said Kate.

'I thought you were getting on quite well enough without me, and another voice would only have confused her.'

'We're getting somewhere, aren't we? We'll find her soon.'

'Yes. But we may have to pull this place apart to do so.'

31

Joyce

Early in the evening, when we get back from work, dear Ruth likes to pour us both a drink, so that we can sit and relax before I start to prepare our evening meal.

I know it's just fruit cordial and soda water, with a few cubes of ice and a sprig of mint, but it feels luxurious, somehow, as though we are lying back in some exotic cocktail lounge, enjoying some far-fetched cocktail. Ruth thinks I don't know that she likes a little splash of gin in hers, but it's a smell you don't forget. That's what Derek used to like when he came home in the evenings, only he liked his with tonic water and a small slice of lemon. It was when he poured himself a second drink that I knew I was in for a difficult time later that evening. But enough of that. He's long gone now, and I have a new life, with no men, or none that I have to take any notice of.

But I wonder why Ruth doesn't want me to know she likes a small gin in the evenings?

We had a little spat the other day. Nothing much. Just a small disagreement, and over something so stupid.

It was at the end of my first day as a Sunshine Angel, just when I thought I was getting on so well. And all I did was mention that my son-in-law was moving to the Maxwell Clinic, recovering from a cycle accident.

Why hadn't I told her about him before? Had I been in

to visit him? What had we talked about? Had I talked about *her*?

Don't be so silly, I told her. He may be Emma's husband, but he's no crony of mine. He may do very well for Emma, but he was brought up in a godless, atheistical household, and he's brought his ideas into the home he's made with my daughter.

Oh, says Ruth. You mean he's the one.

Yes, I reply. He certainly is.

Well, says Ruth. You did quite right, dear, to ignore him. And don't go soft on me now, will you? I don't want you sneaking back to King George Wing for a little chat about the grandchildren.

As if I would!

But it would be nice to have news of the little ones. Maybe Ruth wouldn't mind if I invited them all round for tea.

Maybe not just yet, though. I wouldn't want to upset her again. She can be a bit funny if you don't fit in exactly with what she wants. It's all right sitting here, just thinking my own thoughts, but it would be nice to have a really good chat with someone who thought the same way.

I think I'll get myself a diary. Ruth couldn't object to that, could she? Or just a little notebook, so that I can jot down my musings.

32

Kate

'Well, that was very nice,' said Roz. 'I'm glad to see that you've taken up some good works. A little unselfish hospital-visiting is splendid for your soul, and doubtless for your vanity, but has it done our enquiry any good? Are we any closer to finding Joyce Fielding?'

'Of course we are!'

'Explain it to me.'

'Mrs Bassett remembers her. She says she's been working here.'

'We knew that. At least, we knew that someone called Joyce – and not necessarily our Joyce – has been working here. We don't know whether she's still here. And if she *is* here, just where to find her.'

'Stop being so negative. It's not like you. Well, perhaps it's true we didn't learn anything specific, but it did confirm other reports, don't you think?'

'I think you like Mrs Bassett and want to visit her. That's fine by me, but you don't have to pretend that it's anything to do with Joyce Fielding. So, what shall we do now?'

'Since we're inside the clinic, I think we should go exploring.'

'Good idea. And what shall we do about the sandwich shops? Should we go exploring them, too?'

'I think we could leave those until tomorrow. And I'm

not sure George's regal lady was entirely reliable.'

By which Roz understood that Kate was starting to feel tired. They could wander round the Maxwell Clinic, but she wasn't going to encourage Kate to do anything more than a little light nosy-parkering that afternoon.

'We've looked at the second floor, in both wings, and the third. I imagine the first floor is similar. They have that same antiseptic hospital smell, and I saw elderly, dressing-gowned figures bumbling around. I might even have caught the flash of a Zimmer frame, so I don't think they're going to yield up anything extraordinary. Now, how do you think we reach the more exciting areas?'

'If we go back to the ground floor, and turn right at the bottom of the stairs, away from the eagle-eyed receptionist, we can see what's through the next set of glass doors.'

'I think there's something fishy about this place and I'd like to know what it is.'

They walked quietly and sedately down the main stair-case, and, as Kate had suggested, they then turned away from the entrance hall and reception desk, passing through another set of glass doors into unknown territory. Blue-carpeted corridors stretched in front of them.

'What do we say if someone challenges us?' asked Kate.

'We're looking for the ladies' room.'

'Can't we do better than that?'

'We can say we're looking for Sam, but we've lost our way.'

'Not very original, but it'll have to do, I suppose.'

'This is very plush,' remarked Roz. 'Do clinics often have carpeted corridors? I thought they'd go in for something hard, shiny and easily cleaned.'

'Perhaps this section is for the seriously rich, rather than those being paid for by an insurance scheme. I forgot to ask George, but do you think they have Famous People here?

You know the ones. They're hurried into large cars by their agents and deposited at an expensive clinic for rehabilitation. Whether they have problems with drugs, alcohol or sex, apparently these places can cure them all.

'What do you think lies behind all these doors?' The walls were a restful lilac, the doors painted a gentle dove-grey. There was nothing so vulgar as a name or title breaking the perfect paintwork. 'They look like offices to me.'

'There's only one way to find out,' said Roz. She walked across to a door, knocked, turned the handle and walked in.

'Yes? What do you want?' came the brisk reply.

'Sorry, wrong room,' replied Roz and came out again, backwards.

'You're right,' she said. 'It's an office. Very boring.'

'What sort of office?'

'The sort with a couple of desks, computer terminals, typists' chairs, filing cabinets and in-trays. Someone with neat hair, spectacles and a bossy manner. She looked like a secretary. I didn't see any more.'

'Not bad for three seconds' observation. Let's try another,' said Kate. 'My turn this time.'

She chose a door which, judging by its distance from its neighbour, led into a larger room than those they had already walked past. She knocked and walked right in, just as Roz had done.

'Yes?' The voice was male this time, and not pleased at the intrusion.

'I was looking for Dr Hickory,' said Kate, and came out again.

'Dr Hickory?' queried Roz.

'It was the best I could come up with on the spur of the moment.'

'So what did you see?'

'A group of about ten people, sitting round in a circle on

upright chairs. Some were smoking. All young, all casually dressed. Though the one who looked to be in charge was a little older. Late twenties, maybe.'

'It sounds like a group therapy session,' said Roz.

'You could be right. They looked like a group of bored, sulky teenagers, certainly.'

'We haven't found anything unusual yet, have we?'

'I was hoping we'd come across a room full of padlocked grannies. But we've had no luck so far, that's for sure. I'm not giving up yet, though.'

Ahead of them appeared another set of glass doors. When they reached them they found a notice: PRIVATE. NO ENTRY. VISITORS MUST NOT PROGRESS BEYOND THIS POINT.

'Can we resist a challenge?' enquired Roz, pushing her way through the doors.

'Apparently not,' replied Kate, following her.

Suddenly there was a different feel to the place.

'No carpet,' remarked Roz.

'Music,' said Kate. 'Voices. People talking. The buzz of conversation.'

'Young people, at that,' said Roz.

'Could you tell me what you're doing here?' The voice came from behind them. They hadn't heard a door open, or the sound of any footsteps as the man approached.

'I'm so sorry,' said Roz. 'We appear to have lost our way.'

'You appear to have walked through a door marked NO ENTRY,' he said.

He was fortyish, with dark hair going elegantly grey at the temples, an expensively well-groomed air, and he was wearing the spotless white coat of a doctor who didn't have intimate contact with sick people.

'I was hoping to speak to someone about the . . . difficulty . . . my daughter is having.' Roz spoke delicately, as though not wanting Kate to understand her. She needn't have worried. Kate hadn't a clue what she was talking about.

'The normal course of action is to obtain a letter of referral from your own doctor, and then wait for us to make an appointment for you.' He looked at Kate. 'Since your daughter is over eighteen, she might be expected to do these things for herself.' He was wearing a name tag with a photograph that looked exactly like him, well groomed and plastic. Dr Anthony Haufman, it said.

'I was hoping for a little look round before making an official approach,' wheedled Roz. 'It is so important that dear Kate should find the *right* environment for her problem.' She sighed. She overdid it, thought Kate. 'Money isn't everything, is it?' Roz continued. 'We've spent so much and achieved so little. I thought that if I could just wander round and absorb the ambience, I'd *know*.'

'But that wouldn't be fair to our other patients, would it, Mrs . . . ?'

'Ivory.'

'It would be treating them rather as one might treat animals in a zoo, and that wouldn't be right at all.'

'I do understand what you're saying,' said Roz, moving imperceptibly down the corridor all the time she was speaking. The sounds of music, bursts of conversation, and laughter were growing closer. Haufman looked as though he was about to grasp Roz by the sleeve and detain her forcibly.

Kate took the opportunity to look for one of the Sunshine Angels, but couldn't see anyone except a youth in torn jeans and t-shirt who ambled out of one door ahead of her and in through another.

'Why don't you go back to your doctor, ask him to write to me, and then request an appointment for assessment of your daughter?' Dr Haufman said firmly, ignoring Roz's vague manner and charming smile. 'And I really must ask you to stop now, and not to encroach any further on my patients' privacy.'

'Of course!' said Roz. 'Come along, Kate, we mustn't take up any more of Dr Haufman's time.'

'What exactly is your daughter's problem?' asked Haufman, as they turned back towards the glass doors.

'I wouldn't want to discuss it here, in such a public place,' said Roz reprovingly. 'I'm sure you must understand that.'

Haufman reached the doors ahead of them, held one open, and waited for them to go through before following them out into the corridor that led towards the entrance hall. He obviously didn't trust them. He was going to see them off the premises.

'If you know anything about the work we do with young people,' he said austerely to Roz, 'you will know that it is inappropriate to wander in and out of our clinic without my permission. Our patients are vulnerable – as perhaps your daughter is – and we wouldn't want them to come in contact with someone who might . . .' He paused, as though looking for a polite phrase. 'Someone who might, whether knowingly or not, harm them.'

Then they were back in Reception, walking briskly through the main doors, Dr Haufman watching them leave.

Kate said, 'Apart from post-flu depression, what am I supposed to be suffering from?'

'I'm not entirely sure. It could be a drug dependency. Or alcohol abuse. Anorexia, maybe. Or bulimia. It was very clever of you to look so ill, I must say.'

'Don't worry, it took no effort at all on my part.'

They were standing outside the clinic, on the forecourt. 'Will you make it back to the car, or would you like to wait here while I fetch it round?'

'I think I'll manage to stagger that far. And don't you think I'm a bit old for your over-anxious mother act?'

'Probably. But with that white face and the black circles round your eyes, you could easily be a twenty-year-old who's been abusing various illegal substances.'

'Thank you, Mother.'

33

Joyce

It's funny writing things down after all this time, but it does help to clear my mind. I get confused about things sometimes, so Ruth tells me, and when I see them written down on paper it's easier to understand. I do hope it will be.

I wrote quite a bit when I was a teenager, of course, but then adolescent girls do, don't they? Every evening, up there in my room, scribbling away in the notebook with roses on the cover that Auntie Lil gave me for my birthday. 'You say you want to be a writer,' she said. 'Well, now you can get going.' So I wrote my stories, sitting at the table that Dad had bought in a junk shop and which we painted with white gloss to cover up the scratches. The walls of that room were blue, I remember, a duck-egg blue. I don't think I've ever loved a room as much as I loved that one. The curtains were white with blue flowers and a trellis of green leaves on them. Mum made them for me, with wide blue satin tie-backs, a darker blue than the walls. And she bought me a whitewood dressing-table, kidney-shaped, and made a flounced skirt for it from the same material as the curtains. That room seemed to me like a bower in one of the poems we read at school, all fresh and untouched.

She'd never let me help her with the sewing. I suppose it was because she was such a perfectionist. I could never come up to her standards. Not at that age, anyway. But it was all right by me. I liked things to be perfect, too. And I was content to sit and watch her, with the fabric billowing out behind the needle, and the click and hum of the machine filling the room. I sat and watched her, and that's how I learned to do the things she did. And I always liked things just so, as she did.

Not that I ever did become a writer, even after all the hours of scribbling. Nothing I wrote seemed good enough, somehow, and I never dared to show it to anyone. One word of criticism and I'd have died, or that's how I thought about it then. And then the ambition died. Well, they all do, don't they?

Funny how these things come back to you. Here I am, in a very different room, putting down my thoughts and actions and suddenly I'm taken back to when I was thirteen years old. I haven't thought about it for years. But I can see the blank lined pages of the notebook and feel the silver propelling pencil in my hand, the one I got for being Melanie's bridesmaid, with my name in script down the side. I suppose that notebook would have been dull for anyone else to read, but I wish I still had it. Maybe some of the stories weren't that bad, at that, and I'd like to look again at the girl I once was, captured for ever in the notebook with the pink roses on the cover.

I've got a small, plain notebook this time: I don't want anyone to think it's special. I don't want anyone looking inside. I feel the same about people looking at my work as I did all those years ago. Fifty years ago. A whole lifetime for a lot of people.

I suppose, if I'm honest, what I really mean is that I don't want Ruth reading it. There, I've written it down. It looks so unkind, and to someone I should feel grateful towards. Well, I am grateful to Ruth, but I need this little bit of privacy.

Some of the time I write my diary inside my head. If

Ruth sees me, she thinks I'm just sitting there daydreaming, but I'm not. She'd think I was going as peculiar as some of the old dears I met that first day at the Maxwell Clinic if she knew what I was doing.

This new life of mine reminds me of being a teenager. That, too, was a time when every experience was new and surprising, every day a voyage of discovery. Not that many of the experiences were pleasant, more's the pity. And voyages of discovery weren't much approved of. My parents wanted me to have a nice safe job, and a nice safe marriage, and not look any further than that. But now, at this time in my life, I'm meeting new situations and new people and it's only by writing them down that I can sort them all out. They're the same old mixture, some nice, some nasty.

Not that I need to sort out what Ruth is. She's one of the most straightforward people I've ever met. You look at that round face of hers, with the intelligent dark eyes and the clear pale skin, and you know you can trust her. Everybody feels the same about Ruth. It's lovely to see the way their faces light up when they catch sight of her, and the smiles they can't help giving back in return for hers. She's a jewel, is Ruth, and I'm lucky to have met her when I did. She does worry me sometimes, though, when I feel that *she* doesn't always understand *me*.

I tore the roses notebook up and burned it, ripped out every page, crumpled them up and threw them into the flames, so that nothing of the words I'd written would be left. You couldn't rake them out again and put it back together, I made sure of that. That was after I was married, when I knew what life was about. You lose your silly dreams then, don't you? My ambition to be a writer was long dead. No more thoughts and feelings written down every evening. All that sort of thing goes when you're married. No use being selfish, that's what they all said. You have to put your husband first. I don't suppose I'd have been much of a writer anyway.

When Emma grew up and left home I would have started again, but what's the use of writing if you can't put down what you really think and feel? And I couldn't do that. When someone is peering into your private notebook, looking over your shoulder, asking questions, then you have to watch what you say and write. I found I was watching what I was thinking, even. He had a way of looking at me as if he could get in through my forehead and read everything that was going on in my brain. I could tell by the way he twisted up his mouth that he didn't like what he saw. Well, eavesdroppers never hear any good of themselves, that's what they say. Dreamkiller. That was him. My Derek.

I could have locked the notebook away, but he would have found it, the way he found everything else. Creeping round the place, prying into my secrets.

They all said we were such a devoted couple. It was such a tragedy when he died, and me only in my forties. That's what they said. But I can write it now: I was glad.

There. That's the first time I've ever admitted it. I wasn't completely ignorant when I married him. My mother had given me a book to read, so I knew what to expect. Or I thought I did.

But that wasn't enough for him. He had other ideas. And he didn't like it when I told him it was wrong. That's one thing I do know about: right and wrong.

Enough of that. I said that I would look forward now, not back.

Is it too late? Have I left it too late?

Never too late, that's what they say. I hope they're right.

I put this notebook out of harm's way by standing it on the shelf in my room, in between my Bible and my prayer book. It's funny how even the nosiest people won't look at your Bible.

I don't understand this modern world. It's like a foreign country to me. We thought ourselves so modern then, so up-to-the-minute, so different from our mothers' generation. I'm writing about the nineteen-fifties, before I was married.

Such lovely clothes! I made my own. I was good at that. I still remember the feel of that starched petticoat against my legs, prickling, scratchy, like jagged fingernails. It was made of a fine, soft cotton, with starched flounces of net on the inside, in all different shades of pink.

It's funny to think of it now, but that's how I thought a man would feel. Hard, prickly, scratchy. I never imagined he would feel like rubber.

We were so innocent in those days.

It was his hands, his fingers, that were hard and painful.

'Why do you want to hurt me?' I asked, wondering.

'I don't. Only when you won't let me do what I want to do.'

But I wouldn't. Not even when he hurt me again.

When I was at school, my English mistress always told me that if I wanted to write, I should start with what I knew.

What did I know?

In those days, nothing.

Now, I'm still wondering whether anything I've ever known is true. So I'll start here with the little I do know, the small measure I'm sure of.

This room. This room is more or less square, not very large, not really small. The bed has a light-green cover, the carpet is beige, the curtains have a pleasant pattern of yellow flowers on a dark-green background. There is a bedside table with a mahogany veneer, and an upright chair. And here I sit, in that chair, with my notebook on the bedside table.

And that's all I know for sure.

What else? There must be more.

Very well. There's a mirror, and so I can look at myself. And I wonder, Who is this? Who is she?

Joyce. My name is Joyce. The woman in the mirror has a round face, with the contours starting to sag and little lines radiating out from the eyes and pulling down the corners of the mouth. Eyes, blue. A pale, clear blue, like the eyes of a doll. Nose short and snub, shining because I haven't bothered to put any powder on it today. Or yesterday either, if I'm honest. Mouth. How would I describe the mouth? Discontented, I think is the word that sums it up. Disappointed.

Move on. Hair, a faded brown with streaks of grey at the sides. Waving hair, so pretty once. Perhaps I should have it cut and permed. Would that help? Would that make me look more like the self that lives inside my head?

Probably not.

Isn't she just as real as the dull, middle-aged woman who stares at me from the mirror with her doll's eyes? Ah, yes. But she has wild hair and eyes. Hair that is coal-black and wiry, and eyes that shoot fiery sparks. Green eyes, I think she must have. And scarlet fingernails. With fingernails like that, I could do the scratching for a change. I could score the skin so that scarlet drops followed the trail of the scarlet nails.

Just for a change.

I'm wearing beige cotton twill trousers, the comfortable sort with elastic at the waist, and a pale-green blouse and a navy cardigan I bought in the men's department at Marks. I'm wearing my knee-length dark-green socks and a comfortable pair of beige lace-up shoes. Could you imagine anything more boring? I doubt it, I really do.

34

Kate

The next morning, as Kate and Roz were drinking coffee in companionable silence, the phone rang.

'Hello?' said Kate, answering it.

'Miss Ivory? It's the Maxwell Clinic here. I believe you wished to be kept informed about Mrs Bassett's condition.'

'Yes, I did. How is she? Is she all right? Is she in danger? Do you want me to come over?' They must be ringing her because Anne Bassett was on the point of death.

'It isn't one of her good days, I'm afraid, but there's nothing to be concerned about. Her condition is very little different.'

'So why did you ring?' Kate was annoyed that she had been upset unnecessarily. What with the after-effects of flu and the flashbacks she was getting of her visit to identify the late Mr Bettony, her nerves were all on edge.

'Mrs Bassett said she would like to see you. She spoke to the assistant who was helping with her breakfast, and asked for you. It would be very nice for her if you could manage to get here. Today if you could make it.'

'Oh yes. Of course. When would be a good time?'

'Mornings are better than afternoons. She tends to drift off after lunch. Could you come in at half past ten, or eleven?'

'Yes. Tell Mrs Bassett I'll be there.'

'So you're going back to the clinic,' said Roz, when she returned to the table. 'You really think that place can tell us something, don't you? You just want to beat the information out of one of the smug bastards who work there.'

'It's nothing to do with Joyce. I'm going to visit Mrs Bassett. She's asking for me. I'll go over there after we've cleared up breakfast.'

'And I bet you wouldn't go rushing off like this if it weren't the Maxwell Clinic.'

Kate didn't argue any further, because she knew that Roz was right.

'Do you want to come with me?' she asked.

'Not unless you want me to. I've got a couple of letters to write.'

'I'll go on my own. And I'll be back before lunch. She won't want me to stay long if she's not feeling well.'

'You must wrap up warm, and don't go exploring that great rabbit warren of a place without me to look after you.'

'No, Mother. I'll be good, Mother. I'll wear my muffler and gloves, Mother.'

'I'm glad you're showing me some respect at last.'

At which they both laughed.

It was a misty, chilly day that looked as though it would never get really light. Nevertheless, Kate decided to walk across Port Meadow. She hadn't been taking much exercise since she'd had flu, and she wanted a brisk walk.

When she reached the clinic, she greeted the receptionist almost as an old friend, and then walked up the stairs to the third floor and Mrs Bassett's ward.

'You're looking a bit better today,' said Mrs Bassett when she entered. 'You've got a bit of colour in your cheeks.'

'I was about to say the same about you,' said Kate, pulling up a chair close to Mrs Bassett's head.

'The silly old bat told you I was dying, did she?'

'To do her justice, no, she didn't. She did say you wanted to see me, though.'

'I was afraid I wouldn't get these to you in time,' said Mrs Bassett. She indicated an envelope with a bent index finger. 'You look in there,' she said.

Kate pulled out three slips of paper.

'Well?' asked Mrs Bassett.

'They're tickets for the Christ Church carol service,' said Kate, reading.

'They're for you.'

'All of them?'

'Take two of your friends with you.'

'I will. Thank you very much. I've always wanted to go, but I've never had a ticket before. And I'll take my mother. It'll be good for her.'

Mrs Bassett made an odd croaking noise, which Kate realized was laughter. 'And who will have the third ticket?'

'I might just invite a man,' confided Kate.

'That's good.'

Kate looked at the head on the pillow. The colour and animation were fading from Mrs Bassett's face as she watched. She was tired by their conversation even more rapidly than she had been the previous day. It was time to go.

'I'll come back and tell you all about it,' she said.

'You . . . do . . . that,' replied Mrs Bassett, her crumpled pink eyelids drooping over her blue eyes.

'Goodbye,' said Kate, touching her hand briefly. 'I'll be back.'

She passed the ward sister on her way out, and raised a hand in greeting. As she approached the glass doors, they were pushed open by someone entering the wing. She saw a tall woman in a pink overall and heard the rattle of trolley wheels. The woman's face was in shadow, but Kate noted broad hips, dark hair and a determined tread. Was this the unpleasant Angel that George had spoken to? She paused, meaning to waylay the woman.

'Miss Ivory!'

It was the ward sister behind her. She turned back and the Sunshine Angel overtook her and continued down the corridor. She hoped the sister wouldn't keep her long. If she hurried, she might catch up with the Angel.

'I'm sorry if I startled you this morning.'

'That's all right. I'm glad you rang.'

'So you don't mind if I contact you again?'

'No. Please do. I'll be back to see Mrs Bassett again in a few days, anyway.'

'I'm so glad. It does her a lot of good to have a visitor, and I like to know that I don't need to invent an excuse to call you in here.'

'Goodbye.' Kate hoped she hadn't been too abrupt with the woman. She started down the corridor, in the direction the Angel had gone.

'That's the wrong way. The staircase is through the doors over there.'

Reluctantly, Kate turned back. 'I'm sorry. I lost my sense of direction for a moment,' she said.

She went back the correct way, taking the stairs as usual, rather than the lift. On the ground floor, she paused for a moment. She hadn't managed to catch the Sunshine Angel – she was sure this was the one she wanted to see – but she could have another look at the millionaires' wing. If she met Dr Haufman she would just have to give him a big smile and hope she could come up with a reasonable excuse.

She retraced the route she and Roz had taken, finding the corridor with the plush blue carpet. If I were looking to make myself some money, this is the section I'd make for, she thought. All you could con from the Mrs Bassetts would be their false teeth or concert tickets. If you wanted to make serious money, this is where you'd aim for. And after all, anyone with a criminal turn of mind *would* want to make serious money.

There was the same buzz of noise, sudden bursts of laughter or of rock music from open doors as she reached the furthest corridor.

Then another door opened and a figure appeared and started to walk towards her.

Haufman? A nurse? No, this one was young, male, and thin, with a pale, lined face.

'Hello,' he said, coming up to Kate.

'Hello,' she replied, wondering how to ask intelligent questions of such an unlikely looking source.

'Are you one of the Sunshine crowd?' he asked.

'Sorry?'

'I thought you were an Angel.' He had a standard estuary accent, but could produce enough consonants to indicate that he had probably come up through an expensive private school.

'Are you feeling all right?' asked Kate, as he swayed slightly in front of her. 'Shall I call for help?'

'I'm right as rain.' He scratched his nose, then moved his hand down to scratch his neck. 'Or I will be, when I meet up with my friend Ruthie.'

'Ruthie. Do you mean Ruth? The woman in the pink overall?'

'The woman with the gear,' said the young man. He sniffed, and started to scratch his shoulder.

'You shouldn't be here, Austin,' said a quiet voice from behind Kate. 'Why don't you return to your room and I'll come and see you in a minute.' Dr Haufman waited until

Austin had disappeared from sight, then he turned to Kate. 'Miss Ivory, isn't it?'

'Yes.'

'And still looking around to see if this is the right place to deal with your problem. Or habit. Which is it, I wonder?'

'Actually, I was visiting a friend of mine,' said Kate. 'Up in Prince Albert Wing,' she added for authenticity. 'And on the way out, I just lost my way. Can you show me the way to the exit, Dr Haufman?'

'Certainly.'

He didn't touch her, but she still felt as though she was being frogmarched out of the building.

Well, Dr Haufman, is that what you're afraid I'm smuggling into your expensive clinic? Something for the rich young man with the drug habit? But it wasn't me he was looking for, you see, it was one of your saintly Sunshine Angels.

Oh dear, Joyce. What have you got yourself into?

Is there any chance I'll find you one day, meekly filling sandwiches in a city deli, far away from all criminal activity?

35

Joyce

I'd nearly forgotten what time of year it was.

I was walking through the centre of the town this morning and I suddenly noticed, as though someone had sprung it on me in the middle of August, that we're coming up to Christmas! The streets and the shops are so pretty, with the streetlights and the decorations, and the windows full of Christmas trees and fairylights. And there's me, I haven't bought a card or wrapped a single present. I suppose it's because I've been so absorbed in my work. I mentioned it to Ruth, but she said we should remember it is a religious festival first and foremost, and not give in to the commercialization that is all around us.

Ruth has been very good. Apart from all the excellent work we do in the clinic – and Ruth has more than one place that she works in – she finds time to help me with my spiritual problems. She's never mentioned it to me, but I'm sure she's the brains behind the Sunshine Angels. She's off on their affairs every day, and she often has people to see 'on business', as she puts it. She doesn't take me into her confidence, but I know that she's working selflessly for the good of others.

I've always been a believer, and a churchgoer, but Ruth has pointed out how worldly the organized Church has grown in these recent decades, and I can only agree with her. They condone all sorts of wickedness these days, and you never hear a word preached against it from the pulpit.

But I'll have to speak to her about Christmas. I can't let the children think their granny has forgotten all about them. I've still got my pension, and I can afford a little something for each of them. It would be all right if I popped round to deliver my gifts, I should think. I needn't stay long, but it would be such a treat.

I'll have to ask Ruth about it. But I can't see what harm it would do.

36

Kate

On her way back from the clinic, Kate walked through the centre of Oxford. The streets were decorated with half-hearted reminders of Christmas, she saw with surprise. There were coloured lights that looked like rampant worms, and Christmas trees, and a Salvation Army band playing carols on the corner of Queen Street.

It had crept up on her, probably while she was in bed with flu, and she just hadn't noticed it.

'It's Christmas!' she announced to Roz on her return.

'Not for another fortnight or so,' her mother replied placidly.

'But we've done nothing about it. Where's our Christmas tree? Where are our presents? Why aren't we knee-deep in wrapping paper and Christmas cards?'

'I believe the envelopes heaped on your desk probably contain cards from your friends,' replied Roz. 'Why don't you open them?'

'Why didn't you tell me they were there?'

'You could hardly get your eyes open during the past week. I thought you'd find them when you were feeling better.'

'I've hardly been down there since I finished writing my last book. I've just shovelled all the post into a pile and ignored it.'

'A bad habit. I can't think where you got it from.'

'Oh my God!'

'What? Have you discovered suddenly that it's your birthday, as well?'

'Don't be ridiculous. I've just realized that Estelle said she was going to read the manuscript I sent her and get back to me. One of those envelopes contains her comments.'

'I'll make us some coffee, and you go and open your post.'

Ten minutes later, Kate had returned to the sitting room with a heap of Christmas cards and a few other envelopes.

'I'll put up the strings and we can start to hang these up,' she said.

'Have you still got the miniature clothes-pegs to do it with?'

'Of course.'

'We could call them an Ivory tradition,' said Roz.

'Like neglecting to pay bills,' said Kate, slitting open a couple of ominous-looking envelopes.

'Drink up your coffee before it gets cold. And I've put out a few biscuits.'

'Won't they spoil our lunch?'

'Where did you get these nannyish ideas from?'

Kate and Roz crunched contentedly for a moment, then Kate opened the final letter.

'Yes,' she said. 'This one's from Estelle.'

'What does it say? Does she love the book?'

Kate read rapidly to the end of the letter and then through it again, slowly. 'She says that it's fine. That she'll send it straight to my editor. And have I remembered, this is the last one I'm contracted to write. And have I done what she suggested and thought of something a little more *modern*, because she doesn't think she can sell another one like this.'

'Why not?'

'The market's difficult, whatever that might mean.'

'So what are you going to do?'

'I'm going to enjoy Christmas. Tomorrow is another day. A new year is starting. And other such clichés. I shall make plans in the new year.'

'Very sensible. More coffee?'

'Yes, please.'

'And you might as well have the last biscuit. You look as though you need a bit of building up.'

'Anyway, I think we should go shopping. I shall have Estelle's cheque in the post quite soon, and we might as well start spending it now.'

'Do you want to do your shopping in Oxford? Or whizz up to London?'

'I'm not sure I'm quite up to fighting my way through the London crowds. Shall we stick to Oxford?'

'It's fine by me. Why don't we spend the afternoon making lists, then get up early tomorrow and head for the bright lights of Oxford?'

'I'd better get my Christmas cards written and posted in the next twenty-four hours, too.'

'I shouldn't overdo it. If you miss this Christmas, there'll be another one along in a year or so.'

Next morning, they were up early so that they could walk into Oxford as soon as the shops opened.

'Don't forget your list,' said Roz, winding a long scarlet scarf round her neck to combat the raw cold of the morning.

'I've got these, too,' said Kate. 'You'd better have one of them.'

She handed Roz a copy of the photo of Joyce that she had had photocopied.

'Just in case we see her in town. She must do some Christmas shopping, and it would be stupid if we walked

227

past her in Debenhams without recognizing her.'

'And I suppose you want to look into all the sandwich shops as well, just to see if you can spot her buttering a ciabatta roll.'

'That's a good idea. Why didn't I think of it?' Kate was checking that the back door was locked. She pulled on a green woolly hat and hitched her large handbag over her shoulder.

'Come on,' she said, and pulled the front door closed behind them as they set off into town.

'Perhaps we should visit Emma again. She must know something she isn't telling us,' suggested Roz, as they turned into the Fridesley Road. They were moving faster than the traffic, they were pleased to notice.

'I expect you're right about Emma. But what would make her change her mind and tell us now?'

'Desperation?'

'Shall we try seeing her this afternoon? After lunch and before the older ones get back from school would be best.' They crossed at the lights and turned left into the Botley Road. The traffic was even worse here.

'We might get more out of the children than we do out of Emma,' said Roz thoughtfully. 'They're usually less aware of the lies they should be telling.'

'Very well. You take the children. I'll tackle Emma. We'll compare notes when we've finished our interrogations.'

'Don't you think you're getting a little carried away with the hunt for Joyce?'

'Not at all. It's time we tried to shake a little more information out of Emma.'

'We'd better crack on with our shopping. I'm going to need twenty minutes with my feet up and a soothing read of *Sporting Life* before I can face another outing.'

'I'll make our lunch,' said Kate.

'You must have recovered from your flu at last.'

'I do believe I have.'

They had reached Queen Street, which was solid with grim-looking pedestrians and a dozen jammed buses.

'When are they going to sort out this traffic?' asked Roz, looking in despair at the scene.

'Next year, apparently. All will be fume-free sweetness and unpolluted light. I can't wait.'

'Meanwhile, I'd better try this nasty-looking shop for bribes for Emma's youngest children.'

'Roz! You can't do that!'

'It's as well to be practical about these things, I've always considered.'

'Oh, very well. I suppose it's what I'd do myself. And while you're doing that, I'll go looking for something pretty and impractical for Emma herself. No cookery books, no button-through cardies, no picturesque tea towels. Something frivolous. That should startle her enough to make her cough up all she knows.'

'I'll meet you in Marks and Sparks in half an hour.'

'But I don't want socks for Christmas!'

'Biscuits,' said Roz. 'And those flaky olive twists, and some interesting fruit, and—'

'Oh, very well. I get the picture.'

They met in the food department in Marks and Spencer half an hour later, and if Kate had peered into one or two sandwich shops along the way, and compared the assistants with the picture in her handbag, she didn't mention the fact to Roz.

They loaded themselves with carrier bags full of expensive food, then looked at one another.

'OK,' said Kate. 'How long will it take us to choose a present for one another?'

'A very long time,' said Roz. 'But shall we say one hour?

I'll meet you in the coffee shop over there. I'll need a breather by then.'

An hour later they were sitting at a table for four. They needed the extra seats for their purchases.

'Do we really know this many people?' asked Roz.

'I doubt it. I think we've been very, very generous to the two or three we do know. And by the way, we haven't even bought wrapping paper yet,' replied Kate.

'Wrapping paper can wait until another day. I think we should treat ourselves to a taxi home.'

'An excellent idea.'

They both dipped their forks into the almond pastries they had ordered, then Roz said, 'What is it about the Maxwell Clinic that fascinates you?'

'I didn't know I was fascinated by it.'

'You think the answer lies there, don't you?'

'Last time I was there, I bumped into Dr Haufman again.'

'You were trespassing in the carpeted corridors,' said Roz accusingly.

'Yes. And I got the feeling Dr Haufman thought I might be providing drugs for his young patients. That's why he was so keen for us to leave the first time.'

'It all sounds very nasty, but what's it got to do with Joyce?'

'Nothing, I hope. But I think it has something to do with those Sunshine Angels.'

'Then it's lucky we haven't actually discovered Joyce there, isn't it? Though I can't believe she'd get involved in anything like that.'

'Not knowingly, perhaps. But suppose she's being used.'

'I think it's very far-fetched.'

'If this is all drugs related, it might explain the murder of Bettony.'

'I can't see that we can do much about finding Bettony's

murderer,' said Roz briskly. 'The day of the amateur sleuth outwitting the police is long past. Let's just concentrate on finding Joyce and restoring her to the bosom of her family before Christmas. We can then enjoy spending our fee in the new year. And in spite of your wild theories, I really don't think she's incarcerated in the cellars of the Maxwell Clinic.'

'I'm not so sure.'

'Drink up your cappuccino. And if you don't want that apricot half, I'll—'

'I do want it.' And Kate licked cappuccino froth off her upper lip and apricot syrup off her index finger. Then she pulled out her mobile phone. 'These things come in useful,' she said, as she dialled and requested a taxi. 'Come on. It'll take us a minute or two to load ourselves up with all our loot, and he'll be here immediately. Or so the woman said.'

'Oh good. And you did say earlier that you'd be making the lunch, didn't you?'

37

Roz

They drove to Emma's in Kate's car, taking the bypass to avoid the centre of town.

'Hello, Emma! Merry Christmas!' cried Kate as festively as she could manage when Emma opened the door. They hadn't phoned first. Kate had said she thought that Emma might well try to fob them off if they did.

'But it's not Christmas yet,' objected Emma. 'You're early, Kate.'

'I believe in being ahead of myself,' said Kate breezily. She thrust a brightly wrapped parcel tied with a cascade of gold ribbons into Emma's startled hands. 'Just a little something to cheer you up,' she said.

Emma didn't open it immediately, but placed it under the Christmas tree, where it sparkled garishly among the other bright parcels. Roz wondered what Kate had chosen in the end. She must remember to ask her on the way home.

'What do you want?' asked Emma warily. Then, 'Can I get you some tea?' she added belatedly.

I was right about the efficacy of bribes, Roz noted, and shot a look of triumph at Kate. Emma hadn't thrown them out the way she obviously wanted to do. Instead, she was about to ask them to sit down.

'Tea?' Kate was saying. 'What a lovely idea. Let's go to

the kitchen, and I'll help you put the kettle on.'

There were two small children and the baby in the living room.

'Don't worry,' said Roz. 'I'll keep an eye on the children for you.'

'And what's your name?' she asked the one who looked like a pugilist.

'Amaryl. But they call me Ammie.'

The one with the rash, thought Roz. Ammie no longer had a rash, but her face was now covered in pink blotches instead. Probably something she ate, thought Roz optimistically.

'We're watching videos,' Ammie said with deep meaning.

'And I'm interrupting you?' asked Roz gaily. 'What a pity! That's what comes of being sociable.'

Ammie stared at her. 'Jack and Tristan will get very cross if I don't press the Play button soon,' she said.

'Very well,' said Roz, picking up the remote control and pressing the appropriate button. 'But I'd like to talk to you, Ammie dear.' She delved into her bag and brought out a small wrapped parcel.

'What is it?' asked Ammie suspiciously.

'Something I'm sure your mother won't approve of,' said Roz. 'And I have several more in my bag.'

Ammie turned her back on the warbling figures on the screen. 'What do you want to know?' she asked.

'I'd like to know which video you were watching the afternoon your granny disappeared.' Roz wasn't going to pussyfoot around with a child like Ammie. She could see the pound signs flashing every time Ammie blinked, and concluded that the child was not exactly sensitive about her grandmother's disappearance.

'We were watching a Disney. We were bored and Tris kicked me. I picked up a cushion to hit him back, and there was a video underneath it. So we put that on instead. It didn't have a name.'

'What was it about?' Roz had a nasty feeling she could guess.

'There were people with no clothes on, but Granny ran in and pressed the eject button.'

'Do you know where the tape is now?'

'Granny took it.'

'And you didn't recognize the box?'

'It didn't have one but it could have been one of Daddy's.'

'And Mummy didn't see this one?'

But Ammie reckoned she'd answered enough questions in return for one unknown present and she stared pointedly at Roz's handbag.

'Oh, very well,' said Roz, pulling another packet out of the bag.

'I hope it's worth it,' said Ammie, trying to gauge from the size and shape what was inside.

'The video,' prompted Roz.

'Mummy only watches videos when they're ours. She doesn't like anything else. I've shown her where Daddy keeps his, though. In his desk. And he locks the drawer. I told her this morning.

'I see.' And Roz picked another small parcel out of her bag. 'That's the last one,' she said. 'And I hope you share them with your brothers and sisters.'

'Not sodding likely,' said Ammie, scooping up all Roz's offerings and leaving the room with them.

At this moment Kate came back into the room, holding a tray.

'Tea?' she said.

I'd rather have some of Kate's single malt, thought Roz, but she smiled and accepted an unwanted cup of tea.

★ ★ ★

'How did you get on?' asked Kate in the car on the way home.

'I didn't learn much,' said Roz. 'I can come to one or two conclusions, though. You're not the only one in the family with an imagination, and mine is working overtime at the moment. How about you? Did you beat anything out of Emma?'

'I was sweet and lovely to my friend Emma as we dropped teabags into the teapot and watched the kettle boil. She was a little inclined to be weepy, and at first I put this down to her anxiety about Sam's health, and the disappearance of her mother. Only it appears that Sam is progressing very well, and in Emma's opinion he may not be as deserving of sympathy as she first thought. As to Joyce, I think Emma is running out of patience and is starting to feel the beginnings of anger.'

'This all sounds very healthy.'

'But not desperately helpful.'

'I'm not so sure about that. If we add it to what I learned from Ammie—'

'I thought you said that Ammie told you nothing.'

'But a very revealing nothing. Just before Joyce disappeared, the children were watching a video. At least, Ammie put a video into the machine, switched it on and then Joyce came in and pressed the eject button. Ammie didn't know what the film was, and hasn't seen it again, but she thinks it belonged to Sam. Immediately after that, Joyce left the house and hasn't been back since.'

'And Emma's pissed off at Sam.'

'Now what sort of film would upset Joyce?'

'From what we know of her, I'd say sex. Pornography. Well, not even that, I should think.'

'So what we deduce is that Sam was hoarding pornographic films – which Emma subsequently found out about

– Joyce played one by mistake, and was so horrified that she rushed out of the house,' said Roz.

'That would explain why Emma hasn't wanted to answer too many of my questions about Joyce and why she left. She didn't want to tell me about Sam's funny little habits.'

'I think she only found out about them this morning. It's left us with the same old problem, though,' said Roz thoughtfully. 'It explains why Joyce left, but it doesn't tell us why she's stayed away. And we're no nearer to knowing where she is now.'

'And we don't know where Mr Bettony fits into any of this.'

'And we haven't found out what she was doing at the Maxwell Clinic,' added Roz. 'If she ever was there, of course.'

'I'm sure she was there,' said Kate, turning into Agatha Street and looking for a parking space. 'I feel it,' she said, reversing fairly neatly into a twenty-foot space. 'And I think she may still be hidden there somewhere.'

'Now you're being fanciful,' said Roz, sliding out of the car and waiting for Kate to fit the steering lock.

'Maybe I am.'

'What shall we do next?' asked Roz as Kate opened the front door.

'I'm going to ring George. It's time we looked at Joyce's flat. And I'm going to invite him to the carol service at Christ Church.'

'Lucky old George,' said Roz, removing her scarlet muffler.

'You're invited too,' said Kate. 'As long as you behave yourself.'

'I'm the best-behaved mother you're ever likely to have.'

Five minutes later Kate said, 'George would love to come to the carol concert.'

'Good,' said Roz. 'And what about Joyce's flat?'

'We can go tomorrow. George's term has finished. He's not a school teacher, apparently, but something in further education.'

'I've never really understood what that was.'

'Sounds impressive though, doesn't it?'

38

Kate

Kate woke to find that during the night someone had taken a large paintbrush and swept a translucent silver wash over the whole of Fridesley. At first glance it looked as if it had snowed, but then, as she rubbed the sleep out of her eyes, she could see that it was frost. Not the sparkling, shimmering frost of fairytales, but an opaque layer that leached the colour out of the landscape. The only colours she could see were the petrol-blue and gold stripes over in the east, where the sun might appear. The vault of the sky was covered with closely packed clouds, the kind that promised a cold, dry day.

As she looked out on the alien landscape, her first thought was of Joyce Fielding. She had to find her. There was something she instinctively disliked about the Maxwell Clinic and she had a constant depressing feeling that Joyce was in danger, and if she didn't get a move on and find her, then it might be too late. Without Kate's help, Joyce might soon be as dead as Mr Bettony.

She shivered. Maybe Joyce was already dead. Maybe she was lying under the concrete of another car park somewhere on the outskirts of another market town.

No! She couldn't let herself believe that.

She stood under the shower to wake herself up, then went downstairs to make coffee and toast.

This was going to be a good day, an enjoyable day, a day spent with George Dolby. They would find some clue to Joyce's disappearance in her flat.

She sighed. She acknowledged to herself that it was unlikely.

They had agreed to take George's car, since it was larger, newer and more comfortable than Kate's. They didn't mention the fact that he was a better driver than she was. Kate, in honest moments, admitted that most people drove better than she did.

George, as usual, was at the door on time.

'Did you mention Leicestershire?' Kate asked him as she walked out to the car. 'Or was it Lincolnshire? Do we need a map?'

'Where did you get that idea from? It's past Milton Keynes, out towards Bedford,' he said. 'It's not nearly as far. And I don't need a map, I know the way. Sam has given me excellent directions.'

'Haven't you been there before?'

'Joyce is Sam's mother-in-law, not mine. I didn't think it necessary to make quite such an effort. And before you ask, yes, I remembered to get the key to Joyce's flat from Emma. We won't need to break in.'

Kate didn't admit that even if they had no key, she would probably have found a way in. It was as well not to confess to her skills as a housebreaker. This was the sort of thing one hid from a man one wanted to impress, she had found.

The flat landscape was still white with frost as they drove out of Oxford, with clumps of bare trees and an occasional barn pencilled in. The clouds were still there, but if one were an optimist they looked as though they might lift and then there would be mild winter sunshine for an hour or two.

'I have one piece of bad news, I'm afraid,' said George, as they drove on to the M40. 'At least, it's unfortunate for me. Emma reminded me that I'm expected at her place for lunch on Thursday, and then I have to keep an eye on the children while she cycles over to see Sam. It means I won't be able to make the carol service.'

'I'm surprised she's still cycling after what happened to Sam,' said Kate, hiding her disappointment about the service. She had been looking forward to a candlelit afternoon with Roz and George, soaking up the warm Christmas spirit.

'Emma is a dedicated saviour of the planet. She wouldn't use a motor car for a distance under twenty-five miles.'

'Maybe we could do it next year instead,' said Kate.

'I'll write it in my diary. At least by then I shan't be expected to look after the infant Dolbys whenever I have a day off.'

The miles disappeared behind them, and they turned off the motorway on to a country road.

'We don't really expect to find Joyce sitting in her flat, do we?' said Kate after a pleasant silence.

'No, I don't think so. And I can't think we'll find anything very useful in her flat, either. I don't think Joyce went in for a secret life.'

'And yet there must be something.'

'I think we should look on this trip as a day off,' said George. 'Let's just enjoy it and consider any information we come up with as a bonus.'

'Good idea,' said Kate, who was all in favour of taking days off. She had decided to take a break in her writing until after the new year, after all. It might as well start here, with George.

'There's a copy of *The Good Pub Guide* in the passenger's side pocket. I've marked one or two we might explore at lunchtime. Why don't you take a look and decide which one to visit?'

It took something over an hour to reach the small, dull town where Joyce lived, time that George and Kate spent chatting about themselves and their lives.

'I can't imagine ever choosing to live here,' said Kate, as they entered the red-brick suburbs. 'What makes someone think, Yes! I'll buy myself a flat in Dullsford and settle down?'

'But then again, why not?' replied George. 'Property prices are moderate, crime rates are low. There's a library, a cinema, and a town hall where you can sometimes catch a decent concert. I'm sure there are plenty of other women like Joyce for her to make friends with.'

'It wouldn't suit me,' said Kate.

'Nor me. But it did suit Joyce. Perhaps she missed it so much that she had to run back here.'

George had turned into a prosperous road, much like thousands of others in towns all over Britain, with plum and sycamore trees along the verges, and gardens with low stone walls and neat herbaceous borders. Somewhere, a small dog was yapping. A tortoiseshell cat sat on a gatepost, enjoying the brief sunshine.

'We're here,' said George. 'Joyce has the bottom flat in the house opposite. She and the owner of the other flat share the garden, but they pay someone to look after it for them.'

'I'm glad about that. I'd hate to see a weed in a road like this.'

'Don't exaggerate,' said George.

'Somehow I imagined her living in a small, purpose-built block of flats, the sort where you hardly recognize your neighbours, let alone say "good morning" to them.'

'I think she knew quite a few people. She doesn't lead a particularly solitary life, you know.'

Kate picked up the tone of mild disapproval. 'I've been making too many assumptions about her.'

George paused at the door to the ground-floor flat. Somehow the house had been altered to provide separate entrances for the two apartments. He fished in his pocket and came up with a key.

'I think we should ring, just in case, don't you?' suggested Kate.

So they rang, and waited for a few moments before George used the key to let them inside.

'Dead air,' said Kate as they walked in. There was a lifeless quality about the air in the flat, as though the action of inhaling and expelling it through human lungs, that had previously kept it alive, had failed. Just inside the door there was a pile of post.

'Some junk mail, the rest are Christmas cards,' said Kate, picking them up. It was the thing in the flat that most brought it home to her: Joyce had left, and had never returned. The postmarks showed that she hadn't collected her mail for several weeks.

'I don't feel like sorting through her things,' said George, as they wandered into the sitting room. 'It's too much of an intrusion on her privacy.'

'I couldn't do it, either.' Kate wondered for a moment how she would have felt, what she would have done, if George hadn't been there to place a restraint on her curiosity.

In fact, there was very little to see. Joyce had tidied and cleaned so that the flat had an impersonal air to it.

'I can't believe there's anything of any interest to us in her cupboards and drawers,' said Kate. She wandered across to the single bookshelf. It contained the same selection of pious works as Joyce's room in Emma's house, all standing in the same straight line.

Kate wanted to ask, Why did we come? but she could see from George's face that he felt the same way as she did.

'At least we know she isn't here. It was an outside chance, but we had to find out,' said George.

'Let's leave,' said Kate, eager to escape from the chilly, characterless rooms. 'I'm starting to wish we'd never come.'

'Don't say that. Now that we've done what we came for, we'll lunch in our country pub with the blazing log fire. We'll find a canal or river bank to stroll along for half an hour. And then we'll make our way back to Oxford, slowly.'

As George was locking up, Kate asked, 'Is it worth asking whether her neighbour upstairs knows anything? We don't want to worry her unnecessarily, but she just might know something we don't.'

'It does seem a long way to come for so little,' replied George.

They walked round the side of the house to the other entrance, and rang another doorbell – brass and porcelain rather than plastic, this time. Joyce's neighbour was a step up the status ladder.

In fact, Joyce's neighbour wasn't another middle-aged widow, they discovered, but a man in his forties, dressed in light-blue trousers and shirt, with fair hair and an excellent sun tan.

'We're looking for Joyce Fielding,' said Kate.

'My lovely friend, Joyce,' said the man. 'But I haven't seen her for weeks. Have you any news of her?'

'We were hoping you'd have some,' said Kate, and she explained who she and George were.

Joyce's neighbour listened, looked them over, and said, 'Stephen Bonnet. The "t" is silent and the stress lies on the second syllable. You both look quite respectable, yet not at all boring, so I shall invite you inside. Wouldn't you agree it's time for coffee?'

The upstairs flat was decorated throughout in white and cream, with natural objects displayed in tasteful groups. There were some very good photographs on the walls. Some landscapes and townscapes, but most were of people. Stephen liked faces, close-up and grainy, or far-off and tiny against plain, textured backgrounds, or surrounded by objects in the middle distance.

'That's what I do,' he confided. 'I'm a photographer.'

He moved into the galley-kitchen, where he could still talk to them while he put the kettle on and ground coffee-beans.

'But I don't suppose you've done any of Joyce,' said George.

'Of course I have! Joyce and I have spent many cosy hours together, and my camera is never far from my hand. She has a really interesting face.'

'She has?' asked Kate, surprised.

'It's the contrast. The opposition, the fight between opposing forces,' said Stephen.

'Then could we look at them?' asked Kate, taking the cup of coffee he passed across to her, and making sure that she spilled none of it on the cream carpet.

Stephen indicated a long, deep, cream linen sofa and invited them to sit down. 'I would love you to see them,' he said. 'Just wait a tiny moment.'

Kate and George looked carefully through the portfolio. It was interesting, thought Kate, the way he had seen her. The sweet little old granny was certainly present, with her soft grey curls and soft blue eyes, but there was more to her than that in Stephen's pictures. A hardness? No, not quite that. More an intransigence. (And there was a word to use in her next book.) And Stephen was right. The expression in the eyes was not the same as that in the lines of the mouth. Joyce was impressionable, perhaps, but she was also stubborn. Just the sort of person who would get a daft idea in their head and then run off with it, thought Kate. And yes, Stephen had caught the steel that ran through Joyce's nature. And Kate had no reason to believe that what Stephen had seen wasn't so. He had been camping it up for her amusement and George's, but he was a very perceptive man, she reckoned.

'How long have you known her?' asked George.

'About two years. No, I tell a lie. It must be nearer three.'

Kate, having put her coffee cup back in the galley, was wandering around the room, looking at Stephen's 'objects'. It was difficult to tell that the season was Christmas, since there were no green branches of holly, no Christmas tree, no scarlet and gold baubles. There was certainly no tinsel and no blinking fairylights. But if you looked carefully, there were a few, very discreet, decorations, mildly indicative of Christmas, mostly in brushed aluminium and bleached wood. And then she found his Christmas cards, built into a pyramid, held in a white metal framework. Stephen's friends were mostly as sophisticated and artistic as he was, she noticed, sending cards bought from art galleries or screen-printed in their own studios. All except for one.

In the middle, standing out like a sore thumb, was a beautiful, sparkling, Dickensian scene, with stagecoach and passengers in some vaguely Victorian costume, and a bright golden festive message emblazoned across it.

'Daringly kitsch, don't you think?' said Stephen from behind her shoulder, noticing what she had found.

'Who sent it to you?' asked Kate. She held her breath.

'Why, it was darling Joyce. Who else would it be?'

'When did you get it?' asked George, staring at the noffensive scene as though it were something from Dante's *Inferno*.

'I don't remember exactly. But sometime this last week, I suppose.'

'If I'm very careful not to disturb the rest of the edifice, do you think I might look at it?' said Kate.

'Be my guest.'

Kate lifted out the card without displacing any of the others. She and George pored over it.

It said, 'To dear Stephen, a very Merry Christmas and best wishes for a very successful New Year, from his very good friend, Joyce.'

'Well?' asked George.

'She's still alive,' said Kate. 'Or at least, she was until a few days ago.'

'I don't suppose you have her address, have you?' asked George.

'I'm afraid not. But I did notice that the postmark was Oxford.'

'Good! That means she's still there,' said Kate.

'I thought she'd gone to help her daughter out,' said Stephen.

'She did. But we've managed to mislay her,' said George apologetically.

'Well, I hope you just get her back again very soon. I'm very fond of my friend Joyce,' said Stephen.

'Is there anything else you can tell us? Anything at all that would help us to find her?' asked Kate.

'Let me think.' They were sitting down again on the natural linen-covered sofa. Stephen had stretched his long legs out on the rug and was admiring his cream kid Italian shoes. 'Yes, well. She said she was going to Oxford to look after her daughter's children. She loved them, apparently, but she wasn't looking forward to spending too much time with them because she felt they were undisciplined. Apparently her daughter – Emma, isn't it? – had been unwilling to apply the same strict methods of child-rearing that Joyce herself had favoured.'

'I'll believe you!' said Kate.

'But your daughter is always your daughter, as dear Joyce might have said, and so she set off with her wonderfully retro suitcase in darling green checked nylon. Her first letter did mention that she was finding the children a trifle tiring—'

'*Her first letter*? I thought you said you hadn't heard from her?'

'I said I didn't have her address,' said Stephen mildly. 'I didn't realize this was going to be some sort of interrogation.'

'I'm sorry. I didn't mean it to sound like that. Put it down to our concern for Joyce.'

'How many letters did you receive?' asked Kate.

'Two or three. I forget now.'

'Did any of them have an address?' asked George.

'No.' Stephen was brief and growing antagonistic.

'Are you sure there was no address? No clue to where she was?'

'Have you still got the letters?' put in Kate.

'So many questions! Well, I'm afraid I threw the letters away after I'd read them. I can't stand clutter, as you may have noticed. Paper is the very devil. I get rid of it as soon as I've dealt with it. I don't remember an address, but if she had given me one, I'd have written it straight into my address book. I'll check for you.'

Stephen's address book was beautiful: dark-green snake-skin, by the look of it, with real-gold lettering and a dear little gold pencil to go with it. Kate lusted after it. It was just her sort of 'object.'

'Here we are,' said Stephen. 'Aren't we the lucky ones! I'd forgotten all about it. Seventeen Carpenter Street, Oxford.'

'So she was there! I was right,' exclaimed Kate.

'You followed her as far as Carpenter Street?' asked Stephen.

'Yes,' said Kate.

'Well?'

'I didn't find Joyce, and there was no sign of her in the house. She must have left before I got there, and the rest of it is a very long story.'

She felt queasy at the thought of Mr Bettony, and she wouldn't want anyone to throw up on Stephen's beautiful carpet, so she said no more.

'Did she send you another address after Carpenter Street?' asked George.

'No, she didn't. I'd have it in my little book, and there's nothing here. What do you think has happened to her?'

'We don't know. And we have no idea why she walked out of Sam and Emma's place without a word,' said George.

Kate didn't confide in them Roz's latest theory about dirty videos. Stephen probably wouldn't like it any more than Joyce had.

'If you ask me,' Stephen was saying with a certain self-conscious drama, 'I think it has something to do with the son-in-law.'

'Why do you say that?' asked Kate guardedly. She had to remember that Sam and George were brothers, and probably quite fond of one another. She didn't want to force Stephen to make any embarrassing revelations about Sam while she and George were at such a sensitive early stage in their relationship.

'I've never met him,' said Stephen. 'But I gathered from Joyce that he was not all she had hoped for as a husband for Emma. Of course, that might have meant simply that he didn't wear pyjamas in bed, or he used the occasional four-letter word without washing his mouth out afterwards. Joyce did have very high standards. On the other hand, it might equally have meant that he had affairs with his students –

male and female! – or made indecent proposals to children in the park.'

'Oh, no! Not Sam!' said Kate quickly.

She was glad that George didn't immediately tell Stephen that Sam was his brother. That would stop the flow of information all too effectively. She said, 'I'd be surprised if he did any of those things. Except the bit about the pyjamas and the strong language. They *do* sound just like Sam.'

'But then, we never do know quite as much as we think we do about our nearest and dearest. One can be sadly disillusioned,' said Stephen, looking as though he might confide his disappointments to them in intimate detail.

Kate rose to her feet quickly, Joyce's Christmas card in her hand. 'I'll put this back,' she said. 'I'll be very careful,' she added.

She walked across to the pyramid of cards. Behind her, she could hear George asking more questions. She could tell from Stephen's tone of voice that he had no intention of giving anything else away. As she went to replace the card, she turned it over. There, on the back, Joyce had written her name and address in her neat, legible, schoolgirl's hand. Kate memorized the address, turned the card over, and placed it delicately back in its place on Stephen's display, then went over to look out of the window.

'I have to admit to being curious, Stephen,' she said.

'Why is that?' he replied guardedly.

'Why did you choose to live here? You look like a city person to me. I can understand that it would suit Joyce, but why did you bury yourself in suburbia?'

'It's so wonderfully quiet,' said Stephen. 'I love immersing myself in my work, and I like solitude. Here, I live in a desert, with no temptations to socialize – except with dear Joyce, and she hardly bothered me at all.' He watched Kate as she went back to sit decorously on the sofa. 'And where else could I afford such large rooms at such a low price?' He smiled. 'And I have a penchant for people and houses which belie their surface appearance. One story on the outside, quite another on the inside.' He and Kate stared hard at one another.

'I think we've taken up enough of your time,' George was saying. 'We really should be leaving, shouldn't we, Kate?'

'Absolutely. You've been so very kind to us, Stephen. And I wonder whether I could just use your bathroom before we leave?'

The bathroom was as elegantly minimalist as Kate might have expected. She sat on the edge of the white bath (Victorian? Reproduction?), took from her handbag the notebook and pencil she always carried with her, and wrote down Joyce's new address before she forgot it, or mistook the house number. It was just possible that they could get there and find her before she moved on again.

Back in the car, George said, 'He didn't tell us all he knew, did he?'

'No. And he wouldn't have given us the Carpenter Street address if we hadn't pushed him.'

'Do you think he's involved in her disappearance?'

'I don't think so. I think he really likes Joyce, and he wasn't entirely certain of us. And I also think he has a mischievous sense of humour. We were being so intense and serious, and he just enjoyed playing with us.'

'I suppose I should have told him I was Sam's brother.'

'I'm glad you didn't. He wouldn't have opened up like that if he'd known. It's just as well he's never met Sam, or he'd have known immediately.'

'Why? Are we that alike?'

'Only superficially,' said Kate, without explaining any further.

39

Stephen

When Kate and George had left, Stephen threw away the dregs of the coffee, washed the cups and saucers, and put them away in the cupboard. He liked washing-up: it relaxed the mind with its repetitive rhythms, and allowed it to float free.

He frowned. His thoughts weren't as serene as he had hoped. His mind was filled with Joyce, and Kate and George. Had he done the right thing?

To begin with, he had thought they were worrying about nothing. Joyce had gone missing, they said, with not a word to her loving family. Well, why shouldn't she? Why should her daughter assume that Joyce was at her beck and call for months on end, to look after those dreadful children of hers? Anyone would get fed up with it. Anyone would skip off to find a more amusing way of spending their time.

Even Joyce.

He had seen Emma, and Sam, too, when they came to visit Joyce. Emma always had such a bossy tone, and poor Joyce always felt guilty about something when she had left. Sam and George were very similar, at least on the surface, as you might expect from men who were brothers. It was ridiculous of them to imagine that he wouldn't pick up on the likeness. Faces were his business and his fascination. It had been amusing to expound his views of Sam, knowing that George was wondering whether or not to tell him of the relationship.

Altogether, he had found Kate and George too earnest, too intense, too humourless. But now it was coming home to him: just suppose they were right and there really was something to be worried about. That last letter from Joyce had worried him at the time.

No. She might not have communicated with her family, nor with Kate and George, but she had written to her dear friend and neighbour, Stephen.

Should he have admitted to keeping her letters? Should he have shown them to his visitors?

No. Letters were private things, not to be shared with strangers. That was the wordless agreement between correspondents. And he liked the sense of power that secrets gave him.

Stephen popped the linen tea towel into the washing machine. That was the secret of immaculate tea towels: you washed them, very hot, very frequently, and never used one for more than a day. Ironing tea towels was another soothing occupation, he found.

Joyce's letters. He went into another room and opened a drawer in his filing cabinet. He still had them, of course he did. Perhaps he had kept them because he had been just a touch concerned about one or two of the things that Joyce had written.

Perhaps there was something just a little louche about this new life of hers, and about her rather butch new friend, Ruth. Joyce was such an innocent. And then there was her obsession with the clinic where she was doing voluntary work. It had such a déclassé name. Something to do with custard powder, or instant coffee. The Maxwell Clinic. Obviously stuffed to the roof with all kinds of rich perverts. But dear Joyce would never see any of it. He had felt so sorry for her, stuck in that gloomy house in Oxford, clearing up after countless young Dolbys, never thinking to complain. She needed a bit of excitement in her life, he considered, and when she told him about the awful video she had found, and how she simply couldn't stay in the same house with people who watched such things, he had to admit to himself that he had encouraged her.

And then she had met Ruth. Ruth, too, had encouraged her to believe that the watching of pornographic videos was the worst of all sins. She had involved Joyce in good works, and had signed her up for some strict sect that cut her off from her wicked family. Stephen hadn't quite believed in Ruth, or in her sect, which appeared to consist only of Ruth herself and Joyce. But Ruth sounded such a change from anyone else Joyce had ever known, that he had considered that she could be nothing but a good influence. The worst things that could happen to you in life were to get set in a rut, and to die of boredom. Joyce had been well on the way to both fates.

He read through all three letters, then put them back in the folder in the filing cabinet.

I wonder what Ruth's game is. I'm sure she's mixed up in something a tiny bit shady. Should I interfere? Should I allow the busybody couple to interfere?

Stephen went back into his living room and poured himself a small single-malt whisky. He didn't approve of drinking alcohol at lunchtime. But it was Christmas, after all.

Then he sat looking through the photos he had taken of his friend Joyce.

No, she needed to be shaken and stirred. If there was a hint of danger in her present life, it could do her nothing but good. She was tough enough to cope with it, he convinced himself. They could all work out their own

253

problems. He would sit back and watch without interfering.

I am a camera, he said out loud. It was a pity someone else had got to the phrase first.

40

Kate

That evening, back in Oxford, Kate wondered why she
hadn't told George about the address on the back of Joyce's
Christmas card. She hadn't told Roz about it, either. Perhaps
it was because she, too, had a mischievous sense of humour.
Perhaps – and this was even more likely, she admitted – she
wanted to amaze them with her intelligence when she found
Joyce all by herself, with no help from anyone else.

'I'm just going out for a breath of fresh air,' she called to
Roz, pulling on her jacket.

'Nothing fresh about that damp mist,' called back Roz.

Kate didn't answer, but just closed the front door behind
her.

The address she had taken from Joyce's Christmas card
wasn't far from Fridesley. She walked briskly towards the
centre of town, then turned right and made her way into a
network of back streets. The houses were tall and there
were few streetlights. No moon or starlight filtered down
between the tall buildings. Out of sight, on her left, she
could hear the soft sound of the river. She turned a corner,
started walking down a wider street, with a small park on
one side, and a row of broad-fronted semi-detached houses
on the other.

Number twenty-four.

She found it, standing behind a privet hedge and with some large and looming tree masking its front door from the street. There were no lights showing, but the curtains were thick and drawn tightly closed. A whole army could have been hiding behind them, or crouching in one of the back rooms.

Kate pushed open the gate, which groaned loudly as though in protest. She knocked on the door.

No reply.

She knocked again.

In the lengthening silence, she pulled out of her handbag the note she had prepared earlier.

Dear Joyce,

I do hope that you are well and happy. I'm sure you must realize that your family are a little concerned about your absence. There must have been some misunderstanding which can easily be sorted out, and I am enclosing a ticket for the carol service at Christ Church as a peace offering.

I do hope that you will use it, and that you will feel able to get in touch with your family again and reassure them of your safety and happiness.

She signed it with her name and added that she was a good friend of Emma's.

Now she pushed the envelope, addressed to Mrs Joyce Fielding, through the letter box and hoped that it would reach her. Even in the dim light, the brass letter-box glittered at her.

The best indication yet that Joyce and her polishing cloth were in the vicinity, thought Kate, and she turned back for home.

As she turned away, she thought she might have seen the

slight twitch of an upstairs curtain. But then again, it might only have been wishful thinking.

41

Ruth

Ruth had gone to the window as soon as she heard the knock at the door. She couldn't see who was there in the dark, so she waited. Ruth only saw people by appointment, she didn't open her door to chance callers.

She heard the soft sigh of the letter as it came through the letter box, and then she saw Kate as she walked back down the path and through the gate, the solitary street-lamp glinting on her blonde hair.

I know you. You're the Ivory woman. I saw you outside your house in Agatha Street, and I saw you again in Albert Wing. I saw you then and I said I wouldn't forget you. I'd know you if I ever saw you again.

Ruth went downstairs and picked the envelope up off the carpet, saw it was addressed to Joyce, and took it into the kitchen. She wasn't afraid that Joyce would notice, for her friend was sitting in front of something nauseatingly festive on the television, busy decorating the small tree she had bought for their living room.

'Lovely, dear. Quite lovely,' Ruth had said, staring at the tree with disgust. And then she had left the room.

In the kitchen, she had first held the envelope up against the light to see what was inside. It was paper with writing on, but folded so that she couldn't read more than a word or two. She then set the kettle to boil, and when she had a good amount of steam coming off it she held the back of the envelope up to it. It only took a minute or two and then she could carefully peel the flap open.

She read Kate's letter, looked at the carol-service ticket, and then got very angry indeed.

Joyce was hers. Joyce had a job to do. And here was this interfering Ivory woman trying to divert her from it. How often did you find someone as naïve as Joyce? The other Angels could identify potential customers and even take the orders, but it was dear Joyce, with her trusting nature and her sunny smile, who delivered the little gift-wrapped packages. She had no idea what it was she was handing over, and she wasn't the sort you would ever suspect of doing such a thing. Her other helpers worked for money, but dear Joyce worked for nothing but her friend's gratitude.

This was the last straw – the one that broke the camel's back. Well, she'd see what she could do about it. Joyce might be useful, but she wasn't irreplaceable, and she wasn't going to have people calling at her door, and putting advertisements in the paper. She liked to live her life in a low-key, private manner, and never call attention to herself.

First of all it was Bettony, with his demands for more money, and his threats. She paid him a huge rent for the Carpenter Street flat, but that wasn't good enough for him. He made snide remarks about what was going on in her half of the house, and then he insulted her with his suggestions about her private life.

She lost her temper with him, she admitted that. It wasn't a good thing to do, but he needed to be taught a lesson. And she could feel another of her rages coming on when she thought about this Mrs Ivory. This was the one who put the ads in the paper, the one who had spoken on the phone, the one who was sending *her* Joyce the carol-service tickets.

This Mrs Ivory needed to be taught a lesson.

She resealed the envelope, waited a short time for it to dry, then carried it into the living room, where Joyce was still listening to the jolly Christmas music.

'Here's a surprise!' said Ruth. 'Something for you, dear.' And she handed the envelope to Joyce.

'A Christmas card!'

'Better open it and see.'

Joyce opened it, read the note, frowning while she did so. She tucked it back into the envelope and looked at the other slip of paper it had contained.

'A ticket for the carol service! It's famous, you know. They say the singing is positively angelic. Oh, how kind of this person – whoever she is.' Then she stopped and an expression of concern came over her face. 'But there's only one ticket,' she said to Ruth. 'I can't go on my own, it would be too selfish. You've been so kind to me, and to everybody, and you must have it, Ruth dear. I insist.'

Ruth smiled a smile that might have seemed forced to a disinterested observer, but which Joyce found sweet-tempered.

'Nonsense!' she said briskly. 'One of your friends has given you a ticket, and you should certainly go. You might never have another chance.'

'But what about you?'

'Don't worry about me, dear. I've been before, you know. The patients are all so generous to us. And if I did want to go – if that would give you pleasure – I do believe I know where I can get hold of a ticket for myself.'

She remembered an elderly patient, going a bit ga-ga now, poor old thing. In Caroline Ward, wasn't it? On his bedside chest was a plastic beaker containing his false teeth. And propped against the beaker were two or three of these carol-service tickets. She could help herself to one that very evening, and no one would be any the wiser.

'We can go together,' said Joyce. 'Won't that be lovely?'

And the meddling Ivory woman might well come across her missing Joyce Fielding in the cathedral, but she might be upset by the condition she would find her in. Ruth was tired of the lot of them, and she was going to act. She was like that. She'd go along for ages, just letting things drift, and then she'd make a decision and act on it. Keith Bettony had discovered that. Joyce Fielding and the Ivory woman would discover it quite soon. Before they left for the concert on Thursday, she would pack something unexpected into her handbag.

She had often noticed that, in a large crowd, when everyone's attention was focused on something else, you could get away with murder, to coin a phrase.

42

Kate

It was a damp, drizzly afternoon when Kate and Roz set off for the carol service.

'At least it isn't cold,' said Roz. 'There's nothing so cold as an English church in winter, I've found.'

'I hadn't noticed you frequenting that many churches,' said Kate.

'Just another of the tiny nuggets of information about my past which you might pick up and ponder,' said Roz loftily.

Kate made a noise indicative of disbelief.

'Shall we take the car?' asked Roz.

'It's not worth it. We may as well walk. We're in plenty of time.'

They set off towards the town centre. After a while, Roz said, 'Are you going to tell me about the detecting you've been doing?'

'What makes you think I've been doing any such thing?' countered Kate.

'It has something to do with the fact that you've been disappearing without explaining where you're going. Then there's the smug expression on your face when you think no one's looking.'

'I think I'm getting somewhere,' said Kate. 'And maybe it would be useful to talk it over with someone. With a colleague,' she amended.

'Get on with it,' said Roz. 'It doesn't take very long to walk to Christ Church.'

'There are several strands that seem to lead to the same place.'

'The Maxwell Clinic.'

'I'll be quicker if you don't interrupt.'

'Sorry.'

'First, Joyce's disappearance. I think you're right. I think poor old Sam, probably frustrated by Emma's overwhelming interest in her children and lack of interest in sex, has been amusing himself with naughty videos.'

'And who could blame him?'

'Joyce, apparently. Now, here comes a little of my novelist's imagination, if you like, but I think Joyce had some unfortunate experience as a girl that made her believe that sex was awful and all men were beasts, well, any man who was interested in sex, anyway.'

'Didn't I manage to instil similar ideas in you, Kate dear?'

'I'm afraid you failed completely. Anyway, struck with the horror of it all – especially since the youngest of her grandchildren were inadvertently on the point of watching the offending video – Joyce rushes out into the night.'

'Afternoon,' corrected Roz, mildly. 'I suppose she could have noticed the card in the window when she was buying milk, earlier. It seems an extreme reaction, but she might have phoned to find out about the room to let.'

'And when she got to the house in Carpenter Street, she was persuaded to stay.'

'How?'

'I don't know, but I'm imagining someone persuasive, manipulative, perhaps a little sinister. Ruth, in other words.'

'Your imagination's working overtime.'

'She took one look at Joyce and knew she could use her. All you'd need is a sympathetic manner and a pot of tea and you'd get the whole story out of her. Ruth could offer her the room, and friendship, and a condemnation of the sinfulness of Sam and Emma and all their brood.'

'What about Bettony?'

'If he was her landlord, he might have cottoned on to what she was up to. I imagine she had visitors at odd times of day and night. Suppose he tried to blackmail her and she bludgeoned him to death?'

'It's possible. Wouldn't all this have occurred to the police?'

'I expect it has done. They're not going to keep us informed about their investigation, are they?'

'What time are we supposed to get to the cathedral?'

'Two-twenty should be early enough for a good seat. I've got time to tell you the next part of my theory before we have to go inside.'

'Hurry up, then.'

'Now, Ruth is in business. It seemed to me that there were two or three wings at the Maxwell Clinic that dealt with all the ills that one might expect: people like Sam and Mrs Bassett, and so on. But even allowing for space for administration, and technicians and X-rays and all the other things so familiar to us from our television screens, there was still a lot of room left for paying customers. Seriously rich paying customers, I'm talking about. Depressed, exhausted, recovering, vulnerable patients. Some of them young. Most of them young. So, if you were in business, like Ruth, what would you do? You'd make sure they had their drugs of choice, that's what. When I went to pick up the carol-service tickets from Mrs Bassett, I explored Haufman's ground-floor wing again. And this time I met a young man who was looking to buy something from Ruth.'

'It is possible that he'd run out of toothpaste,' said Roz mildly.

'He said she'd have the gear, and I don't think he meant toothpaste by it.'

'You could be right.'

'So, I reckon Ruth, and some of her respectable fellow-Angels, are selling cannabis, angel dust, single doses of cocaine, heroin, or whatever else these people want to buy, all at inflated prices.'

'That's evil.'

'Yes. And I don't think Joyce knows what she's doing. It's ironic, isn't it? She thinks she's escaping from The Pit to sweetness and light, and in fact she's involved in something really immoral.'

'Can we walk a bit faster? We've slowed to a crawl and I'm getting a bit chilly.'

'Just one more thing,' said Kate urgently. 'When we went to Joyce's flat and met her neighbour, Stephen, I managed to find a more recent address for her. I went round there the other evening and dropped off a friendly note containing the third ticket for the carol service. Keep your eyes open. She may be here. And if we can rescue Joyce from Ruth's clutches, we can send the police round after the real villain.'

They were approaching Christ Church and Kate broke off to take their tickets from her handbag.

'And why did Bettony's body disappear?' asked Roz, as they walked round to a side aisle and found places to sit.

'Ruth moved it,' said Kate succinctly. 'She went round to clear up – or she sent her minions, more likely – just after I had left.'

'That seems a bit far-fetched,' said Roz, trying to make herself comfortable in the narrow chair.

'Perhaps. But for now, we have to look out for Joyce and plan how we're going to stop her when the service is over.'

But there was much coming and going around them, and people packing into narrow spaces, and deciding whether to remove their coats or leave them on, and it looked as though they'd never see Joyce in all that crowd, even if she had received the ticket, and decided to attend.

It wasn't until the organ had stopped playing, the choir had done their bit with the first carol and the congregation rose to their feet so that they could let rip in their turn, that Kate saw her. She nudged Roz.

'Over there!'

Roz was singing and didn't wish to be interrupted. Two verses slipped by before she saw what Kate was trying to draw her attention to.

'It's Joyce,' she whispered back.

'Is it?'

'I'm sure it is.'

The figure of Joyce Fielding was on the other side of the choir, standing facing them in the opposite aisle.

When they all sat down, they couldn't see her any longer. Kate was on tenterhooks before the next opportunity to stand and sing.

'Wake, O wake!' she carolled. Joyce was still there. Kate risked a wave with her programme, and a bright smile that might, or might not, have been noticeable so far away. At least the white cover of the programme should be clearly visible across the choir, and she waved again, rather more exuberantly. Several people looked in her direction, but she took no notice. If she could convince Joyce that she was there as a friend, and an ally, that was all that mattered. And then she noticed the figure standing beside Joyce. She should have seen her before, for she was several inches taller than Joyce, and wide, and imposing.

Ruth.

She was sure it was Ruth. Light reflected from her glasses as she bent to read the words of the carol. Joyce looked across in Kate's direction and whispered something in

Ruth's ear. Ruth bent towards her to reply. Yes, definitely Ruth. But had Joyce spotted them? And if so, had she told Ruth about it? Perhaps the second, vigorous, wave of the programme had been overdoing it.

'Keep your eye on them,' she whispered to Roz as they were sitting down, waiting for the third lesson to begin. 'And when the service is over, you go for Joyce and make an excuse to detain her, and I'll tackle Ruth.'

If Roz hadn't been absorbed in listening to the reading, she might have pointed out to Kate what a very risky plan this was.

43

Kate

Kate had always enjoyed singing 'O come all ye faithful'. It was the last hymn, and she sang with gusto, enjoying the sound of the trebles soaring above the congregation. She scrabbled in her purse to find a fiver for the collection, and when she had made her contribution, and joined in the next verse, she looked across the choir to the dim aisle opposite to make sure that Ruth and Joyce were still there.

But Ruth was moving. She had taken advantage of the fact that everyone was standing, and turned to make her way towards the end of the row. Joyce was following, but slowly, as though unwilling to leave so early. She even glanced over to where Kate was.

Oh no, thought Kate. You don't get away from me like that. Roz was standing on her left, but the nearest end of her own row was to her right. She started to inch her way past the squashed people, stepping over feet, pushing past overcoats, as she made her way out.

She had noticed that the readers of the lessons had found a way up to the pulpit, so there had to be a way past the pillars, across the choir and into the aisle opposite.

It meant that she had to make her way through bishop and priests and deacons, or whatever the sumptuously dressed, befrocked men were called. She was glad to see that Ruth had been stopped by a press of people unwilling to let her through. There was time to catch up with her if she didn't mind making an exhibition of herself. Well, maybe she did mind, but she wasn't going to let it stop her.

She reached the end of the row and dodged round the side of the pulpit. A couple of small choirboys watched her progress, their expressions startled, but their singing as angelic as ever. Kate didn't bother to apologize for her intrusion, but sprinted through to the opposite side of the choir, avoiding a candle, a deacon and two more choristers as she did so.

'So sorry,' she murmured in the direction of the altar. 'You do understand, don't You?'

Then she had to make her way down another serried row of the congregation, chasing after Ruth. She was vaguely aware of Roz, her face turned in her direction, mouth open, although she had stopped singing. Ruth hadn't noticed her yet, though, she thought. That was one advantage. She certainly hadn't increased her rate of progress through the crowd. She was probably relying on being among the first to reach the door, and then, with the slow progress that the crowd would make through the narrow space, she would be five minutes or more ahead of Kate and Roz.

And then, as Kate moved forward, the light caught her hair and turned it to silver. Ruth was glancing behind her. She noticed the blonde head. And she saw Kate.

At this moment the choir and congregation came to the end of the final triumphant repetition of 'Christ the Lord!' There was a shuffling of feet and they all sank to their knees, except for Kate and Ruth. Kate could no longer see Joyce. Perhaps she had felt she ought to kneel at this point. But she was sure that if she could overtake Ruth, and stop her from leaving, then Joyce would soon be found.

Kate contemplated the line of legs in front of her. If she was careful she should be able to step between them and reach the end of the row. She had to think of it as an obstacle race, she thought.

It was a question of timing, and of adjusting the length of her stride, she decided, as she tripped over a couple of feet, then finally made it to the end without any further mishaps.

Where was Ruth? She couldn't see her anywhere.

There was a problem ahead: a dense crowd of people standing between her and the main door. Ruth must be in there, pushing her way through like a barge through a flotilla of dinghies.

In front of her was a wall of overcoats and mufflers. Heads were bowed and all were diligently saying the General Thanksgiving. Kate shoved and pushed. She used her sharp elbows to get her through. She even kicked at an occasional ankle and heard the yelps of her victims through the words of the prayer.

'It's an emergency,' she hissed. 'Please let me through!'

Luckily, the people around her belonged to the polite middle-classes, who didn't respond in kind when dug in the ribs by a pointed elbow, or kicked painfully about the ankles. Bodies moved slightly. A narrow passage opened in front of her.

And now she was gaining on Ruth once more. She could see the stout figure ahead of her in its dark coat. It was easier moving through a crowd if you were narrow, like Kate, rather than wide, like Ruth.

'So sorry!' murmured Kate, stepping on feet, shoving at winter-clad bosoms and buttocks as she made her way through, always a little nearer to Ruth.

And then, just around a pillar, she caught up with her. For a moment, she wondered what to do, then she caught at the solid shoulder, turning Ruth to face her. She held on to Ruth's sleeve, trying to keep her locked against the broad back of the pillar, and she opened her mouth to shout for help. She didn't care about the shock-horror reaction of those of the congregation who were close enough to see her, nor that of the cloaked and clerical figure standing by the door. All that mattered was to grab hold of Ruth and to make sure that she didn't get away. Ruth was a lot bigger than she was. She would never manage it on her own.

'Help!' she shrieked.

It was odd, but Ruth wasn't trying to pull away from her. She was allowing Kate to cling to her sleeve. Instead of lumbering away, as Kate had expected, she was reaching into her unusually large handbag and drawing something out.

'I brought this for Joyce, but you got in the way, so you can have it instead,' Ruth was saying.

Kate was trying to ask her where Joyce had disappeared to, but she couldn't speak any more, she found. The thing in Ruth's right hand was a long, wicked knife. And Ruth was plunging the blade into her, through the material of her jacket and the shirt she was wearing underneath it, up under her ribs, moving upwards all the time, twisting.

Where's Joyce? she was wondering as the world drowned in pain and blackness.

'We need an ambulance,' Roz was shouting. 'Hasn't anyone got a mobile phone?'

Someone had already phoned, and the ambulance was summoned.

Ruth had disappeared. Joyce was nowhere to be seen. For the moment, no one cared about them. The congregation were politely asked to return to their places and leave the way clear for the paramedics. Roz didn't care about Joyce, Ruth or the bishop and congregation. She was bending over Kate's slumped body, wondering how to stop the bleeding.

The pool of blood was soaking through Kate's coat and forming a dark puddle on the ground.

There were bubbles of blood on her lips, and she was showing the whites of her eyes.

'Kate! She's dying,' whispered Roz. 'I think she's gone.'

'Not yet.' It was a figure in a cassock. 'Stay with us, Kate. The ambulance will be here. It's coming, I promise.'

The ambulance was there in a few minutes, driven fast through the light evening traffic.

Roz was gently moved aside a few yards by one of the bowler-hatted custodians, and could only watch as the paramedics slipped Kate on to a stretcher, then into the ambulance, and started to drip blood from a plastic pack into her arm.

'I'll travel in the ambulance with her,' said Roz. 'I'm not leaving her on her own.'

Seconds later, the ambulance accelerated away, blue light flashing.

She will make it, won't she?

It was the nearest thing to a prayer that Roz had offered up that afternoon.

44

Joyce

Joyce had knelt down with the rest of the congregation for the General Thanksgiving. It hadn't seemed right to her to ignore the final prayers and push a way through to the door, just so that they could beat the crowd and be first out. Ruth could do as she wished, but she was not going to be so irreverent.

And then there was the young woman who had waved to her across the cathedral. She was sure it was the one who had sent her the ticket, and she wanted to see her, even if only to thank her for that. But Ruth said she was obviously deranged. Ruth knew about things like that, after her work at the clinic, but Joyce wasn't sure she was right, even so. There were several things that had come together in her head and made her think twice about a lot of the things that Ruth said.

Now the prayer was over and a single voice was reading the Collect, so Joyce heard Kate's cry of 'Help!' quite clearly. She rose to her feet and started to make her way towards the pillar where the shout had come from. Even at this moment, she realized afterwards, she had been afraid of what Ruth might be doing. She didn't have anything specific in mind, but she did know that Ruth was dangerous.

At last, that was what she knew.

She didn't see the stabbing, but she saw the poor young

273

woman on the floor with the blood soaking through her coat, and matted in her bright blonde hair. And then she saw Ruth hurrying through the open door. No one else was interested in her. They were all concentrating on her victim.

Joyce left the cathedral and followed Ruth, who had turned right and was hurrying towards Carfax. Joyce could see her quite clearly, for there were few pedestrians in the dark street.

But Ruth was a lot younger than Joyce, and she was moving in a very determined way, and she soon disappeared into the gloom. Perhaps she had even gone into a pub, thought Joyce. She couldn't possibly follow her into such a place.

So Joyce walked slowly up to Carfax and stood at the stop until the familiar bus arrived that would take her back to Emma and Sam's house. That could have been me lying on the floor of the cathedral, she thought. She took the knife with her so that she could kill me and leave my body behind in the crowd.

Murder in the cathedral, that's what Ruth had been planning. It was like those films she liked to watch, where the villain lured his victim to a crowded place, like a theatre or the opera. And in the dark, when everyone's attention was diverted by what was happening on the stage, he would strike, and then creep out of the auditorium, leaving his victim to be found when the lights went up.

And the tragedy was that she, Joyce, was still alive, while that poor girl was lying on the cathedral floor, bleeding to death.

'Oh my God! You're back!'

Joyce thought her daughter might faint with surprise when she opened the door. She knew she must be a bedraggled sight by now, for it had started to rain while she was walking from the bus stop, and she had somehow lost her hat and mislaid her umbrella, so her usually neat curls hung in wisps around her pale face.

'Can I come in?' she asked.

And Emma opened the door, and called, 'It's Granny! She's come home!' over her shoulder to the children. Through the open door into the living room, Joyce could see a gaudily decorated Christmas tree, and fairylights, and they looked like heaven to her. And she could hear the wonderfully familiar sound of the Dolby children, squabbling.

It was a lot later the same evening that Joyce thought she should ring the police, and tell them what she had seen in the cathedral, and give them the address of Ruth's flat.

'Let's hope she's still there,' said the sergeant at the other end of the line. To Joyce's ears he didn't sound very optimistic.

'There's something else,' said Joyce painfully. 'I think my friend Ruth was using me.' She stopped. It was distressing to think she had been blind to Ruth's shortcomings for so long. The truth was, she admitted to herself now, she hadn't *wanted* to see. But now she would have to face unpleasant facts. She said, 'I think there are certain things going on at the Maxwell Clinic, where we were working.'

'The Maxwell Clinic,' repeated the sergeant. He spoke as though he wouldn't be surprised at anything Joyce could tell him.

'You'll think I'm a stupid old woman to be taken in by her,' she said sadly.

The sergeant just said, 'Someone will be round shortly to take a full statement from you.'

'You will find her, won't you?'

'We will,' the sergeant replied. 'Eventually.'

45

Roz and George

It was two o'clock in the morning.

Kate had returned from the operating theatre and was lying in a bed in the intensive care unit. There were tubes jutting from her nose and mouth, and wires snaking from her chest to a monitor. Her eyes were closed. She looked so much smaller and more fragile than all the machines that were keeping her alive.

Roz had thought to phone George sometime during the long evening. Kate would want him there. And she was grateful for the company. They were sitting on a small padded bench just outside Kate's room. The overhead lighting glared down and hurt their tired eyes.

'Shall I get you another coffee?' George asked Roz.

'I can't face another beaker of that stuff, ever.'

George took her hand. There was so little to say that was comforting.

'I should have been there,' Roz said, after a time.

'But you were. You were in the cathedral.'

'I mean, in her life. I left when she was seventeen. That was dreadful of me, wasn't it? I've missed half her life! I came back for a while a few years after that first departure, but then I left for another ten years this last time. And then we shared Callie's cottage for a few weeks, and came back to Fridesley together. We were just starting to get to know one another. We were both making an effort, and we were getting there. And now there isn't going to be another chance.'

'Yes,' said George. 'Yes, there will be.'

'No. You get given your chances in life, just the once. There's no reason for Providence to send them round again. You have to grab them the first time they go past, otherwise they're gone for good.'

George wanted to say, What about me? I haven't been given even one chance yet.

They were both silent for a while.

'She survived the surgery,' said Roz. 'That's got to be a good sign.'

The blade had scraped a rib, pierced a lung and damaged the heart. She has a one-in-four chance, the surgeon had said, but George didn't remind Roz of that.

'She's young and fit,' said Roz desperately. 'She *will* make it, won't she?'

'I'm sure she will,' said George.

But what he really meant was, *I hope so. I really hope she will.*

Oxford Mourning

Veronica Stallwood

When novelist Kate Ivory first meets Dr Olivia Blacket, an academic at Leicester College, Oxford, the atmosphere is far from amicable. Olivia refuses to show Kate the fascinating material she is researching, even though it concerns the same esteemed literary figure that Kate is writing about. Determined to nose out the scandals that could provide her with a best-seller, Kate discovers a darker side to Dr Blacket. What are the strange obsessions that haunt her? What is her relationship with Kate's boyfriend Liam? And most of all, who would want to murder her . . . ?

Liam's name heads the list of suspects, but Kate knows that several others were in the vicinity of Olivia's rooms at the time of her death, including a bizarre 'family' of civilised squatters – four men guarding a blank-faced girl. As Kate is drawn into their circle, she struggles to understand a complex web of overlapping lives, and realises that, before she can unravel the truth, her own beliefs and values will come into question . . .

'Stallwood is in the top rank of crime writers' Mike Ripley, *Daily Telegraph*

0 7472 5343 9

HEADLINE

Written in Blood

Caroline Graham

It is clear to the more realistic members of the Midsomer Worthy's Writers' Circle that asking best-selling author Max Jennings to talk to them is a little ambitious. Less clear are the reasons for secretary Gerald Hadleigh's fierce objections to seeing the man – a face from his past – again. But, astonishingly, Jennings accepts the invitation and before the night is out, Gerald is dead.

Summoned to investigate, Chief Inspector Barnaby finds that Gerald's solitary life was as much of a mystery to his well-heeled neighbours as his violent death. The key is surely their illustrious guest speaker – but where is he now?

Now part of the major television drama series, *Midsomer Murders*, starring John Nettles as Chief Inspector Barnaby.

'Plenty of horror spiked by humour, all twirling in a staggering *danse macabre*' *The Sunday Times*

'Very funny, with a brilliant cast of eccentrics' *Yorkshire Post*

'Enlivened by a very sardonic wit and turn of phrase, the narrative drive never falters . . . a most impressive performance' *Birmingham Post*

0 7472 4664 5

HEADLINE

Beneath These Stones

Ann Granger

Twelve-year-old Tammy Franklin has learned too much about death, too quickly. Two years ago she lost her mother to a long, lingering illness and now the body of the woman her father married in an attempt to replace his wife has been found on a railway embankment close to the Franklin farm. This time the death is murder.

As Superintendent Markby, one of the first on the scene, well knows, Tammy now stands to have her father taken from her, for Hugh Franklin is suspect number one in the mind of the inspector to whom Markby has delegated the case. But, despite his need to distance himself from the murder, Markby begins to realise that the truth is destined to be far more complex than he ever envisaged . . .

Praise for Ann Granger's hugely popular bestsellers

'Granger's deft touch raises her above the competition and her finely drawn characters are affecting and believable . . . Something quite special' *Crime Time*

'Ann Granger has brought the traditional English village story up to date, in setting, sophistication and every other aspect of fiction writing . . . sheer unadulterated bliss' *Birmingham Post*

'You'll soon be addicted' *Woman and Home*

0 7472 5643 8

HEADLINE

The Stargazey

Martha Grimes

Saturday night was not a night to be spending alone, riding a bus through southwest London. But had he been anywhere else, he wouldn't have seen her. She came out of The Stargazey on the Fulham Road, pulling up the collar of her fur coat against the cold November evening. He was drawn to her; he couldn't help but follow her.

Twelve hours later the body of a young woman is found in the grounds of Fulham Palace and Superintendent Richard Jury is faced with the embarrassing task of explaining his rather detailed knowledge of her last movements. But when a visit to the morgue reveals that the fur coat in question seems to have come into the possession of an entirely different woman, Jury has some questions of his own.

'Entertaining ... intriguing ... thoroughly researched'
Sunday Express

0 7472 5696 9

HEADLINE